'When Jack and his scavenger hunt team go looking for a Kookaburra on a school outing in Australia, they unwittingly fall into another world, one where everyone has a superpower. Before they can react, the kids are ambushed, captured, and forced to compete in deadly ancient games by the natives. They'll need all their powers in order to face the South African captive team, one led by a young man fiercely determined not to lose. 'The book delves deep into relationships, past trauma, and the need to find oneself while in a world of wonder and control. The author deftly navigates over a dozen strong, well-crafted personalities, their glee at learning they have powers, their resentment to being captured, their quest to get a leg up on the competition, and their horror at the aftermath of the deadly challenges.

'Will Jack's affection for Max get in the way of winning? Is there any hope of defeating the native Invincibles, if they are even able to best the Afrikaners? When the dust settles, will Jack have a team left to take back through the Gateway? In this stunning debut novel, all these questions find brilliant and often surprising answers.'

Brent Meske, author of *Super Nobody* and *The Alpha and Omegas Series*.

'Realm Travellers: *The Ancient Gateway* is a treat for young adults. At a school camp in a forest, the pupils get divided into groups of five. Jack's group includes his best friend Charlie, the shy, bookish Kenny and two girls, Max and Ruby, who each have problem backgrounds.

'Jack's team sets off on a treasure hunt in the forest where four children went missing five years before and were never found. While on their quest, the ground suddenly gives way and they fall into another realm, where their latent skills become enhanced. In order to be released, they must pit their wits against four other captives in feats of historical games and thrilling ordeals.

'This enjoyable, fast-paced book left this adult eagerly awaiting the next installment of The Realm Travellers. Highly recommended.'
Lyn Behan, author of *The Men and The Medium* and *Seeking Samuel Goldberg.*

Realm Travellers

The Ancient Gateway

M.J. Raco

AIA PUBLISHING

To my beautiful father whose creative genes run through my veins, my gorgeous mother who sparked my world of imagination when she gave me my first Enid Blyton book, and to the best husband and family a girl could ask for ... this is for you.

Acknowledgements

A big thank you to my dear friend Carolyn Livingston for her belief in me, and treasured guidance at the onset of my journey.

A warm thanks to Stephen Measday for opening my eyes to the real world of creative writing.

Thanks are also due to Alexandra Nahlous for her invaluable advice, patience, and honesty. And to Brent Meske, Shane Porteous and Lyn Behan, my first readers.

And my biggest gratitude is to my editor, Tahlia Newland. Her guidance allowed my vision to finally become a reality.

I

Tim Tams at 3am

Max

Max sits up in a sweat, her heart pounding. She searches the room, trying to orientate herself, but it's too dark. She sees nothing. Her breath catches in her throat as she tries to calm down. It takes a moment for her eyes to adjust and see that she's safe. It was just another crappy dream. And yet knowing this, strangely, doesn't bring her any comfort. The burden of reality bears down, like a lead weight pressing on her chest, crushing her lungs and suffocating her.

She grabs her pillow, slams it to her face, and screams. And when that's done, she screams some more. All that built up hurt—all that anger—she lets it all out, trying desperately to free herself from the torment once and for all.

And then she falls back, exhausted.

The threat of tears prickles at her senses, but she won't let them fall. She presses the heels of her palms to her eyes, forcing them back.

Her racing heart skips a beat when she realises that her idiotic performance may have just woken her father. She slows her breathing to listen for any movement from the bedroom down the hallway, but there is none. She exhales unsteadily, knowing that she just dodged a bullet.

That's all I need, another reason for him to hate me.

Her thoughts then slip back to the nightmare, and without wishing it, in her mind's eye, she sees the haunting silhouette of her precious mother before her. Once again those pesky prickles return. But she knows that tears won't bring her back; she's gone.

Enough already!

She curses herself for being so weak.

With a trembling hand, she brushes her hair back from her sweaty brow and reaches for her phone. She groans; it's only 3:11am. But she won't be getting any more sleep tonight; this much she already knows.

Emotionally drained, she drags herself out of bed and quietly makes her way past her father's room to go downstairs to the kitchen. If he knew that she was still having nightmares …

God, don't even go there!

Another year of useless therapy … another year of endless gossip … "Poor Professor Rutherford, losing his wife like that … and that daughter of his … you know she has problems, don't you? How difficult it must be for him …"

For him! What about me? Hello. Remember me? I'm still here!

Max squeezes her eyes tight, trying to shut out her demons.

Now, perched on the kitchen stool, she cradles her hot tea, trying to get warm. But the cold she feels doesn't defrost that easily.

From down the corridor, the approaching sound of shuffling slippers saves Max from that dark place. She knows that sound too well, and is selfishly happy to have some company.

Annuska is the closest thing to a mother she has now.

She silently enters and smiles, then wraps her arms around Max, giving her a warm, comforting squeeze. And then all at once, without a single word, a flicker of a flame begins to thaw away the ache deep in Max's chest.

Annuska rests her chin on Max's head. 'So … you vant some TimTams vid dat?' she asks in her thick Hungarian accent.

Max shakes her head.

'But I bought you your favourite … Chewy Caramel,' she adds in a sing-song voice.

Max can't help but smile at her. Annuska is her rock, and right now she's doing what she does best—saving Max from herself.

'Nah, I'm good, Annie. You know I'll end up eating the whole packet. You don't want me turning into a butterball now, do you?'

'A butterball? I never heard such rubbish. You vait here,' she says firmly. 'I get you your biscuits.'

Max holds back a giggle.

'Butterball! *Ez nevetseges!* Annuska mumbles as she loses herself in the pantry.

And suddenly the world seems a little brighter.

Annie has always been part of Max's life. She started working in the Darcy-Rutherford household as housekeeper and cook before Max was born. When Max came along, she fell into the role of the nanny, and now that Grace is gone, she fills the shoes of a mother/grandmother figure.

Max shudders to think where she'd be now if it wasn't for Annie. With all that's happened, she's hit some gutter-scraping lows in the last three years. All too easily, Max's thoughts slip back to her mother.

Annuska gives Max another squeeze. 'I miss her too,' she whispers. Lost in her own thoughts, she combs her fingers through Max's long hair and begins to braid it with familiar ease.

They sit there for a while in a comfortable silence.

'You vant to talk, honey?' Annuska asks.

Max looks intently into her cup, as if all the answers of the world are hidden there, and imperceptibly shakes her head.

'So … your trip is coming soon,' Annuska says with sudden enthusiasm. 'Tell me again vhere is it you are going?'

Her random question snaps Max out of her thoughts. 'Ugh! I forgot about that!' She's been dreading the school camp all year.

'Vhy you sound like dhis?'

Too late! Annie's look of concern, makes Max realise what she's done.

Fix it, Darcy!

'Oh, the retreat!' she laughs. 'Sorry, Annie, I thought you meant something else. Duh!' She smacks herself on the forehead. 'My bad. Yeah, there's a meeting today. They'll tell us more about it then, I guess. Wow, I can't believe it's finally here!' She knows she's piling it on a little too thick and should stop, but somehow, she can't. 'A whole week off school. Whoohoo! No homework, no assignments …'

She's a train wreck, waiting to happen.

She bites down on her tongue to prevent any further verbal vomit, then searches Annie's face, hoping she hasn't stuffed up. Miraculously, her rambling must've worked, because Annuska is smiling sweetly at her once again. She takes in a shaky breath.

That was too close!

'I tink a break vill do you good, sveety. Annuska vill miss you, I know, but dhat's okay. I be happy for my Maxy.'

Max gives her a sympathetic cuddle.

Feeling safe enough to open her mouth again, Max dares to ask a favour. 'Annie, I need the permission note signed, will you do it for me?'

'Vhat? No, Maxy, your Papa vil do it. Vhy not you ask him?'

Ask him? Really?

Max's thoughts slip back to that dark place, and her rage returns.

That would mean that he'd have to be in the same room as me, and, heaven forbid, talk to me! And when was the last time he bothered doing that?

Max forcibly curbs the escalating inner torment threatening to erupt. She looks up and sees Annie's deep concern. She sighs. *Poor Annie; it's not her fault.*

She takes a moment to clear her head.

The thing is, the note still needs to be signed, and there's no way she's going to ask her father, herself. So she needs to somehow get Annie to do it.

'Annie, you're right,' she begins slowly, 'but I

never seem to catch him. You'll probably see him before I do. Couldn't you ask him for me, please?'

Annuska squeezes her pouty mouth. 'You know I cannot say no to dhis face. You're killing me! Okay, I vill ask him before he leaves for work.'

Max lets out a sigh of relief.

'But now you make it promise to me, someting.'

And just like that, all of Max's jubilation plummets. She holds her breath, waiting to hear the terms of the condition.

'Today, after school, ve go shopping and buy you some nice tings for camp. Maybe even some dresses. No more black. Vhy always dhis ugly black?!'

Max's heart seems to stop. She can't even begin to imagine the hideous things Annie will make her buy. Max doesn't do colour, and she most definitely doesn't do dresses.

Annie looks at her with stern determination. 'So, ve make it deal?'

Max quickly analyses this compromise, her mind searching for loopholes. And then she sees a way out. *Okay, this could work. I'll pack the new stuff, but won't use them. She didn't say anything about having to wear them, right?*

'Okay, deal,' Max says. 'Some new things might be nice. But no dresses! I'm definitely drawing the line there.' She crosses her arms across her chest and looks at Annie with stubborn persistence.

Despite this, Annuska's face lights up at the unprecedented victory.

Max does a private happy dance for getting away with it. And before Annie has a chance to become suspicious, Max jumps off her stool, gives Annie a quick hug and a kiss on the cheek, then says she might try going back to sleep.

'You do dhat, sveetheart. Ve have a big day, later.' Annie's voice trails off as Max makes her escape.

2

TOTALLY WOW!

JACK

'Jack, honey, can you hurry the kids along?' Trish Braden calls up the stairs. 'You'll miss the bus if you don't get a wriggle on. And don't forget to take in your permission note.'

Jack bounds down the steps, two at a time, and gives his mum a peck on the cheek before pocketing the note. 'No worries, Mum. We're all good to go.' It's Monday morning, and like most mornings, his mum tries to rustle her horde into action, but he has everything under control.

Moments later the Braden kids overcrowd the hallway, jostling to get through the front door. Their mother hands out lunches in an ordered fashion as they scramble to exit. A quick kiss goodbye, and then there's a mad dash to catch the bus.

'And, Jack,' their mum calls out as an afterthought, 'Dad will pick you up after hockey training this afternoon. Let Charlie know, too, okay?'

Jack turns around and gives her the thumbs-up sign to let her know that he's onto it.

Once safely on the bus, Jack makes sure his brothers and sisters are all settled before he continues down the aisle where he knows his best friend, Peanut, (a.k.a Charlie), will be sitting. He spots Peanut's head of wavy auburn hair a few seats from the back, throws himself down into the empty seat beside his friend and bumps fists with him. 'Hey, Mum says to tell you that we've got a lift after training this arvo.'

'Thanks, mate. Listen, I've been thinking …' Peanut interrupts him, smiling a mischievous, lop-sided grin.

When this happens, Jack knows that he's up to something. He looks at him with one brow raised.

Peanut motions for Jack to come in closer. He looks around to make sure no one is listening, then lowers his voice. 'Hey, I know someone, who knows someone who can get us stacks of fireworks; you know, the good stuff!' He waits to see Jack's reaction, his eyes gleaming with excitement. 'What d'ya reckon? We'll bring some to camp? The girls will freak out when we let 'em off in their tents in the middle of the night.' Peanut's face beams with all the trouble-making he's imagining.

Jack shakes his head and laughs. 'You're nuts! Can you imagine the crap we'll be in for doing that? You know fireworks are illegal, right?' While Jack explains this obvious flaw in Peanut's twisted plans, he notices a sudden vacant expression on his friend's face—his eyes have glazed over, and his jaw has dropped. He waves his hand in front of Peanut's face, trying to break the trance. 'Oi, are you all right?'

Peanut starts to point past Jack, excitedly, trying to speak, but only managing to stammer unintelligibly.

Jack follows Peanut's line of sight and discovers what has him tongue-tied. He's latched onto a girl crossing the road. And not just any girl; this one's a real stunner—tall and slim, with long, wavy, strawberry-blonde hair.

Jack has never seen her at school before. *She must be new.* You don't not notice someone that pretty. And then, before he realises what's happening, Peanut is tripping over himself to get past him. 'Hey, hold your horses!' Jack cries out.

But Peanut is on a mission. In a mad frenzy, he pushes his way to the front of the bus.

'Ouch, you twit!'

'Hey, watch it!'

'Get off, ya nut!'

'Quit it, Peanut!' Everyone in turn yells out as he bowls them over.

Jack can't miss this. He takes off after him.

Peanut reaches the exit in record time and stumbles down the steps of the now stationary bus. The momentum has him tripping over his huge, size-eleven shoes, and he falls, almost flat on his face, at the feet of this mystery girl.

She recoils at his sudden appearance. Her eyes, big with shock, turn red with rage when she hears the bus full of students howling with laughter at what she must imagine is a cruel joke.

It doesn't help any that Peanut clambers to his feet and stands in front of her with mouth gaping, seemingly groping for something intelligent to say, but only managing to blather. 'Hey, wow! Hi! Geez, um, like, totally wow!'

The kids from the bus burst into hysterics.

The girl retaliates, and slaps Peanut's face. Gobsmacked, he watches in horror as she turns in disgust and marches in the opposite direction. He stands there like a stunned mullet, nursing his burning cheek.

Jack can't hold back from giving him a round of applause. He needs to reward that spectacular performance. What he just witnessed was priceless. 'Oh, man, that was too funny. Go get her, Tiger!' He has all sorts of problems holding back from laughing. 'I'll give it to you, Peanut, that's a different approach. Hey, I might give it a go myself one day … not!'

But Peanut is flying high. 'Oh man, I'm in looove! She's someth'n else, isn't she? Gutsy, too, I like that … it shows character. How old do you think she is? She must be a senior. Mind you, I wouldn't say no to an older woman. Do you think she'll go out with me? Pfft … stupid question; course she will. Why wouldn't she?'

Clearly, Peanut has found his tongue, but now Jack can't find the off-switch to shut him up.

The bell sounds for the start of school.

'Come on, Romeo, let's get you to class.' Jack laughs. 'We can figure out the rest later.'

On their way to roll-call, the boys hi-five and fist-bump several of their mates. Being on the school hockey team that's heading for the state championships makes them quite popular.

The two of them are polar opposites—Jack being the more grounded and level-headed one, while Peanut prides himself on being the class clown. Nevertheless, their friendship is solid.

They tumble into roll-call.

'Calm down, class; the bell has gone,' announces Mr McPhee, their roll-call teacher. 'Everyone, please take your seats.'

'Where to, Sir?' Peanut pipes up, holding up his chair.

Mr McPhee looks at him, momentarily baffled.

'Where d'ya want us to take our seats?'

The class sniggers.

Their teacher tries to hide a smile. 'Okay, I'll pay that, Mr Brown. Now, everyone settle down to roll-call.'

Peanut plonks himself next to Jack.

'Okay, class, before we begin, just a reminder that period six has been cancelled this afternoon for the retreat briefing. As you all know, our trip down the coast to Blue Ridge National Park is fast approaching. Are there any more signed permission forms?'

Jack gets up to join a group of kids making their way to the front of the classroom with their notes. Peanut hands him his to take up, too.

'Sir,' Peanut calls out, 'how come we're going there? Wasn't that the place where those kids vanished a few years ago?'

The class become a little rattled at Peanut's statement. A murmur of anxious discussion resonates around the room.

Mr McPhee struggles to quieten them. 'Thank you for enlightening us, Mr Brown. I'm sure you all have nothing to worry about. The National Park is a huge reserve. Those kids that you're referring to went missing somewhere near there, but in an area away from where we'll be staying. I assure you, the campsite at Hangman's Point is very safe.'

'But, Sir …' Peanut begins to protest.

'Mr Brown, there'll be time to answer your questions this afternoon at the meeting. Now, back to roll-call.'

'But …'

'Right; please answer "present" when you hear your name,' Mr McPhee barrels on. 'Arlington, Ruby …'

'Present,' says a quiet voice from the back of the room.

Everyone turns to see who answered to the unfamiliar name.

Peanut almost falls off his chair. The redhead from this morning is sitting in the back corner, obviously trying to shrink away from the sudden attention.

With the mystery of the missing school children forgotten, Peanut, in his excitement, starts to repeatedly hit Jack on the arm. Jack struggles to protect himself from the increasingly faster and harder thumps.

Mr McPhee looks up from the roll to where the new student sits. 'Good morning, Miss Arlington. It's nice to finally put a face to a name. Class, I expect you all to make your classmate feel welcomed. Okay, now settle down and face the front.' Mr McPhee is once again striving to be heard over the hum of private conversations that've just broken out.

'Hey, I missed it; what's her name again?' Peanut asks.

Jack answers him with a shrug of the shoulder.

Peanut looks around, then leans across to ask the girls next to him. One tells him her name is Ruby.

'Ahh, Ruby!' He sinks into his chair as he repeats her name. His eyes once again glaze over.

Mr McPhee continues with the roll-call. 'Braden, Jack …'

'Here, Sir,' Jack answers.

'Brown, Charlie …'

There's a long pause. No answer comes until Jack nudges Peanut with his elbow.

'Yeah, here, Sir,' he replies absently.

Jack stares at him, shaking his head in disbelief, trying to work out who this stranger is.

Roll-call continues: 'Chen, Kenny …'

'Present,' answers a quiet, self-conscious kid with big, thick, dark-rimmed glasses.

'Darcy-Rutherford, Maxine …'

'It's JUST Darcy!' snaps a small girl from the back of the room.

Clearly unimpressed, Mr McPhee looks over his glasses at her. 'Enough with the attitude, Miss Darcy-

Rutherford! Unless you can provide me with official documentation of this name change, roll-call will remain as is.'

Peanut cowers in his seat. 'She's scary.'

Jack has to agree. She really is something else. He often wonders what's behind that tough exterior. He angles his head a little so he can discreetly take her in. She has, as always, her face done up with dark, heavy makeup. Her blackened hair is tied up in a messy ponytail, and her long fringe obscures her face. She's wearing her usual oversized jumper which is, of course, black.

What's with all the black? Who the hell died? Geez, even her fingernails are painted black!

Just then, as though he's read Jack's mind, their teacher gets up from his desk and walks down the aisle towards her. He then stands over her and asks her to show him her hands. At first, she defiantly whips them under the desk, but then arrogantly places them for him to inspect.

Jack's not sure if he's shocked by that or impressed. Clearly, she's making a stand. He's curious to see what happens next.

'That'll be another lunch-time detention for you Miss Darcy-Rutherford, for your obvious disrespect for school rules.' And with that said, Mr McPhee returns to his desk to complete roll-call in time for the bell.

Maths is scheduled for the first period. Jack and Peanut part ways. It's probably the only class the two boys don't share. Jack is in advanced Maths. For some reason, numbers come naturally to him, so he does well without really trying.

He sits next to Kenny, who's a mathematical whiz kid. In fact, he's a whiz at everything—almost a child-genius. Sure, some of the other kids call Kenny a nerd, but that doesn't faze Jack. They're friends, and Jack looks out for his friends.

Jack then notices Max sitting at the back of the classroom. He does a double-take, surprised she's there. *Has she always been in this class?*

She's on her own, and it hits him suddenly that this is a common thread; she's always alone. *Doesn't she have any friends?* Apart from the times he hears her telling someone off, he can't remember ever seeing her talk to anyone. And for some reason, this strikes a nerve. *Surely she has someone! Who does she hang out with at lunchtimes?* He shakes his head and laughs to himself. *Probably with Mr McPhee.*

Jack doesn't know much about her. She's obviously bright, because she wouldn't be in advanced Maths if she wasn't. He scratches his head. He can't recall if she's in any of his other classes, and he wonders why it's only now that he's picking her up on his radar.

What he realises, and it shocks him to the core to admit it, is that he's curious to know more. Just who is this elusive Max Darcy-Rutherford?

3

WHAT A LOSER!

MAX

It's the last period of the day. Max, along with the rest of the year-ten students, heads for the briefing. She watches some of the girls, bunched in their cliquey groups, giggle and gossip mindlessly as they enthusiastically enter the school hall. There's talk about what to wear at camp and who's bringing what. One girl asks if she should bring her hair straightener; another asks if anyone knows if there's free wi-fi where they're going. One of them is on a mission to get Jack Braden to finally notice her.

'Yay! Retreat. Can't wait!' Max mimics sarcastically.

It surprises her that even the boys appear just as excited. A few of them in front of her jostle to get ahead in the crowd. Peanut is virtually stepping over everyone, vying for some kind of pole-position. His friend, the notable Jack Braden, and Tony Marciano from Ten-F are hot on his heels.

'Oi, Peanut, wait up! Man, he's been disappearing on me all day,' she hears Jack grumble.

'Geez, he's fast! If only he was that quick on the field.' Tony laughs.

'I tell you, as soon as he catches a glimpse of a certain person and her strawberry blond hair, he's a goner.'

'C'mon, hurry up, we need to stick together if we want to be put in the same group.'

Max watches on with morbid curiosity as the two boys catch up to their friend.

'Man, I've never seen you move so fast!' Tony laughs.

Peanut grins. 'Must be the power of looooove.'

Jack shakes his head. 'You know what? You're an idiot!'

Max smirks. *Yeah, I won't argue with that!*

'Okay, Year Ten, let's settle down now; we've a lot to get through this afternoon.' Their year coordinator, Ms Cartwright, commands their attention from the front of the hall.

The group becomes quiet.

'Now, firstly, it goes without saying that consent forms must be signed and handed in if you wish to attend camp. Tomorrow morning is your last chance to return them if you haven't already done so.'

Max sits at the back of the hall. Ms Cartwright going on about the forms, reminds her of the debt she owes Annie. *Shopping! Argh, what a nightmare!* 'But a deal's a deal,' she tells herself.

Ms Cartwright continues, 'We'll be staying at Hangman's Point Campground, Blue Ridge National Park. Information on the campsite is detailed in the parent handout you'll each be taking home at the end of this meeting.'

Max's annoyance escalates as Ms Cartwright continues with the details.

I'm so over this! What a waste of time. What do they think they'll actually achieve by this hippy retreat? A soul-searching journey of discovery? Bonding and reflection are seriously overrated. I should know!

She rolls her eyes as she visualises them all sitting around a campfire, holding hands, a flower in her hair, singing *Kumbaya*. 'And then what? We'll all live happily ever after? Teachers are delusional.'

'... and the lists for your allocated buddy-groups are up on the board behind me, to be viewed after today's meeting,' Ms Cartwright continues. 'We've devised these as a safety precaution. They will assist the teachers in the event of an emergency. Please familiarise yourselves with your team members. Note that the lists are final and non-negotiable.'

'What!' Max jumps up in disgust. *God, they treat us like five-year-olds!* 'We don't even get to choose? Whatever happened to democracy?' she protests loudly.

Everyone turns to stare at her. Max looks imploringly at their vacant expressions. *Come on! Don't let them get away with this. Use your voice! Back me on this one!*

But all she gets is stunned silence.

She's appalled. Not a moan, not a peep of a protest. Nothing! *So that's it? We're going to be dumped into random groups, and you're all okay with that?*

'Non-negotiable, Miss Darcy-Rutherford,' Ms Cartwright repeats.

One by one they turn back to face the front. *Un-be-lievable!* Bitterly disappointed, she plonks herself down again.

The meeting comes to an end. The kids jump up and stampede to the front of the hall, tripping over each other to get to view the lists. Max notices Peanut, streaking ahead, trampling everyone to reach the board in record time, as if his life depended on it.

'What … a … loser! I'll bet you any money I get stuck with an idiot like him.' Unable to stop herself, she continues to watch him, curious to see his reaction to the mandatory grouping. To her shock, he fist-pumps the air and hoots with exhilaration. And then she notices that most of the kids hi-five each other, then laugh and chatter with excitement, clearly okay with what the teachers have done.

She shakes her head. 'Are they nuts?' *Obviously too stupid to be opposed to this totalitarian crap!* She sighs, resigned, and reluctantly drags herself to the back of the dwindling crowd. 'God, I'm dreading to find out who they've lumped me with.'

She then notices some of the kids at the board pointing and laughing at something written there. They immediately stop when they see her and quickly get out of her way.

Yeah, that's right, move it!

They fall back, but linger, gawking at her, clearly waiting for something to happen.

Far out; what's with these morons! She returns their stare with a dagger-sharp glare. Usually this method of confrontation deters them. And it does. They quickly scatter.

She scans the list and her heart suddenly seems to stop.

Oh God, kill me now!

GROUP A:
ARLINGTON, RUBY ELISABETH
BRADEN, JACK WILLIAM

BROWN, CHARLES LINUS
CHEN, KENNY (KEUNG)
DARCY-RUTHERFORD, KATHERINE
MAXINE ELOISE

Max is mortified. Her whole ridiculous name is up there for the entire world to see. And anyone who isn't half blind can see her name transmitting like a beacon, taking up a complete line, screaming 'spoilt rich bitch!'

And she thought the day couldn't get any worse.

4

Toughen Up

Jack

They've just left the meeting and are on their way to hockey training. Jack is making an effort not to laugh. 'Linus?' he teases. 'Are you serious?! No wonder you've kept that one from me. That's gold!'

'Yeah, yeah, whatever. As a kid, Mum had this thing about the comic strip; you know, Charlie Brown, Linus …'

'Your mum is a crack-up. Imagine if she'd called you, Snoopy,' Jack teases, then dives to avoid a punch.

'You're lucky I'm in a good mood, mate, otherwise I might be tempted to flatten you right now.'

But Jack can bet that won't happen because Ruby Arlington's name made it onto their list.

'Hey, what d'ya think about Max being in our

26

group?' Peanut asks, suddenly serious. 'And did you catch that name? Katherine, Maxine, Eloise Darcy-Rutherford. Talk about stuck-up!'

Jack confesses he was just as stumped when he saw it.

'She's weird!' Peanut says in a lowered voice. 'We all heard her in the meeting. What the hell was that all about? You know, I'm not that keen she's in our group. I wish we could swap her with Tony.'

'Well, you know that's not gonna happen.'

'She'd better not stuff up our trip.'

'Stuff up our trip?' Jack laughs at how ridiculous that sounds.

'Mate, don't laugh; I'm serious. I'm telling you; she's psycho!'

'Hey, back up a bit! You can't say stuff like that. You don't even know her.'

'Does anyone really know her? And what about that death-stare? You can't get anywhere near her without copping it. I'm not ashamed to admit it, but I'm a bit of a chicken when it comes to her. I'd rather take on a team of Fijian Islanders in a hockey grand final than bump into her in a dark alley. I've said it before, and I'll say it again, she's scary! I'm telling you; nobody likes her.'

Jack can't argue with that, but he won't ever admit it to anyone. 'I wonder why she's so weird about her name,' he says instead. 'I mean, she always gives old McPhee a hard time about it. Her name's Katherine, just like my sister, Katie. That's a nice name.'

'That's just it, isn't it? It's a "nice" name for a "nice" girl. Problem solved,' Peanut says proudly. 'Anyway, she doesn't look like any Katie I know!' And with that twisted logic, Peanut seems to have confidently justified his argument.

'Hey, but it's great that Kenny's in our group, though,' Jack says. 'I think it'll do him good to hang out with us. It might help him come out of his shell a bit. You know, he's a real interesting kid.'

Peanut's eyes light up—obviously having a lightbulb moment. 'Hey, yeah, awesome! He can help with the fireworks. Imagine the stuff he can get his hands on!'

But Jack isn't making the connection. He looks at Peanut with a please-explain expression on his face.

'What? He's Chinese, isn't he?' Peanut says, clearly offended that Jack can't see the genius in his thinking. 'For someone who's supposed to be so smart, sometimes I wonder about you. The Chinese—' he explains slowly, his hand gesturing for Jack to catch up with his thinking—'they invented fireworks, so … he knows people!'

Jack chokes on a splutter. 'You're kidding me, right? Did you get dropped on your head when you were born or something?'

'Hey, what did I say?!'

'Mate, you can't go saying stuff like that!'

For the first time, Peanut looks a little lost for words, clearly not seeing what Jack is.

'Come on.' Jack laughs at him. 'Let's get you to training. I reckon we need to work on toughening you up a bit.'

'Toughen me up? What for?'

Jack tries to hold back a smirk. 'Mate, you seriously need to man-up. I wouldn't be telling anyone that a girl, who's all of five-foot-nothing, scares the crap out of you.'

That shuts him up, good and proper.

5

First-Aid-Kit on Steroids

Max

Today is day one of retreat week. It's 5 a.m. and Max needs to be at school soon, so she reluctantly drags herself out of bed. She's been lying there for the past hour and a half trying to come up with an excuse to prevent this other kind of nightmare from happening. But she can't put it off any longer.

She stops and studies her reflection in the bathroom mirror, searching for anything that might get her out of going, like a rash or a tumour. But there's nothing, only smudged black eye liner and remnants of yesterday's mascara.

I really should've taken that crap off last night.

She reaches for her wipes. 'Hold on, what's that?' She rubs at her lids with excitement. 'Is that a stye?' She takes a closer look and rubs a little harder, then sits back disappointed. No, she couldn't even conjure up a simple stye. She sighs and makes a note to pack some antibiotic eye drops just in case.

Father would be so proud!

She realises that she's fighting a losing battle and resigns to finishing packing her kit. Her new things are stuffed into the bottom, followed by her regular gear. Max finishes by placing a ghastly pink sweater on top, just in case Annie checks her bag.

On top of the jumper, Max packs her well-equipped first-aid kit. She wasn't joking about the antibiotics. As much as she hates to admit it, Max is a product of two brilliant doctors, so medicine and healing run deep through her veins. That first-aid kit would have any hypochondriac green with envy.

'Sveety, are you up?' Annuska whispers at Max's door.

'I'm almost done, Annie.'

Max opens the door to let her in, then plonks herself back down on her bed, yanking on her Doc Martens.

'Your papa had to go to vork early and asked me to say goodbye.'

Max stops lacing her boots and bites back the

angry reply that she knows she'll regret saying.

'He says to vish you a safe trip, and dhat Mortimer vill take you to school dhis morning.' Mortimer is her father's driver.

'Okay.' Max had no delusions of a teary, father-daughter farewell. But she's a little shocked, and grateful, that he thought to arrange a lift for her. She wasn't looking forward to making her way on her own so early, not with such a heavy backpack.

'I asked your papa if he minded doing us dhis favour.'

Max grits her teeth. 'So much for thinking that the great Professor Rutherford would consider his daughter before his practice for a change,' she grumbles under her breath.

'Vhat, honey? You say it someting?'

Max clamps her lips shut and shakes her head.

Annie's eyes narrow. 'Maxy, vhy are you vearing your old tings?'

Max looks down at her Wolfmother T-shirt and black jeans. 'The new stuff's here, look.' She opens her backpack for Annie to see. 'I figured that we'll be setting up when we get there—you know, putting up our tents, starting up a camp fire, that sort of thing—and I didn't want to get them dirty.'

Annie relaxes. 'Ah! Dat's my sveetheart, alvays being dhe clever one.'

'Come, I have all night been cooking, and now you eat.' Annuska gets up and scurries toward the door. 'Oh,' she cries out, throwing her hands in the air, apparently heartbroken, 'vhat vill you do! Five days vidout eating Annuska's food! Maybe I make fresh Kifli before you go,' she adds, her expression lifting in excitement. 'Dis is good idea, yes? You must eat; you are too shkinny!'

Max watches as she shuffles away, eager to feed her.

She's going to miss her Annie. Tears prickle her eyes as she hoists her kit over her shoulder and reluctantly follows.

6

Touch Down!

Jack

Jack and Peanut have arrived at school already. Peanut is bouncing off the walls, eager to get started. He's pacing back and forth, biting his fingernails.

Jack has never seen him so rattled. 'Mate, what's gotten into you?'

'Hey, it's okay for you, Mr Nothing-Phases-Me!' Peanut snaps. 'You're not the one that needs to make a good impression on the girl of your dreams.'

'Are you still going on about that?'

'For your information, I haven't been able to get anywhere near her. It's like she's got this freaking force field around her. She's impossible. I just want a chance to show her how much of a catch I am.'

Jack laughs.

'Mate, I'm not kidding,' Peanut says seriously. 'Some best friend you are! If you had my back, you'd be using that brain of yours to help me make it happen.'

'Peanut, just be yourself. Anyone who knows you can't help but like you. If she can't see past that stupid first impression, then you've got to ask yourself, is she really worth it?'

Peanut stops to consider this. 'You know something? You're right. Maybe it's her, not me. Yeah, that's it,' he says, instantly relieved. 'What's there not to like? I'm funny, smart, and a legend on the field. What more could a girl want? And to top it off, I'm pretty hot—even if I say so myself.'

'So why are you chasing her? Sounds like you've already found your perfect match. Why not ask yourself out?' Jack sniggers. But he sobers up quickly when he sees that Peanut isn't seeing the funny side of his joke. 'Look.' He sighs. 'If you want my advice, you've gotta ease it up a bit; you know, don't lay it on so thick. You can't go shoving crap like that at them. Girls hate that sort of thing.'

Peanut's face lights up. 'Yeah, yeah, now you're talking! That sounds like a plan. Hey, how come you know so much about this stuff?'

Jack shrugs, at a loss to understand why Peanut can't see that it's a no-brainer. He watches the cogwheels turning as Peanut plans his next move.

'Yep, okay. Now I've got it. I'll back off a little, like you said, then slowly inject a bit of my legendary charm to hook her in. And then, boom, she won't know what hit her!'

Jack splutters on a laugh. 'Um, mate, back it up a bit more and you're there.'

The school drop-off zone becomes congested with parents and kids saying their goodbyes. Teachers give orders to the rabble, trying to stream-line the process of getting the trip underway. They take the roll, mark off names and students begin to board the buses.

Jack, sitting with his friends, waits patiently for his turn. His eyes light up when he notices a wicked black Aston Martin Rapide roll into the drop-off zone. And his curiosity spikes when he sees that it's Max's ride. He also notices that nobody gets out of the car to give her a hug goodbye, and for some reason that disturbs him. He watches her struggle to hoist her heavy backpack over her shoulders—the sight belies her small frame. She is, as always, dressed in black. Her dark hair is tucked under a baseball cap with the rim worn low, obscuring her face. She keeps her head down, avoiding any eye contact.

Jack's relief at seeing Max turn up surprises him. He shakes his head, trying to make some sense of this, then he notices the new girl, Ruby, arrive and join the queue getting onto the buses. Peanut is right; he owes his friend some back-up where she's concerned, so he spends a moment watching her, trying to work her out. He senses something strange about her, but he's not quite sure what it is. Unlike Max, Ruby's gaze goes everywhere, constantly on the lookout, analysing everyone. She appears to be on high alert, her body responding to every sound and movement. It's exhausting just watching her. No wonder Peanut hasn't had any luck getting near her. She's unapproachable.

He and Tony join Peanut as he jumps in line a few kids behind Ruby. They hang back a bit with Peanut. He's trying to act cool and clearly hoping to get a spot near her.

Ruby moves to the back of the bus, sits down and places a large bag next to her, openly warning anyone thinking about sitting there that the seat is taken and they should move on. But Peanut tries his luck, anyway, gesturing to ask her if he can sit there. She all but growls at him, and turns away, giving him a silent but definitive, no. Peanut reluctantly takes the seat behind her, looking very much dejected, and Tony sits next to him.

As Jack is about to join his friends, Mr McPhee calls down the bus, 'Two to a seat. Miss Arlington, please remove your bag for Mr Braden.'

Ruby reluctantly gathers her things, and Jack unwillingly sits there. He can almost hear the explosion of silent death threats aimed at him from behind, and can feel the daggers thrown at the back of his head. He knows exactly what's going on in Peanut's mind—he's cursing Jack for supposedly making a move on his girl.

As the bus pulls out of the school, Jack takes a moment to work out what to do next. He avoids looking behind him. He'll give Peanut some time to calm down.

He then braces himself, determined to make the most of this unexpected turn of events. 'Hi, I'm Jack,' he says to her casually, then smiles. Ruby hesitantly returns the smile. He's a little shocked to see that the 'force field' she radiates is actually penetrable. He hears a half-suppressed moan from Peanut's direction. Ignoring it, and with a new-found confidence, he pushes on. 'So … are you new to the area?'

Ruby looks at him, her expression guarded. 'No, I've just changed schools.'

'How come you left?'

Her eyes turn to slits. 'That's none of your business!'

And just like that, his window of opportunity slams shut. She turns away in disgust, and makes a show of sitting as far away from him as possible.

Shocked by her outburst, Jack starts to backpedal. 'Hey, I didn't mean anything by it. I was just making small talk.'

But Ruby moves even further away from him.

He tries again. 'I just thought we'd get to know each other, you know, since we're in the same buddy group an' all.'

Ruby looks at him from the corner of her eye, taking a moment to size him up. Eventually, she sits back in her seat, looking less tense.

Jack feels this is a prompt for him to continue. 'Okay, let's try again. We'll each say something random about ourselves. I'll go first.'

At this, Ruby seems to relax a bit more.

Jack tries not to think about what's going through Peanut's head right now. He'll deal with him later. He begins by talking about his family. Then strategically moves the conversation to his love for hockey, thinking this would be a good opportunity to introduce her to his hockey mates, who are of course, sitting right behind them.

At the mention of hockey, Ruby's face shows a spark of interest. 'Hey, I played hockey at my old school.'

'Get out! No way! Were you any good?'

Ruby turns to face him, excitement gleaming in her eyes. 'Well, I don't mean to brag, but my team won the state cup last year. How good is your team?'

Jack can't believe his luck. *Don't stuff it up now!* 'We hold our own. We're pretty strong in our attack.'

'Yeah? I play up front. What's your position?'

'Centre-mid ...' Jack hesitates, taking a moment to psych himself up for what he's about to do next. His heart is racing, and his palms have become sweaty. He takes a deep breath to calm his nerves. *Okay, here goes. Play it cool, you only get one chance at getting this right!* 'Um, hey, have you met my mates? They're on the team, and both play up front, too.' Jack braces himself as he twists in his seat and motions for Ruby to look behind.

Clearly having forgotten who was sitting there, Ruby enthusiastically turns to meet Jack's friends. She stops cold when her eyes land on Peanut. 'You!' she hisses before turning her back to him again.

'Hey, what'd I just do?' Peanut protests wounded. 'You're not still going on about the other day, are ya? Give me a break!' His face turns red, and, as Jack knows him so well, he can see that Peanut's about to explode. 'Look, I just wanted to meet you, and okay, I stuffed it up, I'm sorry, all right? The kids on the bus know what a clown I am, and were laughing at me ... ME, not you! I've been trying to apologise, but you're as impossible to corner as a circular room.' His freckles blend into his flushed skin as he lashes out some more. 'How about you build a bridge and get over it! And besides—'

Ruby's unexpected burst of laughter stops him. She turns around. 'As impossible to corner as a circular room? … Build a bridge and get over it?'

Peanut is momentarily gobsmacked by her reaction, but quickly recovers, 'So ya like them? Hang on, I've got better ones!' The floodgates to Peanut's repertoire of famous one-liners opens.

Touch down!

In all his life, Jack has never been so happy to hear Peanut's ridiculous ranting. The ice has melted; the shield has been penetrated. His job is done. His best mate thinks he's a genius, and now knows he wasn't trying to crack onto his girl. He can let go of that breath he was holding, sit back and enjoy the banter between them.

They're like two peas in a pod.

While Peanut, Tony and Ruby talk hockey tactics, Jack glances around the bus looking for the other two group buddies, Kenny and Max. Even though he's still a little apprehensive about Max, he figures that he might try to get everyone together now—saves any awkwardness later. He spots them up the front, so he musters up his new-found courage and approaches her.

7

Retes to the Rescue

MAX

Max is reading her book and notices that Jack, one of the boys in her buddy group, has asked the person next to her to swap seats with him. Her nervous neighbour doesn't need too much prompting to vacate.

He then stands there, waiting. She does her best to ignore him, hoping he'll go away. But to her dread, he doesn't. After what seems like a moment's hesitation, he casually plonks himself down and half turns to face Kenny who's sitting in the seat behind.

'Hi, guys,' he says enthusiastically. 'Hey, I was wondering if you wanted to join us at the back? You know, get the group together before we reach camp?'

Max rolls her eyes and inwardly groans. *Really! Just who does this guy think he is? "Mr in charge of the social committee" or something?* She continues to read.

'Might be fun,' he persists.

She lets out an annoyed sigh and scowls at him, hoping he'll take a hint.

'So what d'ya reckon?' he asks again, completely undeterred.

This shocks her to the core. *That death-stare never fails!*

Kenny stands, looking eager and ready.

They both stare at her, waiting.

What? No way!

Kenny smiles at her in an encouraging way.

And just like that, she finds herself backed into a corner. *Arghhh, great! Thanks heaps, traitor!* She anxiously racks her brain, trying to come up with an excuse to get out of going … but nothing. 'What, me? Um, I don't know.' She looks at Kenny's hopeful face. 'Well, I suppose. Maybe. What the heck; okay.' *Why prolong the inevitable, right? Just rip off the Band-Aid quickly.*

The boys head off.

Max's heart pounds erratically. The thought of hanging out with her peers is making her palms sweat, and her stomach threatens to hurl. This is exactly what she's been trying to avoid the last three years. But there's no time for a panic attack. She reins in her insecurities, puts on her mask of indifference and braces herself.

She focuses on the one consolation in this whole messed up predicament—Kenny. Although at this moment, he's a renegade rat, she's somewhat grateful that he's in the same buddy group. She shares most of her classes with Kenny, and she rates him. And he seems to like Jack, so she figures he can't be all that bad.

But even knowing this, Jack still makes her a little uneasy for reasons she can't explain. She's caught him staring at her at times. Hiding behind her long fringe gives her a pretty good vantage to observe what's going on around her—more than people realise. There's nothing offensive or aggressive about the way he looks at her, it just makes her feel weird.

Max tries to shake off these confusing thoughts.

She closes her book, grabs her things and grudgingly heads to the back of the bus. The new girl is already getting acquainted with Peanut and Tony. As she approaches, Tony gets up to let Kenny have his seat while he goes in pursuit of his own buddy-group. Jack offers Max his spot next to Ruby, while he stands, making the introductions.

Ruby withdraws at the sight of her. It's such an

obvious change to the small group, that it has Jack and Peanut exchange questioning looks.

Thankfully, Peanut cracks a joke, breaking the awkward silence. 'Hey, did you hear the one about the two cows in the field? Well,' he begins, 'one cow says to the other, "I'm really worried about catching that mad cow's disease." "I'm not," says the other. "Why wouldn't you be worried?" asks the first. "Because I'm a chicken!"'

It's such a lame joke, that everyone can't help but laugh. Even Kenny who can be super shy doesn't hold back a chuckle.

'I wonder what the camp food will be like, I'm starving!' Peanut says randomly.

'You had a huge breakfast only an hour ago, mate,' Jack reminds him.

'Yeah, but that was an hour ago. I'm a growing boy; I need food!'

'You'd do well at my place,' Max mumbles quietly to herself.

'Why is that?' Jack asks.

Max almost dies on the spot. She didn't think anyone heard her. *Crap! What am I supposed to do? Oh God, and now they're all looking at me!* There's no getting out of it; she knows she's got to say something. 'Um, well, Annie, our cook, loves to feed everyone. The second she gets a whiff that you're hungry, she drags you to the kitchen and stuffs you until you're ready to puke,' she blathers.

They stare in awkward silence.

Max squirms in her seat. 'Um, so … I guess that's why,' she adds, mortified that she blabbed so much. Her heart races, and she begins to feel really uncomfortable with their staring. *Geez, what did I say?* 'Um, she even made me pack a stack of food for the trip. I've got some Retes if you want to try some,' she offers quietly.

'Whoa! Back up a sec, let me get this straight,' Peanut says. 'You've got a cook? Man, you guys must be loaded!'

Max groans and sits a little more rigid in her seat, inwardly cursing herself for letting this bit of information slip. Above anything, she hates people knowing anything about her. She, of her own doing, has just revealed something very private. *What- an -idiot! And what the hell am I supposed to say now?*

'And you've got food?' Peanut says, suddenly more interested in being fed.

Max grabs that life-line. She dives into her bag and produces Annie's Retes for everyone to share.

'Oh, man; I'm in heaven!' Peanut moans after the first bite. 'This Annie of yours, does she do home delivery?'

Everyone laughs at this, setting that fumbled

declaration right. Even Ruby's coldness towards her seems to have thawed a little.

Max withdraws from the group and takes the opportunity to watch the other four as they interact. Peanut, clearly is the larrikin of the group, quick with the jokes and one-liners, and if she's not mistaken, he's doing his best to impress the other female member. Ruby on the other hand, although laughing at his jokes, seems less keen. She's working hard at establishing a friend-zone with him.

Max notices that Ruby seems a lot more comfortable talking to the boys than she does her. She makes very little eye contact and avoids initiating conversation. It might be the whole 'black' thing that's intimidating. Max isn't too sure, but there's something about Ruby Arlington that prickles at her senses. She holds herself very guarded, especially, Max realises, around her.

She watches as Kenny laughs at Peanut's shenanigans. She's never seen him so relaxed. It makes her feel good to see him having a good time. Kenny too often has his head stuck in a book.

Max allows herself to look at Jack. Something about him makes her withdraw deeper. She can't put her finger on it, but with him, more so than with the others, she finds herself holding back from engaging. He laughs at his friend's bad jokes. He's protective of a kid who's otherwise an easy target for bullying. He goes out of his way to look out for the new kid on the block, and now he's trying to befriend the school freak. Nothing seems to faze him.

Max then realises that he's smiling at her. She's been so caught up with her own thoughts that she was oblivious to what was happening around her. Her breath hitches, and she can feel her face flush with embarrassment. His staring makes her feel uncomfortable. She quickly looks away and tries to focus on what's being said within the group.

Peanut and Kenny laugh at something Jack said, and Ruby nods in agreement. But for the life of her, Max can't follow any of it. She tries to shake the fog from her head, and with determined interest, attempts to study the dynamics within the group.

All eyes are on Jack. And with sudden clarity, she sees that they all gravitate towards him, like he's the magnetic centre of this thrown together, eclectic group. And like them, although trying to resist it, Max finds herself being drawn to him too.

8

SUCK IT UP PRINCESS

JACK

Jack sits back in his seat, his spirits high. The camping trip has started off well. He looks happily out the window, noticing the perfect weather. The trip was nearly cancelled due to several days of torrential rain in the area, but today, there's not a cloud in sight, and better still, a perfect forecast for the rest of the week. It being a little cooler at night this time of the year, he's looking forward to sitting around the warmth of a campfire at the end of the day.

Just after 10:00 a.m., the buses turn into the car park at Hangman's Point. Jack shivers a little as they alight from the buses. The air is fresh this morning.

'Man, it's cold!' Peanut whines, rubbing his arms to stir up some heat.

Jack laughs. 'Suck it up, princess.' He grabs his backpack and joins the others as they follow the teachers heading towards the campsite. The track is well established, so the trek is easy enough. They cross a wooden bridge that bypasses what must normally be a small stream, but since the recent wet weather, it's become more like a rambling creek.

The sounds of the forest are peaceful and calming. Jack loves hearing the birds calling out to each other from the treetops, and the unseen animals scurrying in the bushes—most likely some lizards being disturbed while trying to warm themselves on the rocks.

The temperature drops noticeably the deeper they go into the forest. The sunlight barely filters through the canopy of the trees, making it considerably darker at certain places. But up ahead a clearing is bathed in sunlight, creating a golden oasis.

Jack takes in the campsite and nods his approval. Toilet and shower facilities border the space, and there's a covered barbeque and eating area.

Max comes to an abrupt halt ahead of him. 'Home sweet home,' she moans sarcastically. Clearly, she's seeing things differently to him.

'Not a fan?'

She studies him for a few seconds before replying. 'It's my first time camping. You?'

'Me?' he asks, surprised that they're having an

actual conversation. 'We camp all the time. Dad calls it walkabout—his way of paying homage to Mum's Aboriginal heritage. We've been to some amazing places all over Australia. Sometimes we rough it, where there's just a hole in the ground for your business, and the creek for a wash. Other times we've stayed in cabins with all the mod cons. It's an adventure no matter where we end up. I love it.'

Ruby approaches with the others. 'How about you, Ruby?' Jack asks. 'Ever been camping?'

'It's really not my thing. I'm not good with creepy crawlies.'

'Fear not, sweet maiden! I'm here to protect you,' Peanut says gallantly, moving closer to her.

Ruby retreats a few steps, puts her hands up in a defensive gesture and laughs off his advances, saying that she can look after herself. 'Thank you, anyway.'

Ms Cartwright announces that they'll stop to prepare morning tea before they set up their tents. Everyone helps. Some clear and clean the sheltered eating area, while others go back to the buses with the teachers and help carry the food hampers and boxes of necessities to the campsite.

Soon the horde of hungry teenagers are tucking into lamingtons and scones loaded with jam and cream. Hot chocolates and teas hit the spot, washing it all down.

'Man, I'm stuffed,' Peanut moans, rubbing his belly.

'Anyone would think you haven't eaten for days, the way you inhaled those lamingtons,' Jack teases.

'It's the quick or the dead. You'll learn real fast, my friend, that nice guys finish last. You snooze, you lose.'

'All right already. Enough with the clichés; I get it.' Jack chuckles, then leans in and says quietly, 'And next time, Sir Galahad, you might want to offer that the girls go first, instead of bowling them over to get there before them. Might make a good impression on you-know-who.'

Mr McPhee clears his voice, trying to get everyone's attention. 'Right, thank you, Year Ten for helping with the morning tea. Over the next few days we'll all need to chip in for everything to run smoothly. Both Ms Cartwright and I have organised a roster for the daily chores. I'll have it pinned up on the notice board over to the left where you can all refer to it later. There you'll also find the daily-activities timetable. If we can keep you all in your buddy-groups for these activities, it will simplify things from the teacher's point of view. Now, boys will set up over there on the left, and girls, to the right. Once you've all pitched your tents, we'll get started with the campfire.'

Jack and Peanut are done in no time, so they go to help Kenny who's finding it a challenge. Jack looks across the way to see how the girls are coping. They haven't started yet, and both appear a little uncomfortable around each other.

'Stop worrying about them, mate, and give us a hand,' Peanut yells. 'They'll work it out.'

Jack hopes so, for all their sakes.

9

MEAN GIRLS

MAX

'Hey, Ruby, I think I need some help,' Max says reluctantly. She figures she can't go the whole week without at least trying to make some kind of connection with the girl. 'I won't lie, I'm completely hopeless when it comes to this sort of thing.'

Ruby looks at her, eyes wide like a deer in the headlights. After a moment she replies, 'Um, me too.'

'My tent hasn't seen the outside of its packaging since it left the factory.'

Ruby laughs. Something in that admission appears to have softened her aversion to Max. 'Maybe we can set up together.'

Max, true to her word, is hopeless with her tent, so Ruby steps in to help, and together they manage to get both tents set up next to each other.

'You know, you're really not that scary,' Ruby acknowledges once they're done. 'I'll admit, I didn't know how to take you at first, but you're not so bad, just different.'

Max looks at her with her brows raised. *Wow, don't hold back! Tell me what you really think!*

'Oh, don't get me wrong—different in a good way,' Ruby adds quickly. 'You've probably noticed that I don't warm to people easily, but with you, it's not so difficult somehow.'

Max is floored by Ruby's frankness. She studies the girl for a moment and is surprised that, for the first time in a long time, she can feel a connection too. 'Um … thanks; I guess.' Max smiles tentatively. 'Yeah, I'm not that scary. I just like keeping to myself, that's all. And being like this,' she gestures to her appearance, 'keeps people away.'

'You know, I kind'a get it.'

'What's your story? Does moving schools have anything to do with your trust issues?'

'Wow, how did you pick that?' Ruby says, surprised. 'But you're right, that's pretty much it.'

Max can see Ruby contemplating how much she should reveal. It looks like Max isn't the only one keeping her private life guarded. She may just have a lot more in common with Ruby than she originally thought.

'Um, yeah, it's got everything to do with it,' Ruby reveals. 'You see, I had a tough time at my last school because of a stupid mistake I made … anyway, to cut a long story short, that slip-up made me a target, and girls, who I thought were my friends, surprise, surprise, turned out not to be. It got so bad my parents had to pull me out.'

Ruby appears to get lost in her thoughts. After a moment she takes a deep breath and lets it out slowly. 'It turned my world upside down. From then on I learnt to keep my mouth shut, to trust no one, and to always look over my shoulder.'

What the hell happened to her? It distresses Max to see her so affected, but she doesn't let on how disturbed her words make her feel. 'Well, that kind'a sucks. Yeah, girls can be pretty mean.'

Ruby discretely turns away and swipes at a wayward tear.

Max softens towards her. 'You know something, I'm glad we're here together.'

Ruby smiles.

They then head towards the crowd forming around the campfire site. Max can see some of the kids gathering twigs and bits of wood for the fire later tonight. She notices Jack, Peanut and Kenny amongst those kids and offers to help.

10

There's no 'I' in Team

Jack

Jack sees that the girls have made a connection. Both girls look a lot more relaxed with each other. Ruby's guard seems to have come down and she has Max laughing at something she's just said.

'She's actually quite pretty when she smiles,' he says to himself.

Peanut, overhearing the comment, challenges him. 'Pretty? Mate, she's not just pretty, she's hot! And if I catch you checking out my girl again, I might have to fight you for her. You know, I did see her first ...'

'Not Ruby, Max!' Jack says defensively.

His remark floors Peanut. 'What? Who? Max?'

Now Jack regrets saying anything. 'Look, forget it; I don't even know where that came from.'

Peanut puts his hand on Jack's forehead. 'Nope, no fever. Can't be heat stroke, we haven't been in the sun. Maybe it's dehydration! Here, you should have some water.'

'Knock it off, Peanut! I was just saying.' Jack smacks Peanut's hand away.

'Yeah, you were just saying, only a few days ago, how scary she is.'

'Hey! I think I remember you calling her scary, not me!' Jack reminds him. 'Anyway, just let it go, will ya, I don't even know why I said it.'

'I know, right? Max pretty? Now Ruby is what ya call pretty. She's got hair that's like, wow! And her smile, Oh my God. Man, did ya see her smiling at me on the bus? And she laughs at my jokes. She just gets me. And to top it off, she plays hockey! She's the full package!'

'Okay, Peanut, I get that you're into her. So don't stress about me getting any ideas. She's a nice girl an' all, but like you said, you saw her first.'

Thankfully, Jack sees Kenny coming, and he's only too keen for a diversion. 'Hey, Kenny, what's that you've got there?'

'I came across a box full of steel-wool when we

were cleaning the barbecues earlier. You know it's flammable. We can use it as tinder to help start the fire later.'

'Far out; I did not know that. You're a fountain of knowledge, Kenny,' Jack says in awe. 'That's pretty cool.'

'Nah, it's nothing,' he says modestly. 'I just like to read up on stuff that interests me, that's all. And because of the camp, I've been researching a few things.'

Kenny's eagerness to learn blows Jack away. 'We'll take your lead, then.'

Jack and Peanut help Kenny prepare what's necessary to get the fire started. The other kids gather enough kindling to last the rest of the week, and soon the fire-pit is ready and waiting to be lit later when the sun goes down.

But now, it's time for lunch. While some of the groups get busy preparing the barbeque sausage sizzle, Jack and his group sit out and take a break.

Unable to sit still for too long, Peanut jumps up and wanders over to the notice board. 'Sick! We're playing beach volleyball after lunch.',

'Awesome!' Jack jumps up to check the schedule.

'How good are you at volleyball?' Peanut asks Ruby as she joins the boys. 'I guess with your height, you'd be a natural. So you can partner with me, then.'

He turns and looks down at Max, who's standing on the other side of him, and frowns.

'Hey, what's that look supposed to mean?' she snaps.

Peanut suddenly appears very uncomfortable. He's dug himself into a hole, and Jack's going to enjoy seeing how he'll get himself out of it. He looks on as Max prepares to make Peanut regret that look he gave her, and the insinuation that came with it.

'You shouldn't judge a book by its cover!' she blasts him. 'I might not be able to spike a ball over the net, but I've been known to set up a decent volley. And my serves aren't too bad, either. Don't underestimate me,' she warns. 'All this pent-up aggression has to come out somewhere!'

Jack snorts and tries to hold back from laughing out loud. 'You go, girl!' he utters under his breath with new-found admiration.

Peanut didn't see that coming. It takes him a few seconds to fight back. 'Hey, what did I say? Geez a person can't even look at someone sideways without them biting their head off!'

Max and Ruby look at each other, then burst out laughing.

'Oh my God, that's classic!' Ruby wipes the tears from her eyes. 'The look on your face, Peanut, is priceless. You idiot, Max was only stirring. But she's right, you really shouldn't be that quick to judge a person. As it happens, I've never played, but I'm willing to give it a crack … partner!'

Peanut squirms. It's obvious he's reconsidering his hasty offer.

Jack knows that when it comes to competitiveness, Peanut takes the cake. 'Boy, you've really done it this time!' he says with a grin.

Once lunch is over and the clean-up's done, the groups head down to the beach. The kids sit around the court, eager to start. They take off their shoes and sink their toes into the warm, inviting sand.

'Before we start,' Ms Cartwright says, 'we're changing the rules a little. There'll be unlimited interchange so everyone has a turn, and we'll be playing doubles. One set, first to twenty-one. The best team from each round will play each other in the finals later in the week. Okay, let's get started. Who wants to go first?'

Peanut stands up like a shot, and before they know it, their team has been nominated.

'What?' Max says in surprise, then adds sarcastically, 'I guess a democratic vote is out of the question, then.'

Peanut appears to have caught Ms Cartwright off guard, too. 'Well, okay. I guess we've got our first group, then. What's your team called, Peanut?'

'The Immortals!' he tells her excitedly.

'Arghhhh! Clearly another unanimous decision.' Max says dryly. 'Peanut, will you quit doing that!'

Jack laughs quietly to himself, appreciating Max's dead-pan wit. 'Yeah, he takes a bit of getting used to. Too much adrenaline, I think.'

'Okay, who's up against the Immortals?' Ms Cartwright continues.

A group of five kids come out of a quick team discussion and volunteer themselves.

Max turns on Peanut. 'That's how it's done! We're a team, we should be making these decisions together. I vote we have a group leader. What do you think?'

Peanut volunteers immediately, but Max challenges him with her own nomination. 'All those in favour of Jack being our group leader, raise your hands.'

Three hands shoot up, and before Jack has time to even blink, the decision is made.

'The majority rules,' Max says. 'Jack, it is.'

Jack isn't the only one left speechless. Peanut clearly wasn't expecting the blindside. His impression of a fish out of water is priceless.

Ms Cartwright calls up the teams.

Jack snaps to attention and has his group huddle together to discuss strategies. He suggests that Peanut and Kenny play first. Kenny's a fair table-tennis player, so Jack figures he might be okay with volleyball. Peanut is a gun when it comes to any sports, so by starting with two strong players, Jack hopes that they'll be able to intimidate the other team.

Two of the other side's tallest players walk onto the court; both look like they've played before. They win the coin toss and serve first. The ball flies over the net. Peanut sets the ball to Kenny, who jumps up and spikes the ball over to take the first point.

'Yes!' Jack punches the air with excitement.

'Whooohooo!' the girls both cheer.

Peanut and Kenny high-five each other and move to take the next serve.

The other team come back fighting, and the teams soon equalise. Jack keeps the Immortals on a constant rotation. He's a little surprised to see that Max is as good as she said she was. Like Peanut, he had his doubts because of her height. But during the game, she proves time and time again that she does, in fact, have a terrific serve and can set the ball up beautifully. Ruby loses them a few opportunities in the beginning but comes back firing.

The opposition proves competitive, but it soon becomes clear that their first two players are the only ones that can play. As a result, they minimise interchange and eventually fall apart from exhaustion.

In the end, Peanut and Ruby win them the first

round. Tired but elated, the team sit back and enjoy watching the rest of the groups compete.

The afternoon passes quickly with much laughter and chatter. Most of the kids aren't too competitive, but have fun, providing comic relief for everyone.

II

KUMBAYA

MAX

Dinner preparations are underway. While some of the kids busy themselves with the campfire, Max and her group help prepare dinner. Tonight, they're having spaghetti with meatballs.

Fifteen minutes into the preparation, Peanut starts to whine. 'C'mon; we must've made a million of these already. This is taking forever. I'm exhausted. And when can we eat? I'm starving!'

Max chuckles. 'You're kidding, right? We've only just started. These things take time. You obviously don't help much at home.'

'Me? Help with the cooking? No way. Mum does that.'

'Not fair; I always have to help,' Ruby moans.

'You guys sound like it's a big deal. I always help, Annie. She's the best. I've learnt so much from her.'

'So you're a budding chef, then?' Kenny asks, surprised.

'Oh, I don't know about that, but I do love cooking.'

'What do you want to do when you leave school?' he asks, appearing genuinely interested.

'Who? Me?' He catches Max off guard. 'Um, well, I don't know …' She squirms a little, not feeling comfortable talking so openly. 'Maybe … I'll give medicine a go.' Talking about herself proves to be harder than she imagined it to be. She feels her face burning up with embarrassment.

'Wow, I did not see that coming,' Ruby says.

Apparently neither did anyone else. Everyone stops, all eyes on her.

Max's palms start to sweat from all the sudden attention. She takes a deep breath to calm her nerves, and then, finally, she pushes past that wall she's been hiding behind, 'Yeah, I know, right?'

'You wanna be a doctor?' Peanut laughs.

His reaction offends her. 'Hey, don't make it sound like it's the most ridiculous thing you've ever heard,' she snaps at him.

Peanut recoils at the attack.

'Max, I've no doubt you'll get there,' Kenny says

in her defence. 'You're always getting good grades in class.'

'Thanks, Kenny,' she says meekly. But she doesn't let Peanut's ribbing deter her from going on. 'You see, Mum and Dad both studied medicine, so it kind of runs through my veins—excuse the pun.' She half-laughs at her attempt at humour. 'My mother was a doctor, and my father is a professor of Ophthalmology.'

'A professor of what?' Peanut blurts out.

Max rolls her eyes. 'Well, in simple terms,' she taunts him, 'he's an eye specialist.'

'Max, what do you mean, your mum "was" a doctor?' Jack asks.

Max freezes at the unexpected question. She's said too much. She's let slip something that's been private for a long time. But now she can't take it back. Panic sets in.

Jack frowns. 'Hey, sorry, just tell me to mind my own business.'

But it's not Jack's fault; he couldn't have known. She needs to stop freaking out every time someone asks her an innocent question about her mum. It's time to stop hiding in her past and knock down those walls.

She's about to take that giant leap of faith when she recalls something she'd sneered at the other day—*sitting around a camp fire, all holding hands and singing "Kumbaya"* … She laughs at herself. 'Geez, I didn't even make it to the campfire.' The look of confusion on everyone's face amuses her further. 'It's just something in my head. But, hey, I'm not nuts, okay?' she adds quickly. 'I'll explain that one later. Right now I think I need to clear up a few things.'

She keeps her eyes down, focused on her boots, then takes a deep breath and allows herself to freefall. 'Mum died when I was twelve.' She doesn't stop to gauge anyone's reaction. 'Dr Grace Maxine Darcy was beautiful and super smart. We had a happy family— Mum, Dad and me. We were the three musketeers.

'It was a car accident. Mum was hit by a drunk-driver, and, in a nutshell, she died and he lived. Mum had just dropped me off at school. They say I'm lucky to be alive, but I guess that's debatable.' Tears sting her eyes—the pain just as raw today as it was three and a half years ago. She chances a look at the team's reaction and forces a smile, then lets out a deep breath and shrugs her shoulders, unable to say another word.

Jack pulls her into an embrace. He doesn't say a word; he doesn't need to. She tries to push out of his arms, but he tightens his hold. Slowly, one by one, the others join him in a big group hug. Max feels her defences wavering, and eventually they crumble.

After a long while, with smudged mascara and a few black tears trailing down her cheeks, she looks up into the faces of her friends. There's no overbearing sympathy in their eyes, just understanding. And for that she will be eternally grateful.

12

PEANUT'S PRIORITIES

JACK

Jack wakes, excited about the day ahead. The teachers have planned a treasure hunt. But it's not the day's activity that has him feeling uplifted, but last night's revelation, which explained so much. He was right; there is a lot more to Max than what they see. Her wounds run deep. And he's starting to understand why she is the way she is.

He can't imagine a life without his mother. She's the glue that keeps his family together. Which leads him to suspect something else. Last night, Jack picked up on a few things that Max said, or rather, didn't say. Does saying, 'We *had* a happy family,' mean that now she doesn't? His thoughts go back to yesterday morning when he saw how alone she was.

Does her aversion to being called Darcy-Rutherford have anything to do with this hunch?

Shaking his head free from this current train of thought, Jack finishes packing his backpack with a few necessities, then joins the rest of his team ready for breakfast.

'Man, what is it with this place? I'm starving again,' Peanut says.

Jack grins. 'Must be the fresh air. I'm surprised you're hungry at all after the number of meatballs you scoffed down last night.'

'Oh man, they were soooo good. Quit it, Jack, my mouth's watering. I wonder what's for breakfast. Mmm, smells like bacon and eggs. Cool, I'm in heaven!'

After breakfast, the groups assemble around last night's campfire, eager to begin the treasure hunt.

'Okay students, are your teams ready?' Mr McPhee asks as he hands out the check-lists. 'In a few minutes, you'll be setting out into the forest looking to mark off certain items on this list. In order to avoid teams bunching up, each group has a different starting point. The team with the most questions checked, in the quickest time, wins.'

Jack and the group scan the check-list, looking at what they need to search for.

Mr McPhee gives the signal to go, and there's a

chaotic scramble as the teams disperse into the forest looking to solve their first clue.

'Okay, guys, we need to start on task fifteen,' Ruby says.

#15: The one that laughs last, laughs longest. Find the tree that has our feathered friend protecting her nest. What makes this tree so special?

Peanut grimaces. 'What? How the heck are we supposed to find that? Man; talk about trying to find a needle in a haystack! How about we skip to the next clue?'

'For crying out loud! Will you be quiet!' Ruby yells at him. 'How is anyone supposed to hear anything with you shooting your mouth off? It's not rocket science, you know. We just have to listen out for a Kookaburra's cackle.'

'Talk about stating the obvious, princess,' Peanut snaps back. 'I mean, Kookaburra's are a dime a dozen in a forest like this, how do we know which one has a nest?'

'Look for the tallest trees,' Kenny says, 'somewhere near running water. That's where they prefer to nest.'

Ruby and Peanut look at him like he's just grown another head.

'What? I can't help knowing things.'

They step back, startled by Kenny's outburst.

'Good on ya, mate,' Jack says with a grin. 'You

tell 'em!'

'Hey, you've impressed me!' Max says with admiration.

Kenny relaxes and chuckles to himself.

Jack navigates the group towards the stream they crossed yesterday on their way to the campsite. At the stream, they climb higher in search of taller trees, then they stop and stand quietly, listening.

'Imagine if we came across a dead body out here,' Peanut says randomly.

'Why would you even say something like that?' Ruby says in exasperation.

'Well, look at this place. You could hide anything in here, and nobody would ever find it. What about those kids that went missing a few years ago?'

'You're not gonna start on that again, are you?' Jack warns.

'Why not? Crusty McPhee gave me the brush off the other day, remember? Beats me why they've picked here, of all places, to take a bunch of kids for camp.'

'I meant to ask you about that,' Ruby says. 'I don't remember what happened. It was a while ago, right?'

'Five years ago,' Jack says. 'Four kids disappeared one day. They just vanished off the face of the earth, never to be seen again.'

Ruby rubs her arms. 'Wow, that gives me the

creeps.'

Max shivers a little, too. 'How awful. What do you suppose happened?'

'Do you think they were kidnapped?' Kenny asks.

'Could've. Who knows,' Peanut says. 'Imagine, someone might be lurking in the bushes right now, waiting to pounce on some poor unsuspecting sucker lost in the forest. You'd better stick close to me, Rubes. I'd hate to turn around and find that you've vanished. Now that'd just suck.'

'Enough with the spooky stories, guys, we're supposed to be looking for kookaburras,' Max reminds them.

Amongst the twitter and chirping of the forest birds, they finally hear the recognisable cackle they're after.

Peanut's eyes light up. 'Bingo!'

'They're not that close. We'd better pick up the pace,' Jack suggests. 'You don't want us coming last because of your stupid ghost stories, do you?'

Peanut takes off as if he's competing in a cross-country track event.

'Make sure the bogeyman doesn't get you?' Ruby calls out after him, her eyes twinkling.

They quicken their step.

They climb higher up the wall of the gully, keeping the stream in their sights. Wet, slippery slopes make it difficult to scale, and they're off any discernible track, making it worse. But they persevere and continue through the dense foliage.

Jack notices that Max is having a little trouble keeping up. She trips over vines and exposed tree roots, and struggles to get through the thick vegetation. He debates whether he should offer to help. Not wanting to tick her off by inadvertently insinuating that she's not handling it, he decides not to—against his better judgement. He keeps going, but a sudden yelp from behind makes him turn. He finds Max lying flat on her back, jeans muddied, cap askew, and a look of defeat plastered on her face.

He takes the few steps required to slide down to her. 'You okay? Look, how about I carry your backpack for a while, just until we reach the top.' He picks up her bag and realises why she's having so much trouble. 'Bloody hell, what've you got in here? This must weigh more than you do.'

She grimaces. 'Um, yeah, that. I kind of packed some food and my first-aid kit.'

'Oi, what's keeping you two?' Peanut bellows from further up the slope. 'We're almost at the top.'

'Max packed half a pharmacy and three-quarters of a pantry in her backpack! I'm giving her a hand. We'll be up there in a minute,' Jack calls up.

Peanut's abrupt appearance down the slope,

makes Max yelp in surprise.

'Did someone mention food? Don't worry, I've got this.' Peanut takes her bag. 'Man, what's in here? This weight had better be the snacks and not your first-aid kit!' he grumbles. 'Don't anybody say I never pull my weight around here.'

As he makes his way back up the slope, he calls back to Jack, 'You, my friend, can be the knight in shining armour, and help the damsel in distress.' And then he disappears up the incline as fast as he appeared.

Jack pulls Max up off the muddy ground. 'Don't worry about him. He's an idiot.' Together they climb to the top, where everyone has stopped to catch their breath and take a quick drink. Max picks up her backpack from where Peanut left it and struggles to manoeuvre it onto her back again.

'How about I hold onto this for a little while longer?' Jack says, gesturing to Max's backpack.

She smiles in appreciation.

He hoists it over his shoulder where it hangs lopsided next to his own day pack, then he sets off with the others following.

They walk along the lip of the ravine, and Jack notices that the earth under their feet is unstable. The recent heavy rain has made this section particularly precarious. Cautiously he leads on, ready to warn of areas that appear dubious. But before Jack can yell out the danger, a huge portion of the earth under their feet gives way, and all five of them fall on an avalanche of rocks, dirt, rubble and debris.

Jack grabs hold of the strap of Max's pack but it flies from his hand as he tumbles downward, his body beaten by everything in its course. Images whoosh past him as he rolls on and on. And suddenly he's airborne. His arms and legs scramble to secure contact with anything solid. Then oomph! He hits the ground with such an impact that it jars his leg. A loud crack, and sudden excruciating pain, renders him momentarily gasping for air.

He lets out a tortured scream, and then clenches his teeth to stop himself crying out again. The pain is unbearable; he can hardly breathe. He tries looking around to see if anyone else is hurt, but the shooting pain in his leg puts an immediate halt to that idea. He can't move.

'Peanut! Anyone! I need help!' There's no reply. He starts to panic. 'Guys, is everyone okay?' He takes in a deep breath, trying to calm himself. He needs to find the others.

All of a sudden, an overwhelming blanket of warmth envelopes him, and for some unknown reason, he feels an odd sense of calmness and reassurance. The tension he held while gritting his teeth slowly releases.

A great spark of heat flickers from within his core and radiates to the rest of his body, dissipating the pain. Cautiously he sits up and leans on his elbows to look at his injured leg. He gasps in horror. His right lower leg has snapped in two, the shin bone protruding at an unnatural angle. Amazingly, the skin isn't broken, but what's more amazing is that an injury like that should be unbearably agonising, but it's not.

'What the …?'

The sound of scrambling, fast approaching, distracts him.

13

WAR PAINT AND WARRIORS

MAX

'Jack, are you alright? Oh my God, your leg!' Max stares at his broken leg in disbelief. But she quickly snaps out of it and manages to tear her eyes away from his injury long enough to look around for her backpack. She hopes she has something in her first aid kit to help him. Strangely, though, she realises, he's not showing any signs of distress.

'I don't get it; aren't you in pain?' She shakes her head, trying to unscramble her addled brain. 'Don't be ridiculous, of course he is, just look at his leg,' she argues with herself before turning away to look for her bag. 'Hang on a sec. I might have something

79

that'll help.'

'Don't worry about it,' he says. 'Where are the others? You'd better find them; they might be worse.'

She turns back. 'But what about you?'

'I'm okay; I promise.'

She hesitates and studies his face. 'It's shock. It has to be.'

'Max, just find the others. Please!'

She realises there's no sense in arguing. 'Okay, I'll be right back. Don't move!' She runs down the slope and spots Ruby racing towards her. She looks a little worse for wear, but otherwise okay.

'Max, help!' she yells. 'Kenny's down there, but he's not moving!'

Max takes off after her.

She finds Kenny lying motionless beside a large boulder. She falls to his side and checks for a pulse. 'Thank God he's alive.' Then she searches for broken bones. There's nothing obvious, but she notices a lot of blood on the back of his head. She places her hands gently around the wound, feeling for any breaks there. 'He's got concussion,' she says with confidence.

'How the heck do you know that?'

She experiences a moment of disorientation, as if her world tilts on its axis. 'Wow, that's weird. I, I don't know, but somehow I just do.'

She continues to examine Kenny's head, and an

unfamiliar tingling in her fingers alerts her to the overwhelming heat radiating from within her gut and extending to her finger tips.

Kenny stirs. His eyes open. He looks up at her and smiles. 'Hey, guys, why the long faces?'

'Kenny, are you okay?' Ruby cries. 'We thought you were dead!'

Kenny lifts himself up and sits, looking dazed.

'How's your head?' Max asks, confused over what just happened but relieved to see he's conscious. 'You really cracked it on that rock. There was stacks of blood, but I think the bleeding's stopped now.'

'Oh man, that was just too freaky,' he says to himself, tentatively touching the back of his head. 'Nah, I must've been dreaming.'

Ruby frowns. 'What do you mean? What happened?'

He laughs. 'You won't believe it, but there was this place. It was white and fluffy like a cloud. Then out of nowhere, I saw this brilliant white light. I became so mesmerised by it, like it was calling me. But before I could go to it, something distracted me. I felt this warmth wrap around my head. It was so peaceful and safe, and then I opened my eyes and saw you, Max.'

Did Kenny almost die?

Emotion overwhelms Max. Her eyes sting with the threat of tears. To stop herself from crying, she looks away and shakes the disturbing thought from her head. She can't let herself believe that.

'Come on; we need to find the others.' Ruby's anxious voice snaps Max back to what's happening.

'Crap! Jack! I've left him up the hill with a broken leg.'

'A what?' Ruby and Kenny exclaim.

'Ruby, can you help Kenny on your own? I need to check on Jack.'

She scrambles back up the incline and finds him lying where she'd left him. 'Ruby and Kenny are okay, but I haven't found Peanut.'

She kneels besides him and looks again at his broken leg. 'How is it you're not screaming in agony?'

'I dunno. It hurts, but, for some reason, I can cope. We'd better go look for Peanut.' He tries to get up, but she places a hand on his chest, forcing him back down.

'Where the hell do you think you're going? You've got a broken leg for crying out loud. Don't move!'

Jack holds up his hands. 'Okay, I get it. Relax already!'

'Look, when Ruby and Kenny get here, we'll send them to look for him. And then we'll work out what to do about your leg.'

She wonders how on earth they're going to get Jack up and mobile. 'Wait, I've got some analgesics for the pain.' She looks around for her backpack and spots it a short distance away. A few moments later, she's handing him some pills.

'Really, I'm okay, I don't need them …' he begins, but stops when she gives him a pointed look. He doesn't argue anymore, and takes them.

She notices his leg swelling and turning blue. She needs to do something quickly; but what? Instinctively she places her hands on the break. Heat radiates from her belly and spreads to her finger tips causing them to tingle in that strange unnatural way again.

What the hell's that all about?

Jack moans.

She jerks her hands back in fright, and immediately notices that the tingling stops.

'No, it's okay.' His reassurance distracts her from her bafflement. 'There's this weird sensation coming from your hands,' he explains. 'I mean good weird. I can't explain it, but it feels right.'

For some inexplicable reason, it feels right to Max, too.

Ruby and Kenny turn up and gasp in horror when they see the state of Jack's leg.

Max dares to continue, trying to keep her focus on what's happening with her hands. Heat continues to radiate from her core, and, miraculously, the swelling starts to subside, and the colour in his leg returns. Then right before their eyes, the broken bone clicks into place.

Kenny's jaw drops. 'What the hell just happened?'

'It must be that weird, tingly heat coming from your hands, Max!' Jack says.

The others stare at her in shock, unable to utter a single word. And Max is just as stunned as they are.

'Jack, what you're describing—you know, about the heat,' Kenny says hesitantly, 'I felt the same thing when Max fixed my head.'

Jack's look of confusion has Ruby quick to explain what happened to Kenny earlier.

But Max isn't ready to take the credit for his miraculous recovery. 'I don't think it was anything I did, Ruby; he just snapped out of it, that's all.'

'But look at what just happened! How do you explain that?'

She has no answers. What they witnessed is beyond anything that makes any sense to her at all. That said, she's still curious to see if what she's done has made any difference. So, with Kenny's help, she raises Jack to his feet.

He tests his leg by bearing a little weight on it, and then he takes a step. 'Is this for real?' he says, his expression ecstatic. 'It's fixed!'

Suddenly they hear something thrashing through

the forest, coming towards them at speed from several directions. They look around, on high alert, but no direction is free of the threat. Running isn't an option. Max's heart is pounding as whatever's about to attack grows rapidly nearer. She huddles in closer to the others and braces herself.

What happens next is beyond what any of them could've ever imagined. From the depths of the woods, six massive, battle-ready, fearsome-looking warriors appear around them. They look ancient with horned helmets on their heads and their faces painted with war paint. Animal skins drape their huge, muscular bodies, and they look murderous.

Max whips her head around, searching for a way to escape, but there's no way out; they're trapped.

Each one of these warriors looks as dangerous and frightening as the other. They drag in huge mouthfuls of air, their chests heaving from the run, menace clear in their dark, penetrating gazes.

The biggest one advances towards them. He's as wide as he is tall. His bare chest shows scars of past battles. His eyes are cold and hostile, and his nostrils flare like a just-raced thoroughbred. His presence, almost regal, commands respect.

'We are the Gate Keepers,' he says in a deep gravelly voice with a thick accent she can't place. 'We protect the passages to our world. You are trespassing and thus forbidden to venture further. You must state your intentions before our leaders, The Ancients. If you resist, you will be killed.'

14

'What The...?'

Peanut

The ground beneath Peanut's feet gives way, and before he knows what's happening, he's tumbling towards the bottom of the ravine. His body cops a beating from the bushes and rocks as he accelerates downward. Finally, he smacks into a tree, knocking the wind out of him.

Disorientated, his head spinning, he struggles to get up. And when he does, what he sees leads him to think he must've hit his head in the fall. First Jack, then Max, followed by Ruby, and finally Kenny all vanish before his very eyes. One second, he can see them tumbling down the slope, the next, they're gone.

Impossible!

He shakes his head and looks again. But there's not a single sign of them. He races after them, not losing sight of where they disappeared, thinking he must be mistaken. But he's not. He comes to an abrupt halt, gasping with disbelief at what he sees.

'What the …?'

A shimmering, ghost-like, diaphanous curtain floats before him. He can barely see it, but it's definitely there, suspended in front of him, seemingly untethered—a whisper of a veil.

He walks cautiously around it and discovers that he can see through to the other side from every vantage. He's pretty sure he saw the others tumble through this apparition. No, he's absolutely, one-hundred percent positive. But how can this be?

'Jack, mate, can you hear me?' he calls through the veil, feeling a little stupid doing so. 'Nah, surely, they're hiding from me.'

Questioning what he saw, he searches the forest, looking for any movement or sound that indicates they're playing a trick on him. But he finds nothing. He's completely alone.

He tracks the projection of the avalanche of rubble and sees that it ends at the foot of this enigmatic spectre. There's no other explanation for it. *They've vanished! They've fallen through this 'thing' to God knows where.*

Peanut calls out in a sudden frenzy, 'Jack! Jack! Are you okay? Ruby! Max! Kenny! Guys, answer me! Crap, what do I do?' He begins to panic. 'Think. Damn it! Why can't I think?'

But he realises he's going nowhere by freaking out.

'Okay, okay. Calm down. What would Jack do? Think! Think "help," think "phone." Phone! That's it; I'll call for help.' He pats down his clothes in search of it, but comes up empty. 'Where is it? I had it a minute ago!'

He scans the area, thinking it must've fallen out of his pocket in the tumble down the slope. Kicking and clawing at the fallen debris around him reveals nothing, but he spots his backpack, runs to it and yanks at it, hoping that the phone is concealed beneath it … but, nothing. He searches the area again, and then, to his relief, spots it a few metres up the slope. He sprints to it, slides to a stop and groans when he sees that it's smashed, crushed beyond repair.

'No, no, no, no, no! This cannot be happening!' He's very close to having a melt-down, but the reality is that his friends might need him. So he takes in a few deep breaths and channels composure. 'Okay, the phone-option's out. You've gotta think of something else.'

He wanders around aimlessly, tapping his

forehead to prompt a solution.

Do I go for help? That's an idea. But how long will it take? They might be hurt on the other side of this 'thing' and need me now. And if I leave, how am I supposed to find it again? I can barely see it as it is, and I'm standing right in front of it! And will it still be here when I get back?

He's suddenly not so keen on that option.

Or do I chance it? Do I just go through, find them, and bring them back? But what if we can't get back? And what if they're dead? Geez! What if it kills me, too? Oh crap; I can't do this. I need Jack. He'd know what to do.

His thoughts ping around in his head. He starts to hyperventilate, then doubles over, trying to slow his breathing. Deep down he knows what he needs to do. He looks at the veil waving before him, beckoning him to enter. His friends are missing on the other side of this ghostly veil. He has no other choice.

Despite his apprehension, he approaches it, shuts his eyes tight, says a quiet prayer, and then steps forward, through and into the unknown.

15

SOMEONE'S IDEA OF A BAD JOKE?

JACK

Jack looks on in disbelief at the scene before him. They're surrounded, covered from every angle. His senses are on overdrive, and he searches frantically for a possible escape, ready to make a run for it any chance he gets.

Just beyond the warriors in front of him, he sees something that makes him wonder if his eyes are playing tricks on him. The air behind the menacing men begins to waver and take on a shimmering form. And then, to his bewilderment, Peanut appears out of thin air. Jack needs to blink and look twice to believe what he's seeing. Peanut, with his eyes closed, has just stumbled through this apparition.

The commotion he makes draws the Gate Keepers' attention. 'Seize him!' the head guard commands.

In that split second, several things happen: Peanut's eyes pop open; he realises the danger and makes a run for it; and the gate keepers, en masse, take chase.

Jack sees their chance to escape. 'Get the hell out of here!' he yells.

In a burst of confusion, he, Kenny, Max and Ruby dash off in the opposite direction and disappear into the depths of the forest.

'Imbeciles! They are escaping!'

Jack barrels through the forest, trying to keep everyone in sight. Peanut has half a chance to evade them because of his speed, but Jack isn't confident about the others. Max has a troll-of-a-guard hard on her tail. He can only hope that her small frame will allow her to duck and weave through the forest to get away. He catches a flash of long red hair over to his left. Hopefully, Ruby is using her hockey skills to avoid capture, too. But Kenny isn't so fast, and with two of them on him, he has little hope of escape.

Jack is powerless to help him, because right now he needs to save himself. He's got one of the meanest looking apes he's ever seen breathing down his neck. The adrenalin in his veins pushes him to his limits, and then suddenly those limits unleash. An intense heat from somewhere deep in his gut ignites and radiates throughout his body. He has no idea why, but the heat reassures him and gives him strength. His heart pumps, his gaze darts in every direction, taking everything in, and his legs carry him over vines and tree roots with unexpected ease. That burst of energy pushes him to fight back, to get away.

But a whip cracks and binds his ankles. He jerks to a stop, but his momentum propels him face-first onto the muddy forest floor, halting his escape.

'Got him!' his captor yells, then he drags Jack by the feet back to the head guard.

Jack recovers from the rough treatment enough to push up on his elbows and see that the others have been caught, too. A quick assessment reveals that no one is seriously hurt. Peanut has a gash to his face. Ruby has blood in her hair. Max looks a little dishevelled and scratched but okay. Kenny's shirt is ripped open. He looks terrified but thankfully unharmed.

'You are spirited; that much I will grant you,' the head Gate Keeper says. 'The Ancients will be pleased to learn of this. Your courage will be better served in the arena, I think. But enough! We have wasted precious time; the Ancients are waiting. Artemius, bind their wrists,' he commands. 'Dareios, you will lead, with Miltiades. Kallius and Acacius you will flank the formation while Artemius and I will hold up at the rear.'

The one called Artemius, Jack's captor, immediately takes to the task given to him. Jack looks at each of his friends and tries to relay to them that everything will be all right if they just do as they're told. Thankfully, they nod their understanding.

With their hands literally and metaphorically tied, and the guards in position, the formation moves forward. A low blanket of fog settles around them, which prevents them seeing more than a few metres ahead, but they walk on.

Jack tries to make sense of what's happening. This place doesn't look anything like the forest they were just in. Everything's different, and the eeriness has nothing to do with the fog. The trees are huge—taller, straighter, wider, and nothing like anything he's ever seen. *There's definitely no scribbly gums or kookaburras in this forest!*

Could they've gone back in time? The idea is pretty far-fetched, but what other explanation is there? The men's unusual names, and the strange way they speak makes him think he's not far off the mark with that theory. They dress like ancient warriors, and the guard spoke of 'The Ancients'. *Who the heck are they? And what did he mean by 'better served in the arena'?* Jack's heart pounds faster as his imagination runs wild. *Maybe it's all a prank, someone's idea of a bad joke.* But, somehow, he doesn't think so.

Did he hit his head in the fall? Surely, he'd know it if he had. Or maybe it's just a bad dream. But the tight rope binding his wrists together, cutting into his flesh, tells him that it's all too real—very real.

Jack's mind races. He can't understand any of it, but he knows this much: they're nowhere near home.

They tread toward the unknown, through an unfamiliar environment with people that can, and probably will, hurt them. Still, even knowing all of this, Jack continues to feel unusually composed. He can't understand it, but he's overwhelmed with a feeling of calm.

As they walk, he catches some of the conversation behind him. What he hears is enough to make him question his mental stability. He falls back a little to close the distance between him and the speakers.

'Artemius, can you sense their strengths?' asks the head Gate Keeper. 'The one you took chase on, what power has he?'

Power?

'I cannot be certain, Herodus, but I felt his confidence begin to soar moments before his capture. I had to act quickly before I lost him.'

'As did I. The tall one is gifted with speed, but

hear this; he also has the ability to vanish!'

'No!'

'Yes. As Pius is our Ruler, he began to phase on me. This, we have not witnessed in some time. Of course, he was oblivious to it in the confusion of the chase, so for now we are safe. But remain vigilant, Artemius; he could prove to be troublesome. And what of the others?'

'The female with the fiery hair challenged me. As I tethered her wrists, she repeatedly repelled my efforts with a poorly formed shield. This of course will be of use to them in the challenges if ever it is mastered. As for the smaller female and the Mongol, I cannot say. Their auras did not reveal anything of substance.'

Jack struggles to believe what he's hearing. *Vanish? Shield? What the hell are they talking about? What? They think we've got some kind of super-powers? As if!*

But then he considers the way Max mended his broken leg. Nothing can explain what happened there—no normal explanation, anyway. And then there's the matter of the pain, or—more to the point—the lack of it. He shakes his head. He's just too bamboozled to make sense of any of it.

Jack is so lost in his thoughts that he doesn't realise they've come to a halt. He looks up, and what he sees only adds to his bewilderment. They've arrived at what appears to be an ancient fortress. The walls are so high that it's impossible to see what lies beyond. Jack shares looks of amazement and confusion with the others, but they have no chance to speak—even if they could find words.

The gate keepers march them across a lowered drawbridge, past a heavily guarded archway, and into a large, oval-shaped arena surrounded by tiered, elevated seating—much like an Ancient Roman open amphitheatre.

Jack is gobsmacked, the whole thing looks surreal, like a set from a gladiator movie. Up high, at the far end of the arena, sit a panel of five antiquated men wearing golden crowns and ornate white gowns. They appear deep in discussion.

These must be their rulers. The Ancients.

When the warriors and their captives approach, the rulers' conversation ceases, and they turn to look over the newcomers. The gate keepers advance and bow low on bended knee with their right hand fisted across their chest.

'What have you brought for us, Herodus?' asks one of them.

'My Lords, we have been presented with five new Innocents.'

This news rouses all five, and they share puzzled glances.

'At last, one of our gateways has provided for us!' The man—Jack assumes he's the leader—claps his hands together with satisfaction. 'And yet still nothing from the other?'

'I fear not, My Lord.'

'So be it. We must rejoice in what we are given. Pray tell us, what of their skills?' he asks with eagerness. 'No, wait, perhaps not. It may prove quite entertaining to discover such intricacies for ourselves. Do you agree?' He turns to acknowledge his peers, who concur, nodding with excitement. 'Too much time has passed since the gateways have made us any offerings,' he continues. 'Let us savour it. Our champions grow weary. They hunger for a challenge. Herodus, what of the adversaries? I trust that you have imprisoned those remaining from the previous tournament?'

'My Lord, four from South Africa survived.'

'Ah, an uneven battle. Alas, but that cannot be helped,' he says indifferently.

'I will prepare them at your will.' Herodus awaits his instructions.

'With this appeal, we shall commence the games on the eventide of the full moon. And as is customary, a task will be presented with each new day. At the conclusion of the fifth challenge, the team that dominates will meet with our own champions to fight for their freedom.' He turns to his peers. 'Is this agreed?'

The panel of leaders nod their assent.

At their dismissal, the gate keepers bow to their leaders, then round up their captives and march them towards an entrance under the tiered seating. This access leads to various other passageways and chambers hidden behind heavily fortified doors. They walk deeper under the arena stadium, where the temperature noticeably drops, and the air becomes thick and stale with humidity. Wall sconces, holding ancient torches, provide just enough lighting to allow a safe passage.

The guards eventually stop in front of a door locked with heavy bolts. One of them opens the door and instructs them to enter the room. Jack goes inside first and sees a small barred window letting in a little light and some welcome fresh air. On the floor lie a few hessian sacks over straw. There's nothing more.

'Be warned, there is no escape,' the guard cautions them. 'Any attempt will lead to your certain death. You will remain here until summoned. And if you conduct yourselves well, you will be granted short visits to the outer garden, where again, you will quickly realise that there are no means of leaving. The fortress walls are impossible to scale.' And with that said, he leaves and the door is bolted shut.

For a moment, the five friends stare at each other, not daring to speak.

Peanut breaks the silence. 'What's going on here?'

And then all hell breaks loose, each of them screaming over the other in a confused panic.

Jack tries to settle them so they can try to make some sense of this madness. 'Guys, listen. Hang on. One at a time. Peanut, shut up for a sec. Ruby, quit your yelling …' He's getting nowhere, fast. So he lets out an ear-piercing whistle, so shrill that it commands immediate attention and brings blessed silence. 'Now look, I know we've all got a million things to say, but come on guys, one at a time.' All eyes rest on Jack. 'Okay, firstly, has anyone got anything?'

Once again, the floodgates break, and everyone trips over each other to be heard. Jack shuts them up again, and then, before anyone gets a chance, Kenny puts forward his thinking. 'Guys, listen. I know that this might sound crazy, but my best guess is we've entered another dimension and have travelled back in time.' He looks at his friends with bright eyes, clearly thrilled that he's come up with something tangible.

Wow! Jack gets excited, too. His earlier thoughts weren't so weird after all.

Kenny continues, 'I've read something about the existence of these gateways, or portals, that connect two places through time and space.'

Ruby starts laughing. 'Might sound crazy? Kenny, that *is* crazy!'

'No; listen,' he says, 'just hear me out! Let's look at what we've got here. We're definitely not in the national park anymore—that's obvious—and it seems like we're not even in the twenty-first century anymore, either. These guys don't talk like we do. Their words are almost old English. And just look at what they're wearing. They're draped in animal skins and have horned helmets for crying out loud. They look like Vikings, right out of the tenth century. And what about the buildings? You don't see fortresses and these kinds of arenas nowadays; we're talking early AD here. It's like we're back in ancient Rome. I'm willing to bet that they've seen their fair share of gladiatorial battles in their time. And what about their names? Herodus, Artemius, Dareios Miltiades, Kallius, Acacius, Pius—they sound like ancient Greek names. It's like we've fallen into this eclectic, thrown together, timeless world.'

'Whoa!' Peanut cries. 'Kenny, mate, hold your horses! How ...? What ...?' He waves his hands in front of himself, clearly dumbfounded, searching for the right comment. 'Man, you're just a freak! I mean, how the hell do you know so much about all this stuff?'

'Peanut!' Jack yells at him, offended for Kenny.

'How about using some tact?'

Kenny's face turns as red as a tomato. He looks down at his feet with obvious embarrassment. 'I, I don't know,' he mumbles. 'I just do.'

'Kenny, just ignore that idiot,' Jack tells him. 'For what it's worth, I reckon you might be onto something there. As mad as it seems, maybe we have gone back in time.'

'Now hang on a sec, Jack, I wasn't having a go at Kenny,' Peanut says to his defence. 'I was just stumped with how smart he is, that's all. What he just said; it kind'a explains a lot of stuff for me, too, especially about the portal. Man, when I saw you guys vanish through that weird curtain "thing," I thought I was going nuts. Kenny, your take on what's going on here—gateways and different dimensions—it makes sense.'

'That's what I'm talking about, a parallel universe!' Kenny's earlier enthusiasm returns.

Jack nods. As unreal as it might seem, Kenny's theory answers a lot of their questions. 'Okay, so we've fallen through this portal and landed in this weird ancient world,' he says slowly as he tries to get his thoughts together. 'Now, hear me out for a sec, before I say out loud what I'm thinking, for it to make any sense, I've got to tell you what I overheard the guards discussing.'

He begins by relaying to Peanut what happened with Max and his broken leg, and then he tells them all what the guards said as they walked. He finishes up with his own theory that they've all, somehow, got superhuman powers now.

'Whaaaat!' Peanut shakes his head slowly and stares at him like he's cracked. 'The parallel universe theory, I get, but Max being able to fix broken bones, and all that other crap? Mate, I really think you've hit your head. That's demented!'

'Hey, that's a low blow.' Jack's pride is wounded. 'And what would you know? You weren't even there when it happened, and you didn't hear what the guards said, so how about you put a muzzle on it and just hear me out!'

Peanut starts to laugh. 'Oh my God, you're serious!' He turns to Max. 'Hey, Max, have you got anything in that first-aid kit of yours for this loony? I think he's a sausage short of a fry-up. Mate, I'm seriously worried about you. You call *me* nuts. But you, my friend, take the cake.'

'But—'

'Listen,' he interrupts, suddenly serious, 'don't you think I would've noticed myself going invisible? I can tell you, one-hundred percent, that did not happen!'

'Um, Peanut,' Max says tentatively, 'I think Jack's

got a point. I can't explain what happened with his leg, but it's true, it was broken, and somehow I fixed it.'

'Same thing happened with Kenny,' Ruby adds.

But Peanut isn't buying any of it.

'Look, it's just a theory,' Jack snaps. 'Take it or leave it. But I'm not gonna waste any more time arguing over it. We've got to move on and talk about these challenges that they were going on about—something about a face-off with some South Africans. And it's gonna happen soon. Can anyone remember what they said about the moon?'

'They said the first challenge was going to be on the eventide to the full moon,' Kenny answers. 'Eventide is another word for dusk or nightfall, and the next full moon will be …' He hesitates a moment to calculate it. 'In two days.'

'What?' Peanut says, completely flabbergasted. 'How the heck did you work that out?'

'Whoa!' Kenny stops and steadies himself. 'Now I'm freaking out. That's so weird. I've got no idea how I knew that.'

They're all stunned by his confession.

What's going on here?

'Oh my God!' Max's eyes gleam with excitement.

It looks like she's hatching a theory of her own.

'Kenny, how big "exactly" is the moon?' she asks.

Peanut chuckles. 'Max, are you alright? What's with the random pop quiz? I don't get your point? And come on, I know he's a brainiac and everything, but how's he supposed to know that?'

'Watch, this might just prove something.' She smiles encouragement at Kenny.

For a moment it looks as if Max's question has thrown him, but then he blurts out the answer as if he's always known it. 'The moon's mean radius is 1,737.5 kilometres, therefore 3,475 kilometres in diameter. Its equatorial circumference is 10,917 kilometres ...' Kenny clamps his hands over his mouth, his eyes wide with alarm.

Everyone stares at each other, staggered—everyone, that is, except for Max.

'Now do you see my point?' Max says, clearly thrilled with her discovery. 'Jack is right, we do have super-powers, and yours, Kenny, is knowledge!' Her excitement fizzles when she sees everyone's blank expressions. 'Look, it's obvious. I don't know how or why, but somehow, by entering this dimension, our natural abilities become modified. We become better at what we're already good at.'

It takes a moment for this to sink in, but Jack starts to see where she's coming from. Everyone else, however, stares at her like she's lost it.

'Can't you see?' she tries again. 'Kenny's naturally

smart, so it goes without saying that here he turns into a human Google. Whereas I'm good at anything medical, which explains why I was able to fix Jack's leg. And Jack, you've got this uncanny way of not letting too much faze you. That's why you could cope with the pain when you broke your leg.'

Max continues like a runaway train, 'Peanut, I've heard Jack complain that you're always disappearing on him, so it makes sense that you've got the power to vanish. Believe it or not, what Jack heard the guards say is probably right. And Ruby, that thing about a shield, well, you know yourself that you've had your guard up lately. Wow, I bet you can produce a force field. How cool.'

'No way!' Peanut's eyes grow even wider. 'You mean I can vanish? Majorly awesome! I've always wanted to do that.'

The sudden sound of the bolt releasing the chamber door snaps the friends back to reality. They brace themselves for whatever's about to enter.

16

TROTTER SOUP

MAX

The heavy door opens. Max's heart jumps to her throat as adrenalin races through her veins. She grabs Ruby's hand and backs them up against the furthest wall. Jack stands protectively in front of them, seemingly ready to attack. Peanut and Kenny do the same.

A huge man, carrying an enormous vat, enters. The stench makes Max block her nose to stop herself from throwing up. She can't tell if the smell's coming from the container or him. Another man follows him in. He's bald and carries a big basket under each arm.

Both men wear dirty white tunics splattered with something that looks horribly like blood, as if they've just come from a murder scene. The larger of the two stands well over six-foot tall and must weigh at least two-hundred kilograms. His long, dirty hair falls over his face, obscuring his eyes, and the end of his long beard hangs into the vat he's carrying. His hands, and up to his elbows, are filthy, as if he's had them deep within some kind of muck—probably the contents of said vat.

The other man is, by comparison, smaller, but he's still large, and the scariest looking guy Max has ever seen. One of his eyes is completely white, obviously blind, and a huge, angry looking scar runs from the top of his forehead, across the other side of his face and down to his chin—as if a machete had slashed his face.

'The Ancients have sent food,' the bald man tells them. 'We have prepared a delicacy for you—Melas Zomos.' He motions to the cask. 'The baskets are filled with bread, honey, dried figs and nuts. You will need your strength come the full moon. Now you eat.' With that said, the men leave, and the door is once again bolted shut.

The five friends stare at the offerings, then look at each other.

'Kenny, what's Melas Zomos?' Max isn't sure she really wants to hear the answer, but she's curious to test her theory.

Kenny puts his hand to his mouth as if he's going

to be sick. 'Um … are you sure you want to know?' His screwed-up face tells Max she's not going to like what he has to say. 'You know what?' he continues, 'all of a sudden I'm not so keen on having super powers.' He laughs without humour. 'But because you asked and for some bizarre reason I find I need to answer it, Melas Zomos is a meal favoured by the Spartans, back in the times of ancient Greece, around 400BC. It means "black soup," and, it's made from …' He gulps. 'Pigs' feet, blood, salt and vinegar.'

'I think I'm going to be sick!' Ruby clamps her hands over her mouth.

'And that's their idea of a delicacy?' Peanut exclaims. 'What are they trying to do? Kill us?'

'Remind me to think twice before asking you anything next time, Kenny,' Max says, regretting her impulse to ask.

Jacks covers the vat with the lid from the basket in an attempt to smother the stench, and moves it as far away from them as possible. 'I think we'll all give the blood soup a miss.'

Peanut gawks at Jack, clearly surprised at seeing him do this. 'Man, you made that look too easy. How heavy was that?'

Jack shrugs, unfazed.

Peanut then grabs Max's backpack. 'Hey, Max, got anything left over in this kit of yours?'

'Oh yeah! Thank God for Annie.' Max hands out what she has. 'You know, sooner or later we're going to have to get used to whatever they bring us.'

'I can tell you right now, starving or not, there's no way in hell I'm gonna start eating that crap!' Peanut protests.

'Look, let's face it, we might be here for a while,' Max says to them, then realises that's a very real possibility. 'If we lose these challenges, it might be that we never leave.'

'Never leave?' Ruby cries out in a panic.

Peanut stares at Max in horror. 'What? They can't do that!'

'Peanut,' Kenny says, 'they can do whatever they want. They're calling the shots.'

'Hey, let's just back it up a sec,' Jack says. 'You're forgetting that we've got superpowers now. We just need to learn how to use them, and then we can get the hell out of here.'

This manages to calm them down somewhat.

'Just imagine, Ruby with her awesome shield, and Peanut with his invisibility,' he continues. 'They won't know what's hit them. Guys, we can do this. Let's try to keep it together. Kenny, you said the full moon is in two days; that means we've got a bit of time to work at this. We'll win these stupid challenges so we can go home. Okay?'

Jack's pep talk soothes Max, and her insecurities disappear. All doubt vanishes, and her thinking becomes confident and clear. And, if she's not mistaken, she's not the only one feeling it. She looks around and senses tranquillity amongst them—a peaceful, embracing feeling of invincibility. She's almost certain that Jack tapped into his super-power, and what they're feeling now is the result.

With a new-found belief that everything will be okay, they sit and make the most of the situation. Thankfully the food baskets, along with Max's stash, provides them with something to eat. That no one will eat the contents of the vat is a definite foregone conclusion.

Later on, the guards return to take them outside. They're marched down a few passageways to a heavy iron gate that opens to a large garden. Max breathes in the freshness of the forest and looks around. As far as she can see, the fortress walls enclose the area. As in the forest, the trees here are huge and tall, and the vegetation lush and dense. It feels good to be out of the stale chamber.

'There is no escaping,' the guard again warns them. 'You will find a small lake beyond, which provides fresh water. But beware, the garden is not yours alone.' He then turns and leaves.

'What's that supposed to mean?' Ruby asks in a

whisper, her eyes unnaturally wide. 'Do you suppose there're wild animals in here?'

They all remain perfectly still, listening for any discernible sounds. They hear nothing but the peacefulness of the garden.

'Okay, let's make a pact,' Max suggests. 'We stick together at all times.'

'Agreed.'

They set off to explore, moving together.

'Will ya get a load of those walls?' Peanut exclaims once they come into view. 'They definitely look more impressive from the inside.'

'They've warned us twice that there's no way out of here,' Jack says, 'and going by how high they are, I can see why. I was kind a hoping that we'd somehow find a way, just so we don't have to do these stupid challenges. But there goes that idea.'

It surprises Max that up until Jack mentions an escape plan, out of pure fear, her thinking hadn't ventured anywhere so risky. She'd been resigned to accept the situation and do what was expected of them.

'The way I'm seeing it,' Jack continues, 'they've got us cornered. We've got no choice but to compete. Is anyone seeing this differently?'

Peanut throws up his hands. 'Mate, the walls are too high to get over; the trees are too tall to climb; the guards are too strong to tackle, and if we try to escape, we're goners. Like it or lump it, we've got to go along with what they want. We just need to get this freak show happening, whip these challengers' butts, win the competition and take home the trophy. Simple. There *is* a trophy, right? There'd better be one!'

Jack laughs. 'When you put it that way, we'll be home before you know it.'

'Too right!'

'Okay, let's get to work and focus on these superpowers.' Jack shakes his head and laughs. 'Man; that sounds so weird!'

Everyone chuckles in agreement.

'Anyway,' Jack continues, 'let's take advantage of the space out here. We don't know how big this "force-field" of Ruby's is.'

'What d'ya say, Ruby? D'ya want to give it a crack?' Peanut asks enthusiastically. 'I reckon if you're any good at it, you might just be our ticket out of here.'

Ruby gives him the dirtiest look.

'Just saying,' he laughs. 'No pressure.'

She scowls at him. 'No pressure, he says. Just *how* exactly am I supposed to pluck a shield out of thin air? You may as well ask me to summon a genie. I'd probably have a better chance of doing that!'

Max can't even begin to imagine how Ruby is

supposed to do it. But then a thought comes to her—
something Jack told them earlier that might help.
'Hey, Ruby, think back to when we were caught.
Remember Jack had overheard the guard saying
something about you already radiating some kind of
shield.'

'Good point,' Jack says. 'What were you thinking
at the time?'

'Okay.' She gives herself a shake and cracks her
knuckles in preparation, then takes a moment to
reflect. 'So I was kind of freaking out, I guess, like
we all were, but strange thing was, I felt super angry.'

'Angry? You're so weird,' Peanut blurts out.

'I was pretty ticked off, actually. A bit like now!'
She glares at him, and he backs away. 'Anyway, it
reminded me of what I've been through lately.'

'Try it,' Max says before Peanut has a chance to
pry.

Ruby closes her eyes and frowns in concentration.
'I remember feeling overheated, like my body was
starting to burn up, but for some strange reason I felt
safe.'

Max knows that feeling. She felt the same
sensation when she helped Kenny and Jack.

Ruby squeezes her eyes tighter, making a good
show of really concentrating. But nothing changes.
She sighs. 'This isn't working; I'm hopeless.'

'Look, you were on the right track when you were remembering the "thing" that happened,' Max says, trying to be discreet.

But of course, Peanut can't leave it at that. 'Hey, so, what's this "thing"?'

Max groans inwardly.

'It's okay, Max,' Ruby says. 'Maybe talking about it will bring on this damned shield.'

Max places a supportive arm around Ruby's waist.

'You all know that I've just changed schools,' Ruby begins. 'Well, I moved because some of the girls from my old school were giving me a hard time.'

Peanut's eyes narrow. 'What? Bullying?'

Ruby looks away and nods.

Jack, Kenny and Peanut exchange a concerned look.

Max gives her a reassuring squeeze.

'It was pretty tough. Some of my so-called friends on the hockey team started to hassle me.'

'Why?' Peanut asks.

'I made a stupid mistake—one that I paid for, big time.' She looks away, embarrassed. 'I went out with the ex of one of my girlfriends. That's it.'

Peanut and Jack exchange a look.

'But I honestly didn't know I was doing anything wrong at the time.' Ruby falls silent, her eyes closed, probably reflecting on what happened to her.

Suddenly, a million tiny sparkling lights sizzle around her.

Max sits up, excitement pulsing through her veins. 'Go on, Ruby.'

They watch as Ruby struggles with her memories.

'They started spreading rumours, and the whole school believed them. They said some horrible things about me—things that weren't true—and I lost every friend I had. I put up with their bullying for a whole year. And then one day after school, they cornered me and beat the crap out of me.'

Max is horrified, she had no idea Ruby's abuse became physical.

'I didn't see them coming,' she continues. 'They knocked me to the ground, and then one after the other, they took turns kicking me and belting me with their hockey sticks.' The anger in Ruby's voice escalates.

Tears sting Max's eyes, but she bites down on her lip to stop them falling. She watches closely as Ruby reaches the height of her anger and sparks fly off her in a frenzy. *She must be close.* 'You can do this, Ruby.'

Ruby's eyes remain closed tight, her focus obvious, and her determination even more so. Her face turns red. She's nearly there. And then the sparks vanish.

'I nearly died!' She cups her face in her hands and bawls.

Max wraps her arms around her.

The boys, clearly unnerved by the situation, stand there like statues.

Max glares at Jack for him to help. He snaps out of his stupid silence, and Max feels Ruby begin to relax as the strength of Jack's power takes her pain away. She breathes out a sigh of relief.

At that moment, they hear a rustle nearby. Max sees a flash of movement, but before she has time to say anything, Jack is off and running, giving chase.

'Jack, no!'

But he doesn't stop. They're left with just the sound of his pursuit through the garden.

Max huddles closer to the others and waits with trepidation.

Sparks fly off Ruby.

And then they hear it—something approaching. Max's heart beats frantically, and Ruby's sparks fizz. The sound grows nearer.

Something disturbs the bushes.

And then Jack appears.

Max's heart almost stops. 'You frickin' idiot!' she shouts. 'What the hell did we say about sticking together?'

'Hey, back off! It was a knee-jerk reaction, okay?'

'Jerk, all right. You had us worried to death!' Ruby yells at him.

'Did you see anything?' Kenny asks, diffusing the hysteria.

'No, I wasn't fast enough. Come on, let's go.'

Max grabs his arm in a panic. 'Why what is it?'

'I don't know, but we're not sticking around to find out. We're sitting ducks for whatever's out there.'

And what's out there is anyone's guess.

17

THE ENEMY

ULAN

Oh my God, it's true. More kids have fallen through one of the gateways. We've finally got a chance to go home! Ulan processes this revelation with excitement as she runs like the wind to tell everyone the good news. She sends her thoughts ahead to Banji, her twin, so he can tell the rest of the team what she's learnt before she gets there.

She answers her brother's telepathic question. *'No, I don't think so. Not yet, anyway.'*

Within moments, her gaunt, dishevelled-looking brother appears from the dense foliage, out of breath from running. 'What makes you think that? Did you get close enough to read their thoughts?'

'Yeah, and they're still pretty clueless about

everything.'

They walk back towards the chamber in silence, not needing to talk to know what the other is thinking. They approach a clearing where their two friends wait, eager for news.

'What else do you have?' a very tall, solid, older boy asks her impatiently as she approaches. 'Banji relayed your initial findings, but are you sure they've yet to understand their capabilities?'

'Geez, Ryker, they've only just been captured. They're having enough trouble understanding their new predicament, let alone dealing with any superhuman powers,' she tells him, exasperated.

'Ulan, I'm deadly serious. If they already know something about what they can do, then we're in deep trouble. Don't you get it?'

'Okay, Ryker, don't burst a blood vessel!' Edra, the fourth member of the team, steps between them to redirect Ryker's attack. In doing so, she's more than likely made matters worse. But his foul mood doesn't intimidate her. She confidently stands there, with her impressive height and threatening posture, and eyeballs him without any fear of the consequence.

Ryker is about to lose his head. Ulan needs to diffuse the situation quickly. 'Look, from what I could see, they do know something, but as I was telling Banji, they're pretty naive about things so far.'

'They know? Already?' Ryker groans loudly as he runs his calloused fingers through his long dirty-blonde hair. 'What makes you say that?'

'They were trying to encouraging one of them to project a shield of some kind.'

'A shield?' Ryker grimaces. 'And you don't think that's anything to worry about?'

Banji looks anxiously at his sister. She shrugs her shoulders. 'Well, if it's any consolation, she didn't get anywhere with it.'

Ryker appears to be struggling to keep himself from yelling. 'Can't you see what I'm seeing here?' he asks with forced restraint. 'A shield—or perhaps I should call it a "force-field" just so you can understand the implications of this—will be huge for them, and an absolute nightmare for us!'

'But that's only if she learns to activate it, right?' Edra says.

Ryker lets out a long-drawn breath. 'For all of our sakes, Edra, let's hope she never does.'

Ulan relays the hang-ups Ruby has that prevented her phasing, hoping it might make Ryker think differently.

Ryker's eyes light up. 'This is good. We might have found her Achilles' heel. Ulan, we need to find out more so we can start taking them down ... one by one!'

'And then we can go home!' Ulan grins.

'Let's not get ahead of ourselves here,' Edra warns. 'Taking down one of them doesn't mean we've won. Remember, there are five of them and only four of us. They've already got the upper hand.'

'You're right,' Ryker agrees. 'Vigilant at all times … expect the unexpected!'

'I understand what you're saying, Edra,' Ulan says quietly, 'but for once, in four, painfully long years, there's finally some hope. I just want to go home.' Ulan tries to keep it together. She draws in a deep breath and fights back the tears that threaten to reveal her vulnerability. Just as well she succeeds, because Ryker would never allow it.

Edra reaches out to Ulan and squeezes her hand. 'Okay, so maybe they've got one over us with their extra competitor, but that's not to say that they can beat us. We've been training for this, and we're ready for it.'

'Exactly,' Ryker says. 'We know our powers. We know what's coming. They won't know what's hit them out in that arena. We'll work to our strengths, and our biggest advantage at the moment is their ignorance. We've had time to prepare for this, and I'm confident that we'll get the chance to battle the Realm's champions again, and this time we'll beat them.'

'Yes, but Ryker, we had Jaeger then.'

Everyone falls silent at Banji's mention of their former team mate.

Ulan can't believe her stupid brother. *'Of all the dumb things to say, Banji!'*

He cowers at his sister's attack and shrugs his shoulders, looking repentant.

Ulan glances at Edra to gauge her reaction.

Edra forces a smile and takes in a deep breath, 'So let's do this for Jae, then!'

Ulan squeezes her hand. She knows Edra is hurting right now, and takes a moment to console her. But Ryker sends her a look, making it clear he's waiting to hear more about her findings.

She regroups her thoughts, trying to recall something useful and remembers how Jack was able to alter the team's mood. She begins to tell them, but realises too late that that revelation isn't something Ryker would be happy to hear.

And sure enough …

'Argh! For crying out loud! This is not good!' Ryker throws his hands in the air and storms off in anger.

Ulan shrinks away from his outburst.

He returns moments later, his breathing heavy but controlled. 'Okay, so it is what it is. I need to accept that. What else? Is there anything you can think of that might be used to bring them down? We need to crush them every opportunity we get.'

Ryker's tough approach catches Ulan by surprise.

'Don't look at me like that, Ulan; they're the enemy here. It's either we win, or they do. We've been through too much to let this chance slip through our fingers.'

Ulan flinches from Ryker's attack, but she knows he's right. To lose against the newcomers would mean certain exile into the forest—a fate said to be worse than death. She misses her parents desperately and just wants to go home.

'Okay, so this is the plan.' Ryker, once again, takes control. 'Tomorrow we'll see if we can weed out any more information. I'll join you in surveillance, Ulan. And Banji can remain with Edra to relay what we find as we discover it. That way we'll have everyone's perspective on the discoveries, just in case we miss something significant. Any questions?'

No one says anything. As always, Ryker has everything under control with military precision.

Later on, Ulan lies on her straw-filled hessian sack, looking up at the chamber ceiling, and spends some time reflecting on the day's events. She draws in a deep breath, satisfied, knowing that for the first time in a long time, there's hope.

18

GOOGLE TO THE MAX

JACK

Jack follows the guards down the corridor back to their chamber. A disgusting odour, foul and overbearing, wafts to meet them. Nausea rises in his gut.

'Bloody hell!' Peanut cries out in revulsion. 'What's that smell?' He holds his hand over his mouth.

Poor Ruby can't stomach it. She doubles over and vomits. This sets off a domino effect, firstly Peanut, then Kenny. Jack fights the urge to follow. He rushes them into the chamber, hoping to escape the rancid stench, but finds it's even worse in there.

'Oh, God, Jack, do something!' Max begs.

Of course! Jack gives himself a mental slap on

the forehead. He channels his power and throws a blanket of immunity over his friends. Almost immediately, and with the help of the fresh air from the tiny window, everyone feels a little better, and in no time, they're breathing normally.

'It smells like something died in here,' Ruby says, slowly returning to her normal colour.

'And I thought the stuff in the vat was the worst thing I've ever smelt!' Peanut says, disgusted. 'That beats it by a long shot!'

They sit in the corner of the room, resting their backs against adjacent walls.

'Guys, I think I know what happened,' Kenny says. 'I reckon they've spilt the soup. The straw around the door area has been replaced.'

'Great powers of deduction, Sherlock,' Jack says, genuinely impressed.

Kenny shrugs. 'Yeah, like I've really made a huge difference.'

His sarcasm surprises Jack. 'Hey, what's up?'

'Nothing. It's no big deal.'

'Well, it is a big deal. I wasn't having a dig at you. You know that, right?'

'I know you weren't. Look, I'm just being stupid.'

'Spit it out. Let me be the judge of that.'

'But you'll say I'm pathetic.'

Jack gives him a will-you-just-get-on-with-it

look.

Kenny looks down at his feet. 'I feel like an idiot saying it now.' His face turns red with embarrassment. 'It's just … well, it's just that you guys have got these cool powers, and what have I got? "Great skills in deduction" Big deal! I don't think that's anything to write home about.' He smiles at them awkwardly. 'I guess, I would've liked to have something that was useful, that's all.'

Jack can't believe it. 'Are you kidding me? That brain of yours could be a deadly weapon. Seriously, you're heaps useful!'

'Come on, Jack. You're just saying that.'

'Mate, I'm not.'

'But look at the awesome things you guys can do. So I've got brains; big whoop! Brains aren't going to help us when it comes time to compete, or if we need to beat up a few guards to get us out of here. I'm telling you, you'll soon be wishing I had more than just some grey matter between my ears. Sorry, Jack, but having had my nose stuck in books all my life isn't going to help us here.'

'Kenny, I can't believe you don't see how valuable your gift is,' Max says. 'Knowledge might make the difference between us winning or losing a challenge.'

'Too right,' Jack tells him. 'Besides, we don't know what the challenges are. For all we know, we might be competing in a chess tournament, or a table-tennis match—in which case you'll kill it!'

'And you told us about the full moon and stuff; that's majorly cool,' Peanut reminds him.

'That's right. If it wasn't for you,' Ruby says, 'we wouldn't know that our first challenge is in two days.'

Kenny's face goes a deeper shade of red. 'I told you it was stupid,' he mumbles under his breath. 'I guess I just need to learn to build a bridge.' Their stumped expressions make him laugh. '… as in, build a bridge and get over it.'

Peanut howls with laughter. 'Nice one, Kenny. Stick with me, kiddo, and learn from the master.'

The mood shifts. The friends feel confident, their spirits high.

'Okay. Enough mucking around.' Jack directs their focus back to their situation. 'How about we spend some time working on these superpowers?'

'That reminds me,' Peanut says, his eyes gleaming. 'Jack, you were right about me.'

'I'm always right about you, Peanut, but what exactly am I right about this time?'

'Today, in the garden, I started to phase. It happened after you took off. I started to freak out, and when I looked down, I couldn't see my feet! Bloody hell, can you believe it? I really can go invisible. How mad is that! I wanna try again.' He stands and bounces around with the energy of a five-year-old. 'C'mon, let me have a crack at it again now.'

'That's so awesome, Peanut!' Ruby squeals. It's clear that her opinion of him has escalated ten-fold.

Peanut appears to grow a foot taller.

Jack grins. 'Way to go! Okay, let's give it a go.' He desperately wants Peanut to succeed, not to boost his friend's self-esteem, but because he could prove to be the secret weapon they need.

Peanut closes his eyes to concentrate, and Jack sees Peanut's feet start to fade. *What the …?* His excitement soars. *Come on, Peanut … come on, mate!*

Ruby's jaw drops. 'Whoa! Oh my God, Peanut, you're phasing!'

Her sudden outburst startles Peanut, and he jolts back to reality, along with his feet.

'Sorry, Peanut,' she says. 'I couldn't help it. That was so awesome. Your hands and feet were completely gone, and your body was starting to disappear. You should've seen it. You're so cool.'

If he grew a foot taller before, after praise like that, Jack reckons that in no time, Peanut would be on top of the world.

'Let me try again,' he says eagerly. He shuts his eyes and has another go. And this time, his phasing is almost instantaneous.

'Oh … my … God!'

They're all left speechless.

'What? What's happened?' Peanut's voice comes from a vague silhouette in empty space.

Jack's jaw drops. He can't believe what he's seeing.

'Guys, quit gawking!' Peanut says. 'Can anyone see me? Have I disappeared?'

Jack shakes himself out of his shock. 'Mate, this is so surreal.'

'Yeah, but have I done it?'

'We can still see a ghostly image of you. Can you take it a bit further?'

Peanut closes his eyes once more, clearly determined to succeed.

And then he's gone.

'What the ...' Jack jumps to his feet, choking on the sudden intake of breath. Once he stops coughing he calls out, 'Hey, Peanut, where've you gone?'

No answer.

Jack starts to panic. 'Okay, you can come back now.'

But nothing happens.

'Peanut, quit mucking around! I'm serious,' he yells. He reaches out to where Peanut was last seen standing, but there's nothing there. He looks around, searching, but suddenly, his feet are yanked from under him, and he falls face-down in the straw.

'Whoohoo! I did it.' Peanut's laughter rings in

Jack's ears. 'Man, you should see your faces. I wish I had a camera. This is so awesome. You guys really can't see me, can you? Oh my God the things I could get up to.'

They hear Peanut running around the room, laughing. Jack gets an unexpected punch in the arm. Ruby gets a peck on the cheek. He knocks Max's cap off her head and takes Kenny's glasses and puts them on his invisible face. All anyone can see are the glasses floating in mid-air. It's such a hysterical sight, they all howl with laughter.

'You know we've created a monster, here, don't you?' Jack laughs. 'This kind of power will go straight to his fat head.'

Peanut slowly phases back, doubled over, laughing. 'That was majorly sick.'

Now Jack can see him again, he relaxes. 'Imagine what this could mean.' His mind ticks over with the possibilities. 'Tomorrow, when we're in the garden, maybe you can snoop around and check out what's out there.'

Peanut's face lights up. 'Man, that'll be so cool. I could pretend to be a spy. I've always wanted to be a spy.'

'Let's see if you can do it again,' Jack says. A niggly concern makes him worried that Peanut may have just fluked it.

But Peanut dissolves any doubts by disappearing again, then reappearing on the other side of the room. He does this several times, popping in and out of sight, making everyone's head spin.

'Piece of cake!'

He's a natural. Jack can't wipe the smile off his face.

But remembering what happened earlier in the garden brings Jack back down to earth. 'Okay, guys, we need to talk about this. Today, in the garden, we might have had someone spying on us.'

He has everyone's attention.

'I don't know for sure, but it might've been them—I mean, the other team. So I was thinking, if these are the people we're going up against in the challenges, then it's key that they don't find out about Peanut. In fact, I think we should be careful about letting slip anything about ourselves. From the sounds of it, they've already got the advantage of experiencing these games. We can't afford to give them any more ammo, otherwise we're goners.'

'But if it was them out there earlier, it's too late; we already have,' Kenny says. 'They would've seen Ruby trying to work her shield.'

'Well, lucky for us I'm a slow phaser,' Ruby jokes half-heartedly.

'You'll get it soon enough, Rubes,' Peanut reassures

her. 'And when you do, I'm putting money on it that there'll be nothing else like it. I figure, with your resistance in real life being something else already, imagine how awesome you'll be with superpowers. They'd better watch out is all I'm saying.'

'Thanks, Peanut.' Ruby's face flushes from the compliment.

'You know,' he says hesitantly, 'I never did get a chance to properly say sorry to you for that first day. Don't get me wrong, I did try, but it was impossible to get anywhere near you.'

Ruby frowns. 'I know you did. The truth is, I was trying to avoid you. But you can't blame me; you kind of freaked me out.' She chuckles. 'You jumped at me from out of nowhere—with your tongue hanging out! How did you expect me to react? I thought you were a looney.'

'A looney?'

'Well, I wasn't that far wrong, was I?' she teases.

'Hey, ease up!'

They both laugh. And with that said, the ice between them appears to have well and truly thawed.

'Hey, listen,' Peanut offers, 'why don't you try again?'

'What? The shield? In here?'

'Yeah, I could coach you. Maybe this'll help: I found it easier to phase once I cleared my head.'

Jack snorts. 'That'd be easy enough for you, Peanut, because there's not much going on in that noggin of yours. In fact, it'd be a piece of cake, wouldn't it?'

Peanut vanishes, and Jack realises his mistake too late. Peanut dives on him and starts punching him in the arm.

'Oomph, get off! Hey, quit it.' Jack laughs. 'Okay, okay, I was only joking.' He waves his arms, trying to ward off his invisible friend.

'That'll teach you to talk about cake in front of a person who'd kill for some right now.' Peanut reappears, grinning, then becoming more serious, he turns to Ruby and says, 'Okay, jokes aside; try clearing your head of everything but the shield.'

Ruby stands, takes a deep breath and closes her eyes to block out the distractions. After a few seconds she takes a peep, only to see everyone staring at her. 'Hey, stop it! You do realise you're only making it harder for me? I know how important this is. Believe me; I get it! I don't want to be the one that lets the whole team down.'

'Ruby, you won't let us down; I know it,' Max says. 'Just believe in yourself. You can do it. You were half way there this afternoon. I saw it when Jack took off.'

Ruby takes another deep breath. 'Okay, I'll give

it another go.' With her eyes tightly shut, she tries again.

Within moments Jack sees sparks begin to sizzle around her. 'Keep going, Ruby.' He says quietly. 'Things are starting to happen.'

Her face contorts with the effort she's putting into phasing. But she holds her breath, and her face slowly turns red.

Jack fears she's about to pass out. 'Hey, look, Ruby, you've had a rough day, let's call it quits.'

'Argh! I'm hopeless!' she says in frustration. 'What if the guards got it wrong? Maybe it wasn't a shield they sensed me projecting. Maybe it was sparks they saw and they called it a shield for lack of a better word.'

'Ruby, you're more than just sparks; I'm sure of it,' Jack tells her. 'Like Max said, just trust yourself. You can do it.' But he can see that he's only putting more pressure on her by persevering, so he backs off and suggests that they try again in the morning.

They each grab a hessian sack and try to create an area in which to sleep. The girls huddle in one corner of the cell, while Jack and the boys spread out on the other side. It's quite dark now; the torch provides the only light in the chamber.

But Jack can't sleep. He mulls over everything that's happened to them today. His thoughts spin wildly about what they might have to face in the next few days. Would it be anything like the events of the Ancient Romans, where gladiators faced death by savage animals, with spectators cheering—the bloodier the battle the happier the crowd? Or will it be as innocent as a mental challenge, where the two teams compete in answering questions, or like he told Kenny, playing chess.

Somehow, he doesn't think so.

He puts his hope in the tasks being something less bloody and life threatening. He figures that the other team have competed and survived in the past. *That speaks volumes, doesn't it?* But then again, he hasn't seen the other team yet. For all he knows, they may be built like that guy who brought in that heavy vat of soup. The chance that four competitors that size is a real possibility makes Jack groan.

19.

All You Can Eat Food Fest

Max

Early the next morning, something tickling her neck arouses Max from her sleep. She absentmindedly swipes at it, then rolls over, trying to get comfortable. Moments later she's disturbed again by something crawling up her arm, then into her hair. A quiet squeak in her ear has Max bolt straight to her feet, and within seconds, screaming at the top of her lungs. A mad series of screams follows when everyone wakes to find the chamber floor covered, literally, with hundreds of scurrying mice. They make a frantic attempt to escape the fleeing vermin, but there's nowhere to go. They trip over themselves in desperation to get away; it's every man for himself.

The floor clears as the mice find escape routes. In all the hysteria, Max finds herself huddled in the corner with the others, shaking and reflexively swiping at her clothes at the tiniest sensation.

'Holy crap,' Peanut exclaims. 'What a wake-up call. Thanks, but no thanks; I think I'll pass on that free service each morning.'

They laugh at Peanut's attempt at humour, and very quickly the mood lightens.

Kenny points at the food baskets. 'Look; we left the baskets uncovered. The smell from the spilt soup drew the mice in, but the uncovered baskets of food were an open invitation for an all-you-can-eat food fest.'

'They're so disgusting!' Ruby shivers at the thought of them. 'I'm not going to sleep a wink the whole time we're here; I know it!'

'There's your incentive to get that force field of yours going, right there, Rubes.' Peanut grins. 'That'll keep the mice out of your hair … I wonder if that's even possible,' he says as an after-thought. 'I mean activating our powers while we're asleep?'

'You'll have to experiment later,' Jack says, 'but now we need to figure out what we're gonna do if we get a chance to be outside today. We mentioned sending Peanut to have a snoop around, are we all still cool with that?'

'I'm willing,' Peanut says, looking keen to get moving.

Max hopes they can go out, but not so much for the same reason. She's almost tearing at her skin, knowing that those germ-infested rodents were crawling all over her while she slept. The guard said something about a small lake … that's her only priority at the moment.

After breakfast, to Max's relief, the guards offer to take them outside.

'Thank God,' she says. 'I vote we go for a wash.'

Once alone in the garden, Kenny suggests that Peanut vanishes before they go any further.'

'Good idea,' Jack says. 'We don't want to reveal our secret weapon.'

And since Peanut is itching to get up to some mischief, he phases without any further encouragement.

They venture more, their eyes peeled, looking for signs of the others.

Peanut, being Peanut, makes quite a racquet, so Max quietly says to him, 'Hey, Tinkerbell, you really need to practise being quiet. Just because no one can see you, doesn't mean that they can't hear you. If you're going to be a spy for us, you need to act like one.'

'Oh, right. Point taken. Thanks.'

Jack stops as they approach the lake. 'Hey, guys, I don't think we're alone.'

Max freezes and huddles closer to Ruby.

'What is it?' Peanut whispers.

'I caught some movement over to my right.'

'I'm onto it.' And without a sound, Peanut goes to investigate.

20

SOMETHING'S NOT RIGHT

ULAN

'They're not all there. I can only see four of them,' Ulan says in a whisper. 'I wonder where the tall, red-haired boy is.' She and Ryker lie low, hidden from view, watching their opponents.

'Remain vigilant the whole time, Ulan,' Ryker says. 'Keep your senses alert. What are you picking up from the girls?'

'The shorter one is anxious.' Ulan holds back a giggle.

'What is it?'

'They had a mouse infestation last night. They'll get used to sleeping with mice soon enough, won't they, Ryker?'

But Ryker is all seriousness. 'What more? What's the taller female thinking?'

Ulan turns her attention to focus on the one they call Ruby. She goes into a deep state of concentration and eventually smiles and informs Ryker that the girl is having a lot of trouble producing her shield. 'She lacks confidence,' she tells him, 'and doubts whether she can do it. Her thoughts are plagued by her failed attempts from last night. She feels she's their weakest link.'

'Are you getting anything from her regarding the others?'

'No; she's so bogged down with negativity that I'm not picking up on anything else.'

'What of the two boys?'

'They've been discussing the challenges and are trying to guess what they're up against. Hmm, how interesting; the tall boy, while talking to the Asian boy, is constantly keeping his eye on the girls. He's very protective of them, particularly towards the shorter one. She's actually occupying a lot of his thoughts. She confuses him. He seems a little wound up by her. And now, as the girls approach, his thoughts are becoming quite clear to me, but oddly enough, more unclear to him. I'm really surprised he doesn't get it.'

'He has feelings for this girl.'

'Yeah. Even you can see that.'

'Great job, Ulan. We've learnt a lot. Their emotional immaturity could be their downfall. Have you been relaying your thoughts to your brother?'

'Yeah, Banji and Edra know everything, and they agree with our thinking.'

'All right, that'll do. Let's go before they catch us.' Ryker gets up, ready to leave.

'Wait!' Ulan freezes in place. 'I'm picking up on something.'

'What?'

'Shh!' She remains motionless for a long while, eyes shut, concentrating her full attention on her telepathic ability.

'Ulan, we need to move!'

Her eyes snap open, and she looks around in a panic.

'Now!' he mouths to her.

They quickly and quietly vacate their hiding place.

When they near the others, Banji runs out of the scrub in a panic, and asks his sister the question they know Ryker is anxious to hear the answer to. 'What was that? Whose thoughts were you hearing just then? They appeared muffled and distant. I couldn't quite make them out.'

'They were muffled for me, too. I wasn't sure

where it was coming from. It may have been the other boy of the group, the red-head. He was probably in their cell, and for some reason I was picking him up. I guess that'd explain why the reception was faded and unclear.' As they all know, unless the twins can see their subject, they can't clearly read their thoughts.

'Yeah, I guess.' But Ulan knows Banji isn't convinced.

'We should move it,' Edra tells them, catching up at the rear. 'You'll have to fill me in on that last bit inside where it's safe.'

They leave.

What just happened has Ulan spooked. She and Banji share a worried look. There's a lot that they need to talk about … privately.

21

THE DEATH STARE IN ACTION

PEANUT

Peanut races to his friends, having successfully tackled his first spy operation. He can't wait to tell everyone. He finds them sitting by the lake. 'Hey, guys, you're not gonna believe this.'

'Seriously, Peanut!' Max growls. 'What part of "being quiet" didn't you understand earlier?'

'What?' Max's outburst stumps him for a second. 'Oh. No, it's okay; they've gone inside.'

'They? So we're right, we're not the only ones in here,' Jack says.

'Yeah, and man, you're not gonna believe what they can do!'

145

They share worried glances at this.

'Where do I start? Far out; there's so much to tell you.' He pauses to recollect everything. He's itching to tell them what he found, but he doesn't want to miss anything important.

'Wait, Peanut,' Ruby interrupts him. 'I can't deal with not being able to see you.'

Any organised thoughts Peanut may have had become scrambled. Did Ruby just say what he thought she said? He shakes his head and tries to refocus. He sits down next to her and places his arm across her shoulders. 'Awe, Rubes, you do care.'

'What? No, you idiot.' She throws off his arm. 'It's just that we can't see you, because you're invisible.' Ruby jabs out her elbow, and with great precision, hits her target.

'Oomph!' He cries out before materialising before them. 'Maybe I won't sit so close.'

'Just tell us what you found, you twit,' Ruby groans with frustration.

'Keep your shirt on!' He rubs the area she just jabbed, then begins, 'So they're a team of four, and I'll tell you something for nothing, they look like they haven't seen a bar of soap for a while. Man, it makes you wonder how long they've been stuck here.'

'Peanut, so help me God, can you please just focus.' Ruby gets ready to strike out at him again.

'Whoa! Okay, okay!' His thoughts are bouncing around all over the place. He makes an effort to slow things down. 'So there's this huge, solid dude, called Ryker. I think he's in charge. Man, he's scary. I'd hate to come across him in a dark alley, let me tell you …'

Max's death stare makes him stop, then choose his next words more carefully.

'Ah, okay … and there was this pretty, dark-skinned girl; I think her name is Ulan. She's pretty puny; you could knock her over with a feather. But, Oh my God, you're not gonna believe what she can do!' He stops, suddenly distracted by his own thoughts. 'You know what, come to think of it, even though she's tiny, I reckon she could be the one to watch. She'd be like their own secret weapon … Man, she could …'

Max gives him another pointed look.

'Oh, right, focus,' he reminds himself.

'Tell us, already! What's this "thing" she can do?' Ruby asks impatiently.

Peanut smiles. 'Wait for it …' He holds up both hands, commanding suspense like a well-orchestrated symphony. 'She can read minds!' He looks at everyone's stunned expressions, giddy with excitement that he's been able to shock them.

'No way,' Ruby exclaims. 'Ew, that's creepy, knowing someone's been in your head.'

'She read your thoughts, Max,' he continues, 'and those mice—I'm sorry to be the one that tells ya—but they're here to stay.'

Ruby's expression crumples. 'What! No, no, no, I'm not doing the mouse thing again!' She swipes nervously at her hair and clothes.

'Just keep on working on that shield, Rubes; you'll get there,' he says encouragingly. He then leans in and whispers, 'I've got faith in you, Ruby. You're not the weakest link.'

Ruby's breath hitches, and her eyes well up with tears. She turns her face away, clearly affected by his words. He gives her shoulder a discreet squeeze.

'So listen to this,' he continues. 'Ulan has a twin brother, Banji, and he shares this telepathy thing with her. So while she and Ryker were watching us, she was relaying what they were seeing to her brother, who, in turn was telling the fourth person, a girl called Edra. And by the time they all met up, they all knew what was going on.'

'You're kidding,' Kenny exclaims. 'Just like that, they were up to speed? That can't be good.'

'I know, right? But—and this is a big but—the telepathy didn't work so well on me. I guess because I was invisible. Ulan sensed me around, but she couldn't get a clear read on my thoughts. So even though I was the closest one to them, all she got from me was a confusion of sounds. Cool, hey?'

'So you kind of stumped them,' Jack says. 'That's awesome. And what about the other one, Edra. Did you find out what she can do?'

'No, but when you look at it, we've got five superhuman strengths to their three. That has to account for something, right?'

'Not necessarily,' Kenny warns, 'it'll depend on the task as to how useful our powers will be. Remember, they've already experienced these games; they've got a pretty good idea what's coming. We're still wondering if we're going to have to fight a den of lions or play a game of Family Feud.'

But Peanut doesn't listen. He's still buzzing from his adrenalin-high. He can't believe how easy it was to spy on them. 'Maybe I can find out some more stuff tomorrow. I'll sneak over there before the challenge. Hang on.' He stops as a new idea comes to him. 'What if I can find out what the actual task is? I could sneak out past the guards …' He stops mid-thought again. 'Whoa. Hold your horses. I just had a better idea. What if I find a way for us to get out of here? Then we won't need to do the stupid battles.'

'No!' Ruby's eyes open wide like a startled rabbit. 'You heard what the guard said. They'll kill you if you try to escape. Jack, tell him it's a bad idea.'

'But I'll be invisible, Rubes; that's the point!'

'No, mate, Ruby's right,' Jack says. 'It's too risky. Let's just see what happens tomorrow.'

Peanut feels a little dejected. For the briefest of moments, he had the romantic illusion of becoming the hero. But it's not all bad, he realises. At least now he knows that Ruby cares about him, even if it's just a little. He grows another foot taller.

22

No Holds Barred

JACK

Jack wakes from a fitful sleep, dreading what's coming. One way or another, they're going to face something that'll challenge their lives. What that something is, he's sick to the stomach not knowing. Will they cope? *God, I only hope so.*

What they'll endure today will probably be the toughest test of their lives. He has a task and a half ahead of him keeping their spirits from crumbling. He finds himself hovering over each of them, continuously projecting his positivity.

Last night, they had to endure another mouse-infested night. So when the guards invite them to go outside, Jack jumps at the chance. 'Peanut, you go first. Check the place out and make sure the area around the lake is safe. After that, we'll go and see if we can dig up some more dirt on the others.'

Peanut gladly obliges and returns confirming that it's safe.

The cool morning air and a refreshing swim bring some calm and perspective to the group. Jack finds he can relax a little. So when Peanut takes off for another quick scout, Jack sits back and enjoys the antics of the others.

He laughs as Kenny and the girls chase each other around the lake. He can't believe the transformation in Kenny. *Who would've thought he could come out of his shell so quickly?* It surprises him that Kenny doubts his value amongst the group. But Jack knows better; the importance of what Kenny has to offer will reveal itself before long.

Jack looks at Ruby. *She'll find her form soon enough, and when she does, she'll be, as Peanut said, 'something awesome.'*

Now, Max: she's a little pocket rocket. Her spunk and strength constantly amaze him. He takes a moment to study her and laughs at her shenanigans. She's just fallen into the lake after chasing Ruby with what looks like a frog in her hand. Now she stands waist deep, dripping with water, laughing hard at her own tumble—frog still in hand.

A warm, fuzzy feeling within makes Jack smile.

Until, without a hint of a warning, he finds himself airborne and fast approaching the lake. 'Oi, Peanut! Put me down!'

'You really want me to put you down?'

'You'll give yourself away.'

'No, I won't.'

'Come on, mate, put me down!'

'Are you sure?'

And before he has time to rethink his words, Jack finds himself submerged in the lake next to a hysterically laughing Max.

Jack seizes the moment, grabs Max and dunks her. She comes up spluttering from the shock, then bursts out laughing again.

Moments later, it's a free for all. If you haven't already been dunked, then watch out!

Eventually, they drag themselves out of the water and rest on the bank to catch their breath.

Peanut chuckles but remains invisible.

'I figure this means that the others aren't around,' Jack says.

'I've checked out the place, and there's no sign of them. We can go and have a look again later,' he says to Jack. 'Dry up and I'll take you.'

Jack is happy to laze in the warm sun. The impromptu swim cleansed not only the smell from his clothes and hair, but also rejuvenated his spirit.

Nicely relaxed now, he finds himself dozing.

The sound of restless movement next to him stirs Jack out of his sleep. He turns to his side to see no one there, but he knows it's Peanut. 'What's up, mate?'

'We need to talk. If you're up for it, we'll go for that walk now.'

Jack gets up, then calls out to the others that they'll be back soon.

Peanut remains invisible, so Jack can't read his mood, but he knows something's bothering him. He's just too quiet. Jack watches the trees and bushes move in front of him as Peanut leads.

An abrupt halt makes him smack into Peanut's back. 'Oomph, sorry, mate. How about a little warning next time.' He chuckles.

'Yeah, sorry; I keep forgetting you can't see me. Can we sit here a minute?'

Jack looks at a fallen log and figures that's where Peanut's gesturing. 'Okay, so, what's up? Why so serious?'

'It's something I overheard that big guy, Ryker, say yesterday. I didn't say anything in front of the others because we're mates. And mates oughta tell their mates things straight up, no holds barred, right? Even when they're not gonna want to hear it. Agreed?'

'Yeah, of course; I guess. Hang on, I'm confused. How 'bout you just spit it out.'

'Okay. Sure. After watching you guys, Ryker said something about our emotional immaturity being our downfall.'

'Our emotional what? Where'd that come from, and what's that supposed to mean, anyway?'

'He said that just after Ulan read your thoughts.'

'And ...' Jack gestures for him to go on.

'Your thoughts on Max, mate. They know you've got a thing for her, and after today, I can see why they said it.'

'A thing?' Jack laughs. 'Where's this coming from? And what do you mean, you can see why?'

'Come on, Jack, admit it. You were sitting there watching Max with this goofy smile on your face like she's the sunshine that makes your day. Why d'ya reckon I threw you in the lake? It's so bloody obvious, blind Freddy can see it. I had a hunch before, but decided not to pull you up on it, but now, if this thing between you and Max is gonna be our "downfall," maybe we should nip it in the bud before it stuffs up the bigger picture here.'

This idea surprises Jack. He takes a few moments to digest it, but he's certain Peanut's way off the mark. No way is he into Max the way Peanut says he is. She's interesting, he'll admit to that much, but into her in that way? He's pretty sure he's not.

'Earth to Jack! Can you hear me, Jack? Over,'

Peanut says with a nervous laugh, startling Jack from his thoughts.

'Shit,' he says, 'You scared me. I almost forgot you were there. This invisibility thing takes a bit of getting used to.'

'So what d'ya reckon? Are we good? I didn't mean to piss you off, but we need to keep focused here. We can't afford to have any distractions, right?'

'Yeah, we're good, Peanut. But you're wrong about me and Max. She's a friend, that's all. So don't overthink it. Nothing's gonna happen there, I promise. More to the point, I think we should be worried about this "thing" between you and Ruby. Tell me you're not gonna be "distracted" because you've gone soft on her.'

'You've got nothing to worry about there, mate. Ruby and I aren't gonna happen; she's made that loud and clear once too many times. A guy can only take so many knock-backs before it permanently crushes his ego. She's definitely placed me in a friend zone. But I'm not saying I'm gonna stop trying.' He chuckles. 'You know what? Pretty soon it might get interesting, so watch this space.'

'So I don't have to worry about you being "distracted"?' Jack says. 'You're not gonna be the cause of our "downfall"?'

'Me? Be the cause of our downfall? As if. Oh, ye

of little faith. You guys need me. This thing won't happen without me. Don't ever underestimate the genius of this red head. It'll be me who'll lead you all to victory. You'll see.'

'You know something, Peanut,' Jack grins, 'I reckon you will.'

'Too right I will!'

Jack shakes his head. 'Man, with an ego the size of yours, how can it end any other way?'

23

THE FROG PRINCE

MAX

Today's the day—their first challenge. Max wakes up with her stomach tied up in knots. The guards bring in breakfast, but Max couldn't keep anything down, even if she tried. Thank God for Jack's ability to keep them all calm, because she wouldn't be able to cope without it.

And she's not the only one feeling the pressure. She can see that Ruby's struggling to keep a level head. Jack has got his hands full just with her.

Max's heart breaks a little for her. She can't imagine what this is doing to her confidence—trying to produce her shield and getting nowhere. If only she wasn't so hard on herself. But there's a fine line between channelling her hurt from the past to create something awesome and crumbling into a mess of emotions from the memory of that same pain. Her hurt is too raw and her emotions too fragile to distinguish between the two.

When Jack suggests they go outside for a bit, Max jumps at the chance.

While Peanut scours the garden, looking for the others, Max joins Ruby and Kenny, who sit by the side of the lake. They contemplate jumping in for a swim, but Kenny is reluctant to take the plunge.

'It's too cold; maybe later,' he says.

'Aw, poor baby! Do you want me to get you a blanky?' Ruby teases.

'Hey, not fair. I just feel the cold more than you do, okay?'

'Not enough body fat, that's all. My Annie would say "you're too shkinny! You must eat!"' Max laughs as she mimics her. 'God, I miss her. I wish I could let her know I'm okay.'

'What about your dad?' Ruby asks. 'He'd be worried sick, wouldn't he? I know my parents will be.'

'Mine too,' says Kenny.

'Nah, he'd be too busy to even notice,' Max says quietly.

Ruby shakes her head. 'Come on, Max. Nobody's that busy.'

Just then, a large brown frog swims to the edge of the lake. Carefully, so as not to scare it, Max leans forward, hoping to catch it.

'Ew, gross. Don't tell me you're gonna touch that?'

'What? Don't you like frogs? I think they're cute.' Max leans in a little closer. 'Come on, little guy … I've nearly gotcha … just a little bit more …' All of a sudden, she loses her balance and falls head-first into the lake.

Ruby shrieks with laughter.

Max emerges spluttering, but with the frog in her hand. Max has plans for that frog. And from the look on Ruby's face, she knows exactly what those plans are.

Ruby takes off squealing as soon as she sees Max dragging herself out of the lake and taking chase.

Kenny sits back, enjoying the show. But when Max suddenly turns on him, he takes off, running to get away.

Game on!

One moment, Max is chasing Kenny with the frog, the next she's got Ruby in her sights. The three run around the lake, squealing and screaming, until Max loses her footing and again finds herself waist-deep in the water. She's chuckling so hard that she doesn't see Jack being tossed into the lake next to her until he emerges spluttering. This only brings on another fit of the giggles. Then, before she knows it, she's back under water—courtesy of Jack—her punishment for laughing at his predicament.

Kenny stands by the edge of the lake, watching on in amusement, until Ruby comes up behind him and pushes him in, too.

Ruby takes a run up and throws herself in after him.

Somewhere in all of this, Peanut has joined them. Although unseen, they can hear his laughter.

They enjoy a few carefree moments splashing about in the water, then slowly, one by one, they drag themselves out and lay to rest in the warm sun.

Max smiles as she listens to everyone settling down after all the excitement. It's been such a long time since she's known such happiness; it instantly makes her giddy. It feels so strange that she should feel so happy at this very moment in time. She should be feeling like her world has been turned upside-down, but being with her friends and sharing this moment makes her heart swell. Feeling content in the knowledge that she's with people who care for her, she closes her eyes and drifts into a peaceful doze.

The sound of movement next to her stirs her out of her catnap. Peanut and Jack are having a quiet conversation. They decide to go and try dig up some more information on the challenge tonight, then Jack walks into the garden, seemingly alone.

She takes a moment to reflect on her thoughts—especially her thoughts on Jack. She really had it wrong about him. Initially his 'togetherness' rubbed her the wrong way, maybe because she saw him as her polar opposite. But now she sees him in a different light. There's such a realness, a goodness about him, that she finds comforting—a 'what you see is what you get' kind of guy. She's never met anyone like him before, and his leadership somehow reassures her. Despite only knowing him a short time, she can safely say that she can trust him completely.

But it's more than that. There's something about Jack that has her focusing on him more than she should … the way he makes her feel. She shakes her head. It's all too unfamiliar to her—and confusing. She doesn't understand it, and really, it's something she's not willing to delve deeper into—not now, anyway.

Max takes a moment to consider Peanut. Her opinion of him, too, has changed over the last few days. He's not the loser she once called him. In fact, calling him that was a low blow. She knows it now, and regrets it.

Although outspoken at times, and most definitely self-absorbed, Peanut has his heart in the right place. She's seen a gentleness about him, especially towards

Ruby, which endears her to him a little more. He's not such a toad after all.

And then there's Ruby. Max knows she's found a life-long friend in Ruby. In many ways, they're very much alike, although to look at them, they're chalk and cheese. Max gets her; they just click. She needs to help Ruby realise her full potential. What those so-called friends did to her last year is going to take a while to repair, but Max won't give up; she knows it'll be worth it.

And finally, Kenny. *Kenny's the best.* Max looks at him and sees someone whose confidence is beginning to soar. He used to shy away from being heard, but now he has the gumption to stand up and be noticed.

Good for you, Kenny.

She smiles, thinking of her friends. Feeling this kind of happiness is something Max hasn't experienced in a very long time. She lies there absorbing the warmth surrounding her and soon drifts off to sleep again.

24

FREQUENCY INTERFERENCE

ULAN

Ulan is pacing back and forth in their chamber. Their first challenge is on tonight and her nervous energy is taking its toll. 'Ryker, can't we go out for a bit? I'm sick of being cooped up in here. I need to clear my head.'

'I thought it'd be best to stay clear of the others, but I agree, we need some time-out. Edra, run out and see if it's safe.'

Edra takes off to investigate and returns before the others have had a chance to continue with their discussion. 'Did I miss anything?'

'You're kidding, right? You didn't give us a chance

to take a breath let alone talk about anything!' Ulan laughs.

'You're in good form today, Edra,' Ryker says approvingly.

'I'm just keen to get this started. The faster we finish this, the sooner we can go home.'

'So what did you find?' Ryker asks.

'They're by the lake, but like before, the tall red-headed boy isn't with them.'

Ryker becomes alarmed. 'This can't be good. There's more to it. I can feel it.'

'Don't overthink it, Ryker. It might be that he's sick—maybe even too sick to compete.' Banji smiles. 'Luck might finally be on our side.'

'There's no such thing as luck!' Ryker roars.

Banji cowers from the attack.

Ulan and Edra look at each, alarmed.

'Don't give me that look, you two,' Ryker warns. 'We can't afford to let our guard down, not even for a second. You do that, then you may as well kiss our chances of getting out of here goodbye. Constant vigilance. Remember?'

Ulan keeps her eyes locked on the ground. She's too frightened to look his way.

'Okay, Ryker, we get it. But let's just calm down a little,' Edra dares to tell him. 'How about we go out for a bit while the coast is clear; you know, to help us refocus?'

Ryker exhales slowly and relaxes his clenched fists.

His moods have been explosive lately, and Ulan couldn't bear him taking out his frustrations on them so close to tonight's challenge.

Once outside, with the sun on their faces and the breeze through their hair, their mood shifts, and Ulan relaxes a little.

She and Banji are having a private conversation but stop when they realise that Ryker disapproves of his exclusion. Banji is quick to apologise. 'We were just thinking about tonight, and wondering about the challenge.'

They spend some time talking about the possible options, but Ulan withdraws a little from the group, concentrating on something she's picked up on.

Banji sees this and tunes into her thoughts. 'It's the same muffled thoughts again,' Banji confirms out loud for the others to hear.

'What are you hearing?' Ryker asks, suddenly on edge.

'Like before, I'm picking up on someone, but it's not clear,' she tells them, a little worried.

'That's it; I'm done with this crap. All of you, inside, now,' he orders. 'Someone's out there!'

'I'm onto it,' Edra yells as she takes off into the

garden.

'No!' Ryker calls out. But Edra has gone.

Ulan holds her breath, looking at Banji, not sure what to do.

Ryker begins to follow, but stops when they see Edra return. 'Did you see anything?' he asks.

'Nothing unusual. They're hanging around the lake, like before.'

'Thank God for that.' Ulan breathes a sigh of relief.

But Ryker's on the warpath. He's gunning for somebody. 'You two, what's going on here?'

Banji shakes his head, baffled, and Ulan is too scared to say a word.

Ryker storms off without another word. Once they're back inside, he lashes out: 'What the hell's happening here? You two had better get a grip on this situation. And I mean now!'

This thing Ulan is picking up on is freaking her out. And Ryker's mood swings aren't helping, either. She can't explain what's happening. It's never happened before. She needs to work it out, and fast. She doesn't want to be the one who lets the team down tonight by not being able to lock onto what this "thing" is. She looks at her brother, but Banji's no help. He shrugs, having no idea what they're supposed to do.

25

HOW ABOUT OPTION TWO?

JACK

Jack follows as the thicket ahead of him magically divides to make a path. He and Peanut walk deeper into the garden—leaving their friends lazing in the sun—until Peanut's hand presses against Jack's chest, motioning him to stop.

'We're close now,' Peanut whispers in his ear.

They hear voices in the distance.

'Stay here,' Peanut warns. 'I'll go closer to catch everything. And if you think they're onto us, just run. Get the hell out of here, okay? I'll meet you back at the lake.'

Jack crouches low behind a huge boulder and

quietens his breathing to listen. Their conversation comes to him on a breeze, so he hears snippets of what's being said. It sounds like they're talking about the challenges. One voice dominates over the rest. *That's probably Ryker.* Jack's ears prick when he hears him say something about 'skin pulling,' but he's not able to catch the rest of it.

What the hell!?

He desperately wants to move in closer to hear more and maybe even get a glimpse of this Ryker guy. His curiosity gets the better of him, so he carefully leans forward to make sure the coast is clear, then, heart pounding, he inches towards the voices. Ryker's voice rises, sounding anxious about something, and Jack panics—he or Peanut may have given them away. He doesn't stop to consider anything except getting the hell out of there.

Jack bolts through the garden, back towards the lake. He runs like he's never run before, leaping and dodging like a mad-man, praying that he doesn't get caught. Finally, the lake's in view. He looks back over his shoulder to make sure no one's after him. He's safe.

He throws himself down next to Kenny. Kenny jumps back, startled, and scours the area in alarm.

'It's okay. Give me a sec and I'll explain.' Jack tries to slow down his breathing. His gaze darts everywhere, looking for Peanut. He struggles to hear anything over the thumping of his heart in his chest.

Kenny has turned a ghostly shade of pale. His eyes are begging him to tell him what's going on.

Jack holds up his hand to calm him, but inwardly he's burning, worried sick that Peanut may have been caught.

It feels like an eternity before Jack feels Peanut plonk himself down next to him. 'Man, was that a close one or what?' Peanut chuckles. 'Mate, I didn't think you'd get away fast enough. I thought you were a goner, for sure. I nearly crapped my pants when I saw that girl, Edra, take off. Man, is she fast!'

Anxious, Jack scans the garden. 'Is it safe to talk?'

'Yeah,' Peanut reassures him. 'That thing about sensing me but not being able to read me has them spooked again, so they've gone back inside.'

Jack releases a shaky breath.

'What the hell just happened?' Kenny glares at Jack. 'You gave me a heart attack!'

The sound of the boy's talking stirs the girls awake.

'What did we miss?' Ruby asks sleepily.

'It's all good,' Jack says. 'Sorry about that, Kenny. We came across the other team in the garden again, and we found out heaps. They were talking about tonight's challenge——'

'And we nearly got caught!' Peanut blurts out. 'Man, I thought Jack was toast.'

'What!' both girls exclaim.

Jack shakes his head. 'It's nothing. We got a bit too close, that's all.'

'Of all the idiotic things to do!' Max blasts him. 'What the hell were you thinking?' She jabs her finger into his chest. 'They could've killed you!'

Wow. Where did that come from?

'Look, Max, we went in with a plan, okay? It was a calculated risk, and one that paid off, all right? Tell 'em, Peanut.'

Max stands with her arms folded across her chest in anger. She looks like she's going to burst a blood vessel. Jack can't believe her overreaction.

Peanut begins to fill them in on what they overheard.

When she hears what they've uncovered, Max relaxes her stance.

Peanut tells them that the other team were talking about two of the possible challenges up for tonight. He turns to Kenny. 'What's this "skin-pulling" thing all about? God, I hope it's not what I think it is. It sounds like torture.'

Kenny laughs. 'No, Peanut; "skin-pulling" is

a variation of tug-of-war the Vikings used back in 1000 AD. Instead of a rope, they used animal hides tied together.'

Jack relaxes. 'Well, that doesn't sound all that bad.' He had visions of wrestling with this Ryker dude and having his skin ripped to shreds—something like a Hannibal Lecter scene from the movie *Silence of the Lambs*. 'So, Peanut, you said Ryker was big; just exactly how big?' he asks.

'Oh, man, he's huuuge. You know those guys out of World Wrestling? That kind of big.'

Jack's gut clenches.

'Mate, don't look so worried. We've got this in the bag. Don't forget, there're five of us to their four. Admittedly, they've got Goliath, but we've got you, our very own Incredible Hulk! I saw the way you picked up and moved that heavy vat of soup; like it was nothin'.'

'I don't know, Peanut. I'm not so sure I can compete with the likes of that,' Jack says, suddenly disillusioned.

'How about the others?' Max asks. 'What are they like?'

'The other three don't look like they'd amount to much, especially the twins. They're both puny, so I reckon they'll be a push-over. The other girl, Edra, seems athletic, but she's got speed, not strength. So for this kind of challenge, we've really got nothing to worry about.'

'You hope we don't. Peanut, you can't say stuff like that.' Max crosses her arms again. 'And are they thinking that it'll be this Viking tug-of-war?'

Peanut explains that the other team were only guessing, and that it was only one of the two challenges they were tossing up between, but Kenny interrupts him.

'Um, guys, hold on a sec; there's a bit more to this skin-pulling challenge.'

Peanut frowns. 'What d'ya mean?'

'It's kind of not your average tug-of-war; it's more like an extreme tug-of-war.' Kenny appears reluctant to go on.

They look at him, urging him to continue.

'Um … it's a bit more complicated than just pulling on a rope and winning the advantage.'

'O-kay, so …' Peanut motions for him to get on with it.

'This version involves competing over a flaming pit. The losers often got dragged into the fire and burned to death.'

Jack's heart stops. Any kind of positive energy holding them together at that moment evaporates into thin air. He can see the look of horror on their faces. They're about to go into a state of melt-down. He knows he needs to act, and act fast. He searches for something, anything, to bring back his team's morale. 'What was the other option?' he asks Peanut.

'What? Oh yeah, right. I think they called it Ploater, or something like that. From what I could gather, it's a sport that involves speed and quick thinking.'

Kenny picks up on his lead. 'I think you'll find that it's *Pelota, Pelota-Purepecha* or *Pasarutakua*, if I'm right.' He pauses a few seconds, researching the information coming to him.

A smile spreads across Kenny's face, giving Jack some hope.

'It's essentially a game of hockey,' Kenny tells them, almost laughing with giddiness.

'Now that's more like it!' Peanut fist punches the air. 'Man, you had me worried there for a sec, Kenny.'

Ruby grins. 'Hockey, we can deal with, right guys?'

'Okay, Kenny, tell us what you know about *Pelota*,' Jacks asks. 'How different are the rules to what we know?'

'*Pelota Purepecha* is an ancient Mesoamerican game that originated around 3500 years ago. It varies from traditional hockey in that they use a flaming puck. It's a game that's played at night. Which explains why the others were tossing up between the two challenges.'

'We can all deal with a little ball of fire,' Ruby says. 'What's the worst it can do?'

Jack feels almost delirious with excitement. His confidence escalates and this, in turn, lifts everyone's spirits. 'Tell us more, Kenny.'

'The rules are very similar to what we're familiar with. The objective is to get the ball, called the *zapandukua*, across the opposing team's goal at the end of the field. Each player uses a hockey-like stick, a *jatsiraku*, with which to manipulate the ball. Players aren't allowed to touch the ball with any part of their bodies, including their hands or feet.'

'Okay, because we're all pretty familiar with hockey,' Jack takes over, 'we'll just go over positions and strategies. Any suggestions?'

'Yep, and it's non-negotiable,' Peanut is quick to say. 'I'm up front. There's no way I'm going at the back.'

Jack nods. 'I think that's a given. You and Ruby can be our attack. Max and I will go in defence, and Kenny, you can go in goals. Everyone okay with that?'

'Whoohoo! Man, I'm pumped. Bring it on!'

Peanut yells. 'We're gonna flog their butts! We can't lose.'

Jack can't believe their luck. What are the chances that they're going to compete in a challenge they're good at? And then a sudden dread overcomes him. He remembers the tug-of-war. *God, I hope we're playing hockey tonight!*

26

THE ANCIENT'S CHOICE

The time to compete is fast approaching. Jack has his hands full maintaining any semblance of positive energy amongst the team. The palpable enthusiasm from before is fast dwindling to doubt. His repeated words of support and encouragement are now sounding hollow, even to him.

A meal is sent from the kitchen, but they don't touch it.

'Guys, we need to stay positive. It's just a game of hockey,' he says. 'We can do this.'

Kenny sits cross-legged with his head resting in his hands, his eyes focused on a piece of straw. Peanut stares out the window with a white-knuckle grip on the bars. The girls huddle silently in the corner with Max resting her head on Ruby's shoulder. Jack realises that his words are falling on deaf ears. He needs to do something.

'Does everyone know the words to Nirvana's *Smells like Teen Spirit*?'

'What?' Peanut's head whips around so fast that he almost has Jack laughing.

'Okay, so now I've got your attention,' he says with a smirk, 'there's something I want to run by you guys. You know that thing with the twins, them being able to get into our heads? Well, I was thinking I might have a way to muddle their reception. It may or may not work, but we've got to give it a go, right? Otherwise they'll be able to anticipate our moves, and ruin our gameplay.'

'I didn't think of that,' Peanut says, suddenly very focused.

'Anyway,' Jack continues, 'here's my thinking: if we keep our heads constantly crammed with other thoughts, like with the words to our favourite song, we might be able to jam the twin's ability to read our minds. What do you think?'

But after hearing it said out loud, Jack thinks that this 'great idea' of his kind of stinks. And by the looks on everyone's faces, he's not alone. His confidence takes a rapid nose-dive.

'Really? That's the best you could come up with?' Max laughs. 'Personally, I'd rather Destiny's Child's *Survivor*,' she adds with a cheeky grin.

'Hey, that's a good one.' Ruby hi-fives her. 'Can we share?'

'How about Kanye West's *Stronger*?' Peanut suggests.

Then Kenny adds, 'And Queen's, *We are the Champions.*'

Jack's spirits soar. 'Yeah, that's it! I wasn't sure if you guys saw what I was getting at, but by humming or singing the lyrics, not only are we keeping ourselves motivated, we might be able to block their attempts at reading our strategies.'

'Jack, that's an awesome idea,' Max says. 'You're absolutely right about the twins, they could prove to be a real nightmare.'

Jack's pumped. They're all back on the same page. He feels like he's won a small battle already. Knowing that the guards will be coming for them soon, he calls the group in for a final pep talk. 'So guys, let's try to keep it in perspective here. Remember, it's only a game of hockey. It's not like we're gonna fight wild animals, right? Okay, it's not a game of Family Feud, but it's still a game. We dig deep, and we play hard. We find our strengths and use them to beat these guys.'

He then summons the already familiar heat of his power and radiates his calmness out to blanket the others. He feels an instant shift in their confidence. So when the heavy cell door opens and the head Gate Keeper the Ancients called Herodus enters, the five friends feel ready to take on the world.

They enter the arena to an enormous roar from the crowd in the seats above. It sounds like many hundreds of people have come to watch the game. Another mammoth roar turns their attention to the opposite side of the arena where the guards usher their four opponents.

At the head of the arena, sit The Ancients, dressed for the occasion in what Jack assumes are ceremonial robes. And in the middle of the arena glows a deep fiery pit.

Jack's heart stops.

Even from where they're standing, the heat from the pit reaches them. Jack curses himself to hell and back for being such an idiot in not making a plan for this eventuality. But there's no time for self-recrimination now. He goes into damage control. 'Okay, so it's not hockey, but we can still do this. I'll go up front; Kenny you go behind me; the girls are in the middle and Peanut you're our anchor—'

Kenny interrupts. 'Jack, wait; your thinking's all

wrong. You're our strongest, so we need you to be at the back.'

'Shit, I'm a moron! Of course. Kenny, you'd know what's best; tell us what to do.'

So Kenny takes over. 'Strategically we should put Peanut up front, then Ruby, followed by me, then Max. Is everyone good with that?'

'Okay, that sounds good; what next?'

'There're a few things we need to do. Firstly, the rope has to be properly secured around Jack's waist to improve our leverage. Don't worry, I've got the perfect idea for that,' he tells them. 'We need to hold the rope with an underarm grip and keep our arms extended with our shoulders back. It's crucial that we lean back without pulling. We'll gain stability and momentum by using our thigh muscles to push against the ground. So we'll dig in our heels, keep our feet a little wider apart than shoulder width, and then we'll take small steps backwards. And as we do this, we'll twist our bodies sideways with our chests facing the rope.' Kenny demonstrates.

Time is running out; he needs to push out the instructions. To Jack's relief, he does.

'We work in unison. Jack, you can act as the coxswain, like in rowing, calling out a rhythm for us to move in a coordinated manner. When you feel the other team weaken a little, you call "Pull", and we'll take small shuffling steps back. When you feel them gaining the upper hand, you call out "Hang", and that'll be the sign for us to lean back and dig our heels in.'

Jack looks from Kenny to each of his friends, hoping they've taken it all in, and that Kenny's direction has given them some ammunition to compete with confidence.

Time has run out. The guards shove them forward to present them to The Ancients at the head of the arena. Herodus leads the way.

Jack quickly reminds the group to clear their thoughts as they near the other group. Silently he begins to sing.

Face to face for the first time, Jack assesses that Peanut's description of them was spot on. Ryker is most definitely huge—not only in height but also in bulk. Edra is tall, slender and very athletic looking, with freakishly long legs, and the twins are both quite small, both in frame and stature. He sees them studying each of his friends intently. He prays that his idea to block them is working.

Herodus bows on bended knee before addressing The Ancients. The crowd become silent immediately. 'My Lords, I present you with the challengers for today's event.'

The leader—Jack recalls the gate keepers referring

to him as Pius—stands and directs his speech to the two teams. 'Challengers, we have chosen for tonight's task, the Ancient Nordic sport of Viking Skin-pulling. The two teams will stand at either side of the pit of fire. You will each take an end of the rope, and on my command, will fight to dominate control. The team untouched by the flames, will be the victors.'

The crowd erupts with a chorus of approving grunts, then respectfully becomes subdued and listens as Pius continues, 'But first, let us begin with the ceremony. Bring forth the sacrifices!'

Drums begin to beat at a slow, rhythmic pace, and four cloaked men enter the arena. They're dressed in white with red sashes tied around their waists. Dropped hoods obscure their faces. They march slowly towards the head of the arena. Two guards follow in their wake, leading two oxen. At the base of the podium, in front of The Ancients, sits a small stone basin, blazing with fire.

Ruby's eyes grow wide in horror. 'They're not going to kill those poor animals, are they?'

Kenny wraps his arm across Ruby's shoulders. 'Sorry, Ruby, but this is the sort of thing they did back then. They believed that by doing this, the challenge would be worthy.'

'I can't watch.' Ruby turns away and buries her face against him.

'Neither can I.' Max does the same.

'None of us should.' Jack gets them into a huddle. 'Just block your ears, and keep singing.'

He continues to blanket them all with his positivity. It seems to be helping because he senses a calmness around them. And then a strong, warm energy starts radiating from Ruby. He nudges her, 'Hey, what's happening?'

'What? Oh, I was concentrating on blocking out what's happening over there,' she motions with her chin.

Jack smiles. 'Keep doing what you're doing. I think you're close to producing your shield. Use those feelings to transform that heat into something solid.'

They all watch Ruby, but Jack takes the focus off of her by saying, 'Everyone else just work on blocking your thoughts. The twins are studying us.'

Ruby closes her eyes tight in concentration. Jack watches sparks play around her and prays she can manifest the secret weapon they need to win this challenge. But he keeps that to himself. She doesn't need that kind of pressure right now.

He looks over to the other side and catches Ulan staring at him. He continues to sing, and Ulan turns to her brother with a questioning look on her face. He in turn relays something to Edra and Ryker. Ryker's face turns demonic. Clearly he's not happy with what he's been told.

Jack doesn't let that distract him. He returns his attention to The Ancients. The ceremony is over and men enter to clear the arena. Jack looks towards the spectators. The stadium is now in darkness, but the full moon offers enough light to see that the elevated seats above the arena are full to capacity. The crowd grows rowdy once again.

Jack turns to his team-mates to prepare them. 'Okay, guys, it's show time. We can do this. Now, Kenny, your job is to keep everyone in check.'

Kenny is up and ready. 'Is everybody clear on what we have to do?'

Herodus approaches the two teams, followed by six guards carrying an enormous rope of tied animal skins. They give one end to Jack, the other to Ryker, and then lead the teams to opposite sides of the sunken fiery pit. The trench is approximately six metres in length, three metres wide, and God knows how deep. The heat radiating from it is seriously hot, but Jack doesn't allow himself to think about that. He takes the end of the rope and starts to tie it around his waist.

'Here, let me do it,' Kenny quietly offers.

Jack nods, and Kenny secures it with the confidence and ease of a professional. His know-how on the matter is the only reason Jack is holding it together.

Everyone gets into position. Peanut is the closest to the pit. Ruby is behind him. Kenny swaps with Max, placing her behind Ruby and in front of himself. Jack can see the logic in doing that. He'll be able to keep an eye on everyone that way.

Jack looks across to the others and takes in how they've positioned themselves. Strategically they've mimicked their own positions with Ryker as their anchor, the twins in the centre and Edra up front.

The arena becomes quiet.

Jack's pounding heart seems amplified in the silence. He looks around the arena at the hundreds of spectators. What must they be thinking, seeing five against four, and men against women? They've come to be entertained. They want to see a battle, and in the end, they want to hear cries of pain, as well as those of victory. It makes him sick to the stomach knowing that their fate, whatever happens, is purely for their entertainment.

A red scarf marks the centre of the rope. Herodus positions the scarf centrally across the pit and waits. 'The drum will signal the start of the challenge,' he says.

Jack hears Ryker screaming instructions, but he can't let that distract him. What he needs to do is focus on his power, because up until now, he's been preoccupied with preparing the others. With a sudden urgency, he digs deep into his core, searching for his new-found strength. The warmth circulates rapidly, and an almost painful heat begins to radiate towards his limbs in preparation for the battle of his life. He sees each of his team-mates grinding their heels into the gravel, securing a stable foundation. He does the same.

Kenny continuously shouts instructions: 'Hold the rope with an underhand grip. Keep your feet wide. Dig your heels in and lean back on them. Keep your arms extended, shoulders back. Use your body and legs ...'

Jack feels as if his heart is in his throat. They're ready to battle.

The drum sounds, signalling the start, and Jack's body immediately responds. He's on fire. His body has transformed into an invincible machine.

'Pull! ... Pull! ... Pull! ...' Jack starts the rhythmical calls.

'Shuffle back! Shuffle back!' Kenny yells.

Surprisingly, Jack feels them make some progress, 'Pull! ... Pull! ... Pull! ...'

Kenny keeps at them. 'Shuffle back! Use your legs! Push back! Arms straight.'

But then Jack feels the other team pick up momentum.

'Hang! Hang! Hang! …' he yells the warning.

'Lean back. Dig your heels in. Use your body weight,' Kenny continues.

And in no time at all, Jack feels the give from the other side. *It's working!* 'Pull! … Pull! … Pull! …' he shouts out enthusiastically.

'Turn towards the rope. Use your legs. Take little side steps,' Kenny shouts.

The team responds to the calls as one.

'Pull! … Pull! … Pull! …' Jack feels stronger and stronger. 'Keep pulling!'

'Side steps; lean back; use your body weight; use your legs; keep your arms straight,' Kenny yells, his voice hoarse.

Jack sees sparks of electricity coming off Ruby. She looks like she might be phasing. He momentarily loses focus, and in that split second the other team pick up momentum.

'Hang! … Hang! … Hang! …' he cries out in a panic.

'Lean back; dig in. Dig in!' Kenny yells.

Jack hears the crowd going wild. More sparks fly off Ruby. The competition is neck to neck.

An all-powerful roar comes from the other side. Max stumbles from the unexpected pull. She's quick to recover, but they've lost the upper hand.

'Hang! Hang! Hang!'

They're losing ground.

'HANG! HANG! HANG! HANG!' Jack screams in desperation, but he can feel them being dragged closer to the pit.

Kenny keeps yelling instructions, his voice reaching fever pitch.

Jack throws his entire weight and strength into digging deep into the ground, securing a foot hold. The muscles in his arms and thighs burn. The hide cuts into his flesh, and blood on the rope makes it impossible for him to maintain his grip. All of a sudden, Ruby's shimmering shield evolves and extends back to protect all those behind her.

One last gargantuan roar from the other side of the pit has the red ribbon on the rope favour the other team.

'Oh, God, no! No! Nooo! PEANUT!'

Agonizing, blood-curdling screams from within the pit echo throughout the arena.

The crowd erupts.

27

THE BLAME GAME

JACK

Jack races to the edge of the pit, groping frantically for Peanut. The flames hinder his attempts, burning his arms, chest and face, and the smoke blinds his view. After what seems like a lifetime, he finally contacts Peanut's seeking hand. Jack wastes no time in yanking him out of the pit and tearing off his incinerated clothes.

Peanut's cries of agony pierce him to the core.

Jack turns to seek Max, but she's already at his side. She takes his hands in hers to heal his burns, but he yanks them back. 'Not me! Save Peanut!'

'Listen to me,' she says firmly, 'I need to help you first!' He looks down at his hands and realises her meaning. The flesh of his hands has melted to the bone. He searches her tear streaked face, at a complete loss as to what he should do. Without wasting a moment, she takes his hands in hers and begins. This time, Jack allows it.

Peanut's anguished screams continue. Jack can't bear it; he knows he'll be haunted by them forever.

Jack's burns quickly disappear beneath Max's curing hands. And from that healing, he feels his own power strengthen and surge from within. He projects his invulnerability over Peanut like a blanket of relief. His friend's thrashing, tortured body begins to calm, and his agonizing screams lessen.

Max transfers her attention to Peanut, moving her hands over his charred body. They watch in awe as he miraculously heals. Healthy tissue replaces blackened skin, and melted flesh is restored. Peanut moans quietly now. He's made it through the worst of it. But Jack stays by his side.

Ruby's muted sobs break though the quiet. Kenny sits by her side, consoling her. Jack takes in the arena. The crowd looks on, waiting. Across the pit, their opponents stare, standing rigid. Is it horror he sees on their faces, or is it disbelief?

'We've got to get him away from here. Max, can we move him?'

She nods.

Jack doesn't hesitate, he carefully picks him up

and strides out of the arena, his team with him. In the background, he hears the announcement of victory to the other team. An enormous roar from the crowd follows.

Once back in their chamber, Jack lays Peanut on some clothes Max has pulled out of her backpack.

She continues with the healing.

Peanut remains unconscious.

'Will he be all right?' Jack asks. 'Can you tell? Is there more to do?' His questions reflect the desperation of his thoughts.

'I don't know. Some of the burns are deep. And I really have no control over what's happening here. I guess my instincts will tell me when I've done enough.'

Ruby can't hold it together any more. The flood gates of her suppressed torment breaks. 'Oh, Peanut, what have I done? This is my fault. I'm sorry. I'm so sorry!'

Jack takes Ruby in his arms and holds her tight. 'Max will fix him; you'll see. Everything'll be okay.'

While comforting her, Ruby's words echo in his ears—*this is my fault*. Jack's conscience gnaws at him. It isn't Ruby's fault; it's his! He was the one that played down the whole scenario and told them they were playing a game of hockey.

'Shh, Ruby, don't. You didn't do this. I messed

up, and I'll own it.'

'No, Jack.' Kenny's quick to defend him. 'I should've gone over game strategies. That's my job. I stuffed up.'

'Guys, stop it!' Max snaps. 'Take a look at what just happened here.'

They all stop, silent.

'Nine kids were pitted against each other, for what? For the sake of amusing a bunch of sadists,' she says with disgust. 'We're stuck in a time where this kind of barbaric behaviour is nothing to them. We aren't responsible for what happened here! Yes, I agree, in hindsight we all should've been better prepared for the challenge. None of us is faultless in that, not one!'

And then a barely heard murmur comes from the cindered patient lying in front of them.

Jack can't believe it. Peanut just tried saying something. He looks at the others to make sure he didn't imagine it. He leans closer. 'Hey, buddy. What?'

Peanut slowly licks his parched lips. He's clearly struggling to speak again. The effort makes him choke and splutter.

Alarmed, Jack grabs some water to put to his lips.

After a sip, Peanut swipes at it weakly. 'Did ya see me,' he wheezes, trying again. 'I was freaking awesome.' He chuckles, setting off another bout of coughing.

'You bloody idiot,' Jack says. 'Will you quit with the jokes, already? You're gonna choke to death.' Jack falls back in frustration and rests against the wall. 'I guess this means you're gonna be okay.'

Peanut smiles and weakly reaches out to fist-bump him.

Tears sting Jack's eyes, but he shakes them off and forces a lop-sided grin. 'Oi, and what've I told you about all this bragging? Chicks don't go for that sort of crap.'

Peanut's smile widens.

Jack allows himself to relax a bit more. 'Seriously, though, how are you feeling?'

'Mate, not in front of the girls,' he says weakly before coughing. 'Let's just say …' He pauses to take a raspy breath. 'I've seen better days.' He reaches out and grabs Jack's arm. 'Thanks for taking the pain away, bro. I owe you one.' He carefully takes a few deep breaths. 'Max, how's it looking? Be honest; what are my chances?'

Max looks at him, horrified. 'Stop it. You're not dying on my watch.'

'No,' he says with a frail chuckle. 'I mean my chances with the chicks? I haven't been hit with the ugly stick now, have I?' He laughs at his own joke, but his discomfort becomes apparent when he clutches his chest and moans.

'God, of all the idiots in the world, I had to get stuck with this one!' Max says angrily. 'He's your stupid friend, Jack; do something before I kill him myself.' She turns back to Peanut. 'And as for you, how about you put a muzzle on it!'

But her insult falls on deaf ears. Exhausted from his blathering, her patient falls into a deep sleep. She continues to tend to Peanut's wounds in silence, but an unchecked tear runs down her cheek, revealing her true heart.

Jack slumps back, emotionally drained. Images of what just happened flicker repeatedly in front of him. He presses hard on his eyes, trying to stop the visions. Finally, he lets the tears that have been threatening to fall, fall.

28

ALL'S FAIR IN LOVE AND WAR

MAX

It's well into the night before Max feels the heat in her hands begin to subside. And just in time; she's completely wasted. A weakness like no other has drained her to the point where she even struggles to hold herself upright. Ruby and Kenny have fallen asleep, leaning on the wall against each other. Jack half dozes next to her, fighting to stay awake.

Finally, Max feels confident that she's done all she can.

Peanut is in a deep sleep. He'll carry some permanent scars, especially on his right leg. Max smiles to herself, knowing he'll be happy with that.

Knowing him, he'd want some war wounds to brag about when we get home. And she's pretty optimistic that it'll be *when* and not *if* they get home.

'Jack.' She nudges him gently and whispers, 'Hey, I'm done. He's asleep.'

Jack looks down at Peanut's peaceful face and breathes out a deep sigh of relief. Without a word, he pulls Max down with him and they curl up next to Peanut. Jack's arm is like a vice, wrapped possessively around her middle.

Too tired to question it. Too drained to object.

They sleep.

✑

The next morning, after spending the night with a few of their long-tailed companions once again, the gang sit around having a simple breakfast of dried fruit and bread. Peanut, back to his same ridiculous self, says, 'Hey, Max, I hope you left me some scars. I need something to show the boys when we get back home.'

Max rolls her eyes.

'You're an idiot.' Jack smacks him on the back of the head.

Ruby, sitting close by Peanut's side, says, 'Do you remember anything from last night?'

He shrugs. 'Seriously? Not a hell of a lot. It's a bit of a blur, to tell you the truth. I'll tell you one thing, though; I remember that pain! Man, I'll have nightmares about that for a long time—no kidding. And the moment it stopped, wow … I can't explain it; it was like heaven.'

'That was Jack,' Max tells him.

'But it was Max's quick thinking that helped,' Jack says.

Max and Jack exchange a look of understanding.

'Seriously, I owe you both. Thanks.'

Jack gives Peanut a clap on the back. 'Okay, enough of that; we've got work to do. Today we've got another challenge, and there's no way in hell we're going into it with our eyes shut like yesterday. So no more mucking around. The guards said they'll come for us when the sun is at its highest. I'm guessing that'll be around midday. Is that right Kenny?'

'More or less; it's complicated. The sun's at its highest point at the solar noon, and the exact time of that occurrence varies daily—' Kenny stops and winces. 'Geez, that sounds nerdy even to me. That's embarrassing. I swear I can't control it; it just comes out. Anyway, sorry about that. You're right, Jack; it's around midday. Um, you can keep going now. Don't let me interrupt you.'

They all laugh at poor Kenny. He really doesn't

know where all this information is coming from.

'Okay, so the fact remains,' Jack continues, 'that we don't have much time.' He turns to Max. 'First, I need to know, is Peanut okay to compete?'

She doesn't need to think twice. As far as she can see, Peanut is back to normal. But she leaves that decision up to him all the same. 'I think Peanut is the only one that can answer that.'

'So are you up for it?' Jack asks. 'And look, no one will think less of you if you're not. I mean, we'll be more evenly matched, four against four, so if we have to do this without you, it's okay.'

'What? No way! I'm no piker. Thanks to you two, I'm as good as gold.'

Max smiles, 'So long as you're sure.'

'One-hundred percent. Bring it on. Let's whip some butts!'

'Okay, let's do this.' Jack appears pumped and ready. 'So, Kenny, I'm leaving it to you to fill us in on as many sports as you can research. We need to know everything about every game they ever played back then. The more info we have, the better. We need to be prepared for challenges that they might be better at, so we can work out strategies to beat them.'

'That reminds me,' Peanut interrupts, 'there was something I overheard yesterday when we were eavesdropping. They mentioned a challenge that

Edra was good at. I think it was called "the pits" or something like that. She was saying they'd have it in the bag if that's the challenge they choose.'

'Good one, Peanut!' Max grins. 'That's awesome that you remembered. So, Kenny, what do you make of that?'

Kenny closes his eyes, deep in thought for a few moments, while mumbling variations of the word 'pit'. 'Pit, the pits, ancient game, the *pitz*. That's it.' He opens his eyes. 'It's *pitz*, a Mayan ball game that dates back to around 2500 BC. It's played between two teams and resembles a net-less volleyball game, with each team confined to their half of the court. The playing field is surrounded by six-metre-high walls, and players hit a four-kilogram solid-rubber ball back and forth across the court without it touching the ground, until one team fails to return the ball. But the catch is, you can't use your hands or feet. You can only use your hips, knees, forearms and elbows.'

'A four-kilo rubber ball? Ouch! That's brutal.' Max doesn't want to think what the impact of a ball that heavy feels like.

'What's more challenging is that you eventually need to get that ball through a hoop to win the game,' Kenny adds.

Ruby's eyes light up in excitement. 'I used to play netball, and I don't mean to brag, but I was a damn good goalie. It doesn't sound that hard.'

'Remember, you can't use your hands,' Kenny says, 'and what's worse, the hoop is a solid stone ring perched on the top of the wall, and it's not your typical horizontally placed hoop, as in netball; it's positioned sideways.'

'The hoop is at the top of the wall? What? At six metres? That's impossible.' Now Ruby doesn't sound so optimistic.

'You're right, Ruby; it is nearly impossible,' Kenny replies, 'but you can get points in other ways. You can score by striking the ball against the opponent's wall.'

'Are you kidding me? That ball is a four kilo, solid rubber, pain inducing weapon!' Peanut screeches. 'How the heck are we supposed to do that?'

'There are ways, Peanut,' Kenny explains. 'Traditionally, the game is played wearing protective gear made from animal skins, and a thick yoke worn around the waist which helps keep the ball in play.'

Max recalls one of her favourite movies *The Road to El Dorado*. 'I remember watching something like this on an animated film when I was a kid, but they made it look easy. After hearing what you just said, Kenny, I can't believe it was popular back then.'

Jack nods. 'I'm curious to know why Edra was so keen on this challenge. She has speed—that we know—but I wonder if there's more to her. Kenny, did you say that a team can win if they can pass the ball through the hoop?'

'Yeah, they win outright, regardless of the score.'

'She's got long legs; maybe she can jump and reach the hoop,' Jack guesses.

Ruby snorts. 'It's six metres high. How could she possibly reach that?'

'She's got superpowers, don't forget,' Peanut reminds her.

'Wow!' The impact of Peanut's words shocks Max to the core. 'I didn't think of that. We could be in serious trouble here.'

'If that's true about Edra, then you're right, Max, we're toast.' Jack becomes serious. 'And that's what I'm talking about. If we know their strengths then we can work on obstructing their gameplay. So if *pitz* is one of the challenges, then I don't need to tell you guys that she'll be the one to watch.'

'How about I mark her? I'll use my invisibility.' Peanut's eyes sparkle with mischief. 'Yeah, she won't know what hit her, and I do literally mean *hit* her.' Max's grimace in response to his words doesn't escape him. 'Don't look at me like that, Max. I'm not ashamed to say that I'll stoop to hitting a girl if I have to. This is war. After last night, I'm not holding back.'

Peanut's words shock everyone, but it especially resonates with Max. It goes against everything she knows, everything she's grown up with. But she can't deny it; he's right. To win in the challenges, they need to fight hard. And if it means they need to play dirty, so be it, because it's clear that they won't be going home if they play nice.

Jack asks Kenny to research every ancient sport or game in his mental, Google-like search engine. There's no guessing from which corner of the globe The Ancients will source their next task, so they invest the rest of the morning studying the games of ancient civilizations, hoping to cover every possible challenge that they could face over the next few days. They focus on team-based sports that would be crowd favourites. The bloodier the sport, the more likely it'll be the one chosen.

They realise that they're not playing kiddy games here. The stakes are high. It's no longer about fighting to win the right to go home, it's a matter of survival.

29

Digging a Hole

'Ryker, they've got a healer!' Ulan can't believe it. At last night's challenge, they witnessed something completely out of left field. 'Did you see what she did last night? God, if only we had her on our team when Jaeger was injured. He'd still be alive.'

'Careful, Ulan. Keep your voice down.' Ryker scans the garden, checking to make sure Edra isn't nearby.

But Ulan knows they're alone. 'I'm not stupid, Ryker, give me some credit. I was just saying.' It annoys her that he continually treats her like a child. 'For your information, they're still inside. You forget Banji's in my head most of the time, so I know, okay?'

Ryker relaxes a little. 'Sorry, Ulan, of course you

would. And yeah, I agree, she'd be a great asset to our team. What do you suppose happened last night? Do you think he survived? My guess is he didn't. His burns would've been pretty bad. She'd have to be pretty amazing to bring him back from the brink of death. Let's hope she couldn't.'

Ulan is deep in thought, reliving the horror of what they saw last night. What a tragic result for the other team. *That poor boy.* His agonising screams are still echoing in her ears. 'You know, if it wasn't for you, we'd be the ones that ended up in that pit.'

'To be honest, I wasn't expecting them to be such a challenge.' Ryker shakes his head. 'They had the upper hand more than a few times. Their anchor, surprisingly, had impressive strength for someone his size. I should never have underestimated him. I've preached this to you all often enough, and yet I didn't take my own advice.'

'I think his name's Jack. And did you notice, he's got something more than just strength. We all saw him virtually dive into the fire to get his friend out. Either he's super confident in their healer, or, probably, and more likely, he's got some kind of immunity to pain. Because, did you notice, he was able to transfer this immunity to his friend. The screams stopped almost immediately; remember?'

At Ulan's words, Ryker's expression becomes

unsettled.

Ulan hears a warning from her brother in her head. She lowers her voice. 'They're coming. Just watch what you say.'

Moments later Edra emerges from the garden with Banji trailing. Ulan gives her brother a wink, thanking him for the heads-up.

'So you two finally decided to join us, did you?' Ryker says sarcastically. 'Half the morning's gone already. You do realise that we've got a challenge to prepare for?'

Ulan flinches, hoping that Edra doesn't rise to Ryker's taunting. They don't need any further friction so close to another challenge.

'Quit exaggerating, Ryker. We're here now, so let's get on with it,' is all Edra says.

Relieved, Ulan says, 'Ryker and I were just discussing what happened last night.'

Edra nods. 'We were lucky to have won that challenge. It's a worry that they're so strong already. Did either of you manage to get into their heads and dig up some dirt?'

This piques Ryker's interest, and with all hostility forgotten, he says, 'Good point, Edra. Banji said they were constantly humming or singing. Explain that to me.'

'Yeah, we were confused at first, then realised

that it's a tactic to interfere with our reception,' Banji explains. 'Pretty smart, actually.'

Ryker's expression turns grave. 'But how did they know to do that? I mean, for them to come up with that tactic, they must've known about your powers.' Ryker looks from one to the other, his brow furrowing deeper. 'My gut tells me I was right the other day; we've been spied on.'

Ulan looks at her brother in alarm.

'I mean it, you two had better pick up your game,' Ryker threatens. 'I will not let you ruin our chances of getting out of this hell-hole. You need to get on top of this.'

Ulan cowers, knowing Ryker's just about to lose it. She looks at Banji and silently begs him to re-direct the conversation.

'Um, Ryker, what about the other guy, the Asian boy; what's your take on him?'

'My take? Don't you think that's a question I should be asking you?' Ryker shoots back through gritted teeth. 'What exactly was he thinking when *you* tried reading him?'

Crap! Banji just dug them into a deeper hole.

He hesitates. 'Well, um … the thing is, I couldn't. He was blocking me, with his singing.'

'This damn singing!' Ryker draws in a deep breath, clearly struggling to show restraint. 'Okay …

so what, may I ask, was he singing?'

Ulan's stomach drops. *'Oh God! Banji, tell him anything but that!'*

Banji becomes pale and turns to his sister with desperation in his eyes, but Ulan looks away. She can't bring herself to say anything. And so Banji is forced to go it alone.

Ryker remains seemingly composed after being told, but his lack of response makes Ulan uneasy.

'And that's all you got from him, huh? There's nothing more either of you care to share?' he asks them calmly.

The twins look at each other and shake their heads.

And that's when he loses it.

'Aaaghh! Give me strength!' Ryker's face turns red with rage. The veins on the side of his neck bulge, and he throws up his hands in frustration. 'I need something positive to work with here.'

No one dares to speak.

Banji chooses that moment to remember the shield, but before he has a chance to say anything, Ulan gives her brother a death-stare and mentally threatens him to keep his mouth shut. Not trusting herself to say the wrong thing either, she clamps her lips tightly. It seems that Ryker hadn't noticed that, at the end of the battle, the other team had finally mastered the shield. And there's no way in hell that it's going to be her that tells him.

Last night more than one would have fallen into the fiery pit if the red-head hadn't produced that force field when she did. So, for now, Ulan and Banji agree to keep that bit of information to themselves.

30

BOUNCING OFF THE WALLS

JACK

During breakfast, Jack watches his friends, relieved that things have turned out the way they have. They're safe, and that's all that matters.

When they've finished eating, they go over what today's challenge might be.

'Ruby, have you tried to activate your shield again?' Kenny asks.

'What? When did that happen?' Peanut asks.

Ruby shies away from his sudden attention.

'Wow! So you've done it?' he jumps down and sits next to her. 'How awesome, Ruby. I knew you could do it.'

Ruby shrinks at the praise. This surprises Jack, until he realises that she probably feels she doesn't deserve it.

'Ruby, you need to let it go,' he tells her. 'Stop beating yourself up.'

Ruby sits back and sighs. 'I guess you're right, but it's … '

'Come on, Rubes, show me.' Peanut's eyes gleam with excitement. 'I bet it's awesome. What's it like? Is it anything like Captain America's shield, you know, made from solid metal, or is it like a transparent force-field made of energy-waves? Is it big or small? Can you make it any size you want?'

Jack holds back from laughing. He can't believe Ruby is still punishing herself for what happened last night, because Peanut hasn't even given it a second thought. 'Come on, you'd better show him before he drives us all nuts.'

Ruby smiles. 'Just to shut him up, I'll give it a go.' She stands up, stretches her arms, then cracks her knuckles.

The others step back to give her some room.

She looks at Peanut's excited face and shakes her head. 'Okay, this is for you.'

Her eyes close as she readies herself. The intensity of her concentration as she searches for the required zone is obvious to everyone watching. Stillness surrounds her. Tiny lights start to sizzle around her like fireflies. That sizzling intensifies to electrical sparks, and within seconds those sparks explode with a bang, producing a sphere that fully encompasses her.

Ruby looks out from her transparent bubble and giggles nervously. 'Wow. Look at me; I did it.'

Peanut's jaw drops. 'That's totally sick!'

She squeals with excitement. 'Oh my God; oh my God; oh my God!'

Max moves closer and pokes at it, tentatively at first, then with a bit more enthusiasm. 'Hey, it's really rubbery. I didn't expect that. Ruby, how strong is it?'

'I don't know. How about you throw something at me.'

'Let me have a crack.' Peanut looks around, eager to find something to use, but there's nothing apart from the backpacks and the hessian sacks. So he steps back, then charges at the barrier, ramming his whole weight into it. The only thing he succeeds in doing is ricocheting off the surface, propelling himself into the air, then dropping to the ground like a sack of potatoes.

'What do you call that?' Ruby laughs. 'Come on, grab someone's backpack and go at me with everything you've got.'

Jack can't believe the look of determination on

Peanut's face. If he didn't have so much faith in Ruby's shield, he'd crash-tackle Peanut to the ground to stop him. But, instead, he watches on with interest. Peanut seems intent on making an impressionable impact, but Ruby is more than ready.

Peanut takes an energetic run-up while swinging the bag in the air, then he hurls it at her with everything he has. It happens so fast that Jack wishes he could've videoed it to watch again later. The weapon hits its mark, but the impact repels the weapon back onto the attacker. The attacker, being caught off-guard, has no time to protect the object in the direction of the rebound—that object being his face. They hear a loud crack. The end-result? A broken nose.

'Argh, Ruby! Ya smashed my face up!'

Ruby is horrified. Her shield vanishes with a pop. 'Oh, Peanut! I'm so sorry.'

'Bloody hell! Not fair. I've been copping it, left, right and centre, here. Give me a break, will ya?'

Ruby smothers a giggle. 'A break? I thought I just did.'

Jack, Max and Kenny laugh so hard that they risk ending up actually rolling on the floor.

'Hey, it's not funny!'

'No, mate; it's hilarious!' Jack doesn't hold back.

'Yeah, ha, ha, ha! Have your fun. In the meantime, Max, could you …' He points at his nose.

'You know?'

While Max tends to her patient, Peanut continues to grumble, 'Great mates you all turned out to be. With friends like you, who needs enemies?'

'You kinda asked for it, you idiot,' Jack says with a grin. 'Next time, don't mess with the girl with the shield.'

After that, everyone takes a turn challenging Ruby, and she has everyone bouncing off the barrier in fits of laughter. After a while, even Peanut joins in again, despite the glare he gets from Jack.

After a few goes himself, Jack sits with his back to the wall, watching his friends have a bit of fun. They need to discuss strategies and research ancient games again, but he can't bring himself to ruin the moment.

Max lands next to him after being deflected off the shield and laughs so hard, she can't catch her breath. For some reason, Jack's stomach clenches just looking at her. The girl known for her scary attitude and even scarier death-stare is now rolling on the ground with bits of straw sticking out of her hair and tears in her eyes. She's almost unrecognisable. Gone is everything that once painted her with darkness. And right now, in front of him, is someone vibrating with life. He smiles. And he thanks fate or chance, or whatever the hell it is that's brought them to be in the same buddy-group.

But the sudden sound of the bolt being released to open the chamber door strikes an automatic chord of unease amongst the friends. Grim reality replaces the mood of carefree innocence.

Jack projects a positive aura over them, blanketing them with confidence and readiness. 'Okay, Kenny,' he says, 'as soon as we see what we're up against, you're on. Just tell us what to do. Are you ready, guys?'

The guards usher them once again into the arena. All eyes turn to Kenny. For a moment he looks overwhelmed, but he recovers quick enough and focuses on assessing the altered playing field. The Ancients have erected a court in the centre of the arena. This court measures approximately thirty metres long and eight metres wide. Tall inward sloping walls flank the court on either side. High on each wall sits a vertical stone hoop.

They know this one.

'Right,' Jack begins, 'we've discussed this at length. It's Edra's specialty, so we've got our work cut out for us. Let's go over the rules again.'

Kenny gives them a quick rundown, finishing with, 'And remember, if the ball goes through that ring, it's game-over.'

A pile of protective gear lies to one side of the court. They watch Kenny as he straps on each piece, then follow his example.

'These guards keep the knees and forearms safe,' he says as he straps on the padded leather guards. 'This wooden yoke goes around the waist. Use it to propel the ball.'

The yokes are too big, so they spend a little time adjusting them to fit. Kenny is quick to fashion the alterations using the spare leather guards. They stop when they realise that Ruby isn't preparing herself.

'Hey, Ruby, what's up?' Max asks. 'You're not doubting yourself, are you?'

'Doubt?' She chuckles. 'That word doesn't exist in my vocab, anymore. For the first time in a long time, I'm definitely not doubting myself.'

'What gives?' Peanut asks.

'Let's just say I've come well equipped for today's challenge.'

'Oh, yeah. Cool. Nice going, Rubes. You'll be bouncing that ball off your shield like a pro in no time. They won't know what's hit 'em.' Peanut laughs.

'Peanut,' Jack says, 'like we discussed, your job is to mark Edra. Don't let her out of your sights. You need to block her every attempt.'

'Leave her to me,' he says, grinning. 'I reckon the crowd wouldn't mind it if I bent the rules a bit, do you?'

'And Ruby, you need to chalk up a nice fat score for us while Peanut takes care of that little problem, okay?'

Ruby looks eager to start.

Jack looks across to the other end of the court. Ryker is staring him down. Ulan and Banji are studying them, too. 'Guys, the terrible twins are trying to get into our heads; it's time to block them.'

A horn sounds. The crowd grunts in appreciation and then become silent as Herodus presents the teams to The Ancients.

'Today, for our amusement, the challengers will compete in a sport from the ancient Mayan civilization, *pitz*,' Pius announces. 'After last night, the reigning champions, the South Africans, are ahead. Challengers, be prepared for battle. May the best team win. Let the game begin!'

The crowd roars.

The two teams are placed on opposite sides of the court with a line dividing them. Jack hands the reins over to Kenny, who strategically places each of his players according to Ryker's positioning of his own team. He has Peanut, Ruby and himself up front, with Peanut opposing Edra, and Ruby opposing Ryker. Max and Jack are behind, as are the twins from the other team.

With the sound of a horn, the game begins. A guard throws the ball high into the air from the centre of the court. Peanut races to the heavy rubber ball and whacks it with his forearms joined, across to Ryker who uses his hip to deflect it to Ruby. Ruby has her shield ready and uses it to rebound the ball against the opposition's wall. As quick as that, she scores the first point for the Aussies. The crowd cheers.

Jack looks across to the other team. Ryker's expression says he clearly wasn't expecting Ruby to show up with her shield. Ryker calls his team in for an urgent huddle. Jack smiles; his confidence soars.

Jack has the team regroup. 'Great going, Ruby. Let's get some more points like that.'

'That ball's seriously a deadly weapon,' Peanut warns them. 'Cop that in the face and you're a goner.'

The game continues. This time when the ball is tossed into the air, Ryker jumps high to intercept it. He spikes the ball with his elbows, aiming to ground it for a point. But Ruby, anticipating this, throws herself low enough to deflect the ball from its path. The ball goes to Edra who uses her hip to hit it over Peanut's head to Max. Max uses her hip to deflect it, but miss hits it and the ball falls at Jacks feet. He reflexively kicks it. It's a foul.

The crowd boo and hiss their disapproval.

One point to the South Africans.

The game continues once more. The ball is passed, whacked, deflected and missed. Arms, knees and hips become bruised with every brutal hit of the heavy rubber ball. Ruby wins the next few points by, again, slamming the ball against the opponent's wall. Her accuracy in deflecting it improves rapidly.

Ryker's plan of action changes. It becomes apparent that his new objective is to take out the Aussies, one by one. Each time he connects with the ball, he uses his whole-body weight behind his strikes and sends the ball straight at them. Kenny is his first victim. A blow to his head drops him to the ground like a sack of potatoes.

A point is awarded to the South Africans.

Jack helps Kenny up, but it's a struggle. He wavers precariously, too disorientated to even know which way is up, so Jack exchanges positions with him, leaving Kenny with Max so she can work her magic on him.

Then things turn ugly real fast. Ruby retaliates by sending the next ball directly at Ryker's face. She repels it so hard that they hear a loud crack when the ball makes contact. Ryker stumbles back, a little dazed, wiping at his bloodied face.

One point to the Aussies.

Now in a rage, Ryker fires a bullet of a ball at Jack, who barely has time to defend himself. Jack staggers, winded by the blow, but he forces himself to push through the pain because he anticipates Edra taking advantage and making a move while he's down.

Max is his next victim. A ball fired at Max hits her hard on the shoulder. The impact knocks her to the ground, crying out in pain.

Anger floods through Jack. He doesn't think twice. His only objective is to rip Ryker's head off. But before he can do anything, Peanut and Kenny tackle him to the ground. They struggle to hold him down.

'What the hell are you doing? Let me go!' he yells.

'Mate, stop! You're going to get yourself killed,' Peanut warns him.

Jack stops fighting them.

Kenny slowly backs off, but he looks ready to knock Jack down again if need be. 'He's right, Jack; he'll kill you!'

Jack turns to Max. Her worried look snaps him out of his rage.

'I'm okay, Jack,' she tells him quietly.

He takes a moment to calm down, then turns to look at the other team. His gaze locks with Ryker's. *So this is the way you want it? Well, two can play at that!*

He waits for the next ball to come to him, and when it does, Jack directs it at Ulan. The brutal impact knocks her to the ground, leaving her winded and gasping for air. The look of sheer panic on Ulan's face as she struggles to breathe, however, makes Jack regret his actions. Ryker transforms into the human version of a raging bull. His brow furrows, and his eyes darken and turn into slits. He all but starts to froth at the mouth, snorting, ready to attack and destroy.

There's no two ways about it, Ryker is ready to kill.

'Just play the game!' Edra yells at him.

It takes a few moments for Ryker to regroup, and when he does, the look on his face lets Jack know that this means war. It's crucial, now more than ever, that they keep the ball away from him.

And Ruby does her best to do that. She doesn't give him a chance. With each contact of the ball, she uses her shield to send it over his head to hit the wall, gaining them points with each delivery.

It becomes clear early in the match that Edra's patience with Ryker and his dirty game tactics is running thin. The Aussies are gaining a considerable lead by just playing the game. She motions to Ryker to change places with her, but he ignores her. Jack can see her escalating frustration. The power-dynamics are about to shift.

Edra intercepts the next ball off Ruby's shield, and with the speed and agility of a gazelle, she leaps up high, whacks the ball, and accurately directs it towards the stone ring. Everything suddenly moves in slow motion. Kenny's words, 'If the ball goes through the ring, it's game-over,' echo in Jack's mind.

But Peanut is ready and anticipates Edra's move. He phases, throws himself across the court, clambers onto an unsuspecting Ryker and projects himself high into the air to intercept the ball and change its trajectory away from the ring. The ball falls to the ground, unchallenged.

In the confusion, Peanut succeeds, not only in foiling Edra's attempts, but scoring another point for the Aussies.

Ryker is left mute. He looks at Edra, his expression completely bamboozled.

Edra starts screaming foul-play. She's become wise to what just happened. But her cries fall on deaf ears. The crowd grunts enthusiastically and begins to stamp their feet, clearly unopposed to the dirty tactics.

Ryker and Edra exchange a knowing look, and with a slight nod of the head, Edra prepares for the play.

Jack realises that they're in deep trouble. He calls out to warn his team. But the ball has already been tossed into the air. Peanut, in his visible state, rises to spike the ball. Ryker intercepts it and passes it to Edra. She carefully sets the ball back to Ryker, and he slams the ball straight into Peanut's face. Peanut falls to the ground like a lead weight. Somehow Jack saves the ball and sends it to Ruby, who smacks the ball towards the wall. But, in a flash of speed, Edra intercepts the ball and deflects it to Ryker who in turn sets it back to Edra. She silences the crowd by jumping higher than humanly possible and whacking the heavy rubber ball, with precision, through the impossibly small, stone ring.

The winning horn blows. The crowd erupts.

'South Africans: Two. Aussies: Nil.'

31

POWER BATTLES

JACK

Back in the chamber, the group, now a little deflated, attend to their injuries. Although bearable, Jack still feels the impact of Ryker's hit. It wouldn't surprise him if he had a few broken ribs from the blow he copped. He waits patiently as Max helps the others: Peanut with his broken nose, and Kenny with his fractured skull.

After a quick assessment of his injury, she tells him that he's got internal bleeding. If it wasn't for Max's help, he realises, more than half the team would've been decimated by now—after just two challenges.

'That was brutal,' she growls. 'That Ryker is a creep. He plays dirty. How are we supposed to compete against that?'

'Yeah, we lost, Max, and we came out of it a bit beaten up, but to tell you the truth, I'm pretty stoked with the way we handled it,' Kenny says.

'Too right.' Peanut bounces around, still on an adrenalin high. 'We could've won that one. Man, we were all over 'em. Ruby, you were amazing.'

'And did you hear the crowd, Peanut?' she replies, her eyes shining. 'They loved you. And what about Ryker's face when you used him as a launching ramp? That was classic.'

'Yeah, poor bastard; he really didn't know where to look.'

The image of Ryker's stunned expression makes them laugh.

'It's too bad they know about our secret weapon now,' Jack says on a more serious note. 'And, boy, were they quick to strike back once they realised. Their experience in the arena has made them cunning, all right. If we're expected to beat them, we need to up the ante and be just as ruthless.'

'I'm okay with that,' Peanut says. 'I say bring it on; whatever it takes.'

'Um, about that, Peanut,' Max says, 'now that they know about you, we can't risk you getting hurt. You'd better quit with the spying.'

'What?'

'It's too dangerous. There's no telling what they'd

do to you if you got caught.'

'But Max, how can they catch me?' He grins. 'I can vanish, remember? Duh!'

'Look,' Kenny says, 'we lucked out with what you did before, Peanut, but I'm going to have to agree with Max.'

'You too? No way. I say we put it to a vote.'

He turns to Jack for support, but Jack backs the others. 'You've seen how brutal they can be; they'll resort to anything to win.'

'And not that it'll change anything,' Ruby adds, 'but I'm with them. Sorry.'

Peanut folds his arms across his chest, clearly disappointed. 'But I was so good at it,' he mumbles bitterly to himself.

'Okay, that's settled.' Jack ignores Peanut's last-ditch effort at making a protest and starts the ball rolling on more pressing issues. He needs them to regroup so they can prepare for the next challenge. They start by spending some time going over what happened today.

'It's pretty clear Ryker calls the shots,' Max says.

'I don't know about that,' Kenny counters, 'I noticed Edra doesn't put up with too much of his crap. During the game, she nearly lost it with him a few times when he took charge. She kept looking for opportunities to shoot the ball through the hoop, but he wasn't setting anything up for her. He's got tickets on himself, that's for sure. They could've won that game in the first few minutes without risking the whole team getting hurt. The twins copped a few hits from Jack, and I'm sure they're sorry now because of it.'

'I saw that, too,' Ruby says. 'And it could be a good thing for us. Their power battles might end up being what ruins them. We can sit back and watch them self-destruct.'

Jack snorts. 'If only. But I wouldn't be holding my breath if I were you, because you could be in for a long wait.' And they don't have that kind of luxury. 'Did anyone pick up on anything else from the twins? They don't seem to have anything more than their telepathy.'

'And thank God for that,' Max says. 'I think that's bad enough, don't you? Can you imagine what would happen if they got into our heads? We're lucky your idea to block them works.'

'Yeah, that really was a fluke, though,' he says. 'Let's hope for more breaks like that.'

'Fluke or no fluke,' Kenny says gravely, 'we can't afford to leave anything to chance again. We seriously need to beat them, otherwise we're never getting out of here.'

Kenny's words resonate with them all. They've

lost two out of the five challenges, so they need to win the next three to have any hope of going home. If they lose one more, they've kissed their chances goodbye.

Jack goes to bed late that night with his head spinning from the strategies and tactics they've just gone over the last few hours. They have information overload, thanks to Kenny, having crammed centuries of sporting history into one night. He just prays that when the time comes, that everything will click into place in time to claim their first victory.

32

The Cracks are Starting to Show

Ulan

'Ryker, hold still!' Ulan is down by the lake, cleaning the blood from Ryker's face. 'Wow.' She flinches at what she's seeing. 'I hate to tell you this, but that ball didn't do your face any favours.'

'I don't care what I look like, Ulan. We've notched up another win, and that's what matters. It's all worth it. We only need one more victory, then we can challenge the realm champions, and this time, we'll beat them.' He takes a steadying breath. 'We're one step closer to going home.'

It surprises Ulan to see Ryker so pumped up. He's allowing himself a glimmer of hope for the first time in a long time.

'I know you miss your family, Ryker. I can't even begin to tell you how desperate I am to go home.'

He instantly becomes rigid. 'Drop it, Ulan!' he warns.

His growl almost frightens her, but she wants to reach out to him, to find the old Ryker buried beneath this cold and formidable one. She dares to press further. 'It helps to talk about it, you know.'

He pushes her away and storms off.

She's gone too far. His walls have shot back up. And she should've known better. He isn't the friend she once had. She hardly knows this one. But she does know that this Ryker detests showing any signs of weakness. And just then, without realising it, he revealed some flaws, some fine cracks in this impenetrable armour of his.

Their time imprisoned here has robbed them of what used to be.

'Well, your nose looks broken,' she yells after him. 'Keep the wet cloth on your face; it might help with the swelling.' And then she stalks back inside.

'Leave him, Ulan,' Banji says as she bursts into the chamber. 'He needs to stay focused, and talking about things like that will only distract him.'

'What did I miss?' Edra asks.

'She's been talking to Ryker about home,' Banji

explains.

'Bad move, Lanny. Just leave him. He needs to prepare for tomorrow, and the way he's been acting lately, he needs as much time as he can get. I mean it, if he doesn't hurry up and get his act together, I'm taking over. Tactical genius or not, these erratic decisions he's making are going to ruin it for us. If we're going to have half a chance to get to the final battle, we need the old Ryker back.'

Banji nods in agreement. 'You're right, Edra, things need to change.'

They become silent, each absorbed in their own thoughts on their disastrous predicament.

'How are you feeling after your soak in the lake?' Edra asks Ulan after a few minutes.

'A little better, I guess,' she says tentatively..

'That doesn't sound too good. What's up?'

She seems reluctant to say anything but eventually admits, 'I'm finding it hard to breathe. I keep getting this stabbing pain in my side.'

Edra frowns. 'Don't tell me you've broken a rib?'

'What? How the hell did you keep that from me?' Banji jumps up, fuming. 'And how are we supposed to compete tomorrow?'

'Hey! I'm sorry if I've ruined your plans, Banji.'

Her brother bombards her thoughts with endless questions. She quickly regrets saying anything at all.

'I left him by the lake,' she answers his telepathic attack. 'No, I didn't tell him, and I don't think I will … Why? Just look at your reaction. Imagine his!'

'Lanny, I think you need to say something,' Edra tells her. 'What'll upset him more is if he goes into tomorrow's challenge unprepared.'

Ulan is torn. As much as she's dreading his reaction, she knows they're right. 'It's probably just bruising, anyway.'

'What's just bruising?' Ryker asks as he enters the room, having overheard the tail end of their discussion.

Thankfully he looks like he's cooled down a bit from their last talk, but Ulan silently groans, anticipating his reaction. She was hoping for a little more time to prepare her approach. 'Ryker, please don't get angry again. It's probably nothing anyway.'

'Let me be the judge of that, Ulan.'

So she tells him, then adds, 'Like I said, it's probably from the bruising, that's all.'

Ryker remains silent. His eyes focus on the ground, but his mind appears to be elsewhere. It's hard to know what he's thinking.

Ulan begins to panic and looks at her brother for support.

Ryker looks up. 'This isn't good,' he says gravely. 'We can't have you competing in tomorrow's challenge like this. But I think there's something we can do that'll help. In fact, I'm sure it's what we need to do.'

Her eyes narrow. Ryker is up to something.

Edra sees it, too. 'What are you getting at?'

'Mm?' Ryker responds vaguely, his mind a million miles away.

'Ryker!' Edra commands his attention. 'I can see your mind ticking over with a plan, now spill!'

'Just leave everything to me. I'll fix it.'

His words sound an alarm for Ulan. They don't sit well with her. She looks at the others and sees the dread she feels on their faces.

'What do you mean, you'll "fix" it?' she asks.

He smiles and says calmly, 'I think it's time we paid the other team a visit.'

Edra's eyes go wide with disbelief. 'And do what, exactly?'

'Ask for their help, of course.'

That's something Ulan wasn't expecting to hear from him.

'You know what? I'm getting tired of you not letting us in on your thinking,' Edra says. 'Why are you making these decisions all of a sudden? I really think we need to discuss this as a team. And what makes you think the other team will help us, anyway?' There's a long pause as Edra stares him down.

'I can be very persuasive,' Ryker says ominously.

The way he speaks makes Ulan's hair stand on end, and the three look at each other in horror. Their concern for his state of mind just escalated to a frighteningly macabre new level.

'I don't think that'll be necessary, Ryker,' Ulan says. 'I'm sure I'll feel better in the morning after a rest.' But the only thing Ulan is sure about is that her quietly spoken words have fallen on deaf ears.

33

THE STORM

JACK

Loud claps of thunder and a downpour of rain stir Jack from his sleep early the next morning. He can't tell what time it is, but it's still dark outside. The torches on the wall are burning low, emitting very little light.

Something moves across the chamber. Jack sits upright and peers into the half-light, trying to see what's caught his attention. It's Max. The storm outside muffles the sound of her moaning quietly in a restless sleep. She's murmuring incoherently. Jack clambers towards her on his hands and knees, trying not to stir Peanut, who's asleep next to him.

Max is having a bad dream. She rolls from side to side, her moaning growing louder. The words are a little clearer now. 'No, no! Don't go!'

Jack tries to wake her, but another bolt of lightning and a simultaneous boom of thunder does the job for him. With a strangled cry, she sits upright, terror on her face, and stares through him.

'It's okay; it's me,' he says, trying to reach her.

The emptiness in her eyes fades, and recognition dawns.

A cascade of silent tears trickle down her cheeks, unchecked.

'It's okay,' he repeats, thankful the panic in her eyes has almost gone.

She turns away from him. 'I'm sorry I woke you,' she whispers.

'You didn't; the storm did. Are you all right?'
She nods.

'Do you want to talk? It might help.'

Her posture stiffens. 'There's nothing to talk about; I'm okay.' She swipes at her wet cheeks and forces a smile.

'Max, you're not.' He places his hand over her trembling one to reassure her. She tries to withdraw it, but he holds on tight.

'I just have trouble sleeping when it storms, okay? Pretty pathetic, right?'

'Max, I'm not stupid. Talk to me.'

There's a long pause. For a long time, she's lost in

her thoughts. Jack holds his breath.

She sighs deeply. 'Years of therapy hasn't helped me, Jack. I'm too broken to fix.'

He slowly releases his breath. She's finally letting down her guard. He wants to help, and for some reason he senses that he can. 'Ah, but did your therapists have superhuman powers? I bet you they didn't.'

She half-smiles at his optimism.

He repositions himself and lays down next to her, looking up at the ceiling, his hands tucked behind his head, feet crossed at the ankles. He grabs a long piece of straw, sticks it in his mouth and starts to chew on its end, ready to begin their session.

Reluctantly at first, and then with another sigh of resignation, Max lies down beside him. She stares ahead, not really seeing anything.

Outside, the storm subsides. An occasional faint flash still comes from distant lightning and grumbling from the fading thunder. A chorus of chirps and croaks from the night animals outside floats through the open window and settles within the chamber.

'What do you want to know?' she asks quietly.

Jack wants to know everything. She's still a mystery to him. He's seen thin layers peel away lately, but he knows there's much more to her.

'Your mum, what did she look like?'

Max is quiet for a moment, then says softly, almost to herself, 'I can hardly picture her anymore. I feel like she's fading away, like I'm losing her again.'

Jack remains silent, allowing her to talk.

'Annie says I look just like her. She knew Mum when she wasn't that much older than I am now. She says that apart from our hair colour, we look the same. My mother had beautiful long, blonde hair. To me, she was a princess straight out of a fairy-tale.'

She smiles as she remembers the thoughts of her five-year-old self. 'I loved brushing her hair. She would let me do it while she read to me. It was our special time. We'd sit there for ages.' Max loses herself deep in her memories.

Jack waits.

'You know,' she continues with a sad smile, 'my hair really isn't black; it's light brown, like my father's. I guess I keep it this way to annoy him.'

Jack grins at her attempt at rebellion. But with that confession, he begins to see the deeper layers of Max that she's buried for so long. 'There's that,' he says, 'but I also think you do it because you don't want to be a constant reminder of your mother. You want your dad to see you for you. He loved her very much, didn't he?'

Max is silent.

Jack doesn't need to see it; he senses that what he

said hit close to the truth. Suddenly her fragility is very exposed.

'You said once that you called yourselves The Three Musketeers, but you don't get on now, do you?'

She turns to face him, her look, anxious.

'I kind of figured that one out already,' he says.

Her silence confirms his guess.

'He hardly ever looks at you anymore, does he? You don't even think he loves you,' Jack presses further. He feels her stiffen next to him. Her vulnerability probably feels pretty raw.

He pictures her hurt clearly now. Pieces of the puzzle are starting to fall into place. 'It sounds like he's the one who should be in therapy. He hasn't gotten over your mother's death. You said that you and your mum look alike. I bet he can't look at you because you remind him of her. When your mother had that accident, a large part of your father died that day. He doesn't hate you; he just doesn't know how to cope without her.'

He pauses to let that resonate, then continues, 'He's scared to love you. Deep down, he won't let himself be in a position where he could get hurt again. He's not strong enough to cope with the possibility of losing you, too.' Jack doesn't know where all this is coming from, but it surprises him that it all makes sense to him. He only hopes that it does to her, as well.

Dawn breaks. Faint rays of light begin to stream through the window. Jack turns onto his side to face her. Max remains staring up at the ceiling. A stream of tears runs down her face. She's trying so hard to hold it in, to hold it together. But he can see her control is wavering.

And then it breaks.

He pulls her in close and holds her tight until her silent sobs subside.

'Once this is over,' he whispers, 'when we go home, we'll fix this thing between you and your dad, together. I promise.'

They lie there for a while in the silence, both emotionally drained. Eventually they fall back to sleep.

34

THE LAND OF OZ

JACK

Jack wakes in a fright after being roughly shaken.

'Hey, get up!' Peanut hisses.

He looks around the room, disorientated. The anger he sees on Peanut's face has him even more baffled. A quiet moan makes him look down to see Max asleep at his side. Now he understands. He slowly rolls away, careful not to wake her.

'What the hell's going on, bro?' Peanut says.

'It's not what you think.'

Peanut's expression tightens. 'I thought we dealt with this already. We agreed, no distractions. You said she was just a friend. You promised!'

'Peanut. Let up for a sec. There was a bad storm earlier, and she got spooked, so I dealt with it. She needed to calm down, otherwise she would've woken you all up. That's all. Okay?' he lies.

Peanut studies him for a few moments, before deciding to believe him. 'Mate, you've got no idea what that looked like. Lucky no one else caught you together like that.'

Someone stirs from all the whispering. Jack is only too happy to end the conversation.

'Hey, is that rain?' Ruby asks as she stretches and rubs the sleep from her eyes.

'Yeah, we had a big storm last night,' Jack answers. 'I'm surprised you didn't hear it.'

'I was exhausted from yesterday, and dead to the world.'

Kenny stretches and yawns loudly. 'Yeah, me too.'

The conversation stirs Max to wake.

'I'm glad some of us slept through it.' Jack gives Max a private wink.

Kenny scratches his head. 'You know, come to think of it, I do remember hearing some rumbling last night, but I thought it was my stomach.' He laughs. 'I'm so hungry. I hope they're bringing us something decent this morning. I swear, I think I've lost five kilos already. What I'd give for some steamed dumplings right now, or fresh *jianbing*.'

'Don't talk about food,' Peanut moans. 'I've never been so hungry in all my life. I reckon I'd even give that blood soup a go, right now.'

Ruby pulls a disgusted face. 'Ew, gross!'

'Yeah, you've got a point there, Rubes; I'm not that desperate.'

When the food finally arrives, they rummage in the basket to find something edible. Thankfully the dried fruit, cheeses and bread have been a daily offering. They avoid anything that smells weird, or has beaks, eyes or claws.

While they eat, they brain-storm one final time, knowing they'll be called on soon.

The rain continues outside. Not as heavily as before, but steady.

'Do you think they'll call it off?' Ruby asks hopefully.

'What? The challenge?' Peanut laughs. 'We're not in Kansas anymore, Dorothy!'

'Oh, you're sooo funny! We can hope, can't we?' she snaps at him.

Just then, a guard enters the chamber with the bald helper from the kitchen. They've come to remove the breakfast things.

'Sir … excuse me, sir,' Ruby begins.

The guard turns to Ruby, looking surprised that she's addressing him.

'Can you tell me, will today be cancelled?'

The guard looks even more confused.

Undeterred, Ruby continues, 'You know, because of the rain?'

The guard baulks at her question, then does his best to hide a smirk. He turns to the kitchen hand, who quickly looks away, trying to mask a snort with a cough, then after a glance back at Ruby, the two of them belt out thunderous roars of laughter.

This startles Ruby, then, as they continue snickering, her shock turns to anger. Outraged, she spontaneously summons her shield and repels them both out of the room. She immediately realises what she's done and, horror stricken, says, 'Oh, no! Hey, I'm sorry, all right? I didn't mean it.'

Her regret is short lived when she hears them continue down the corridors in such hysterics that they're no longer able to walk two feet without doubling over, howling.

'Have you ever heard of anything so ridiculous in all your life?' cackles one.

'Cancel the battles? Because of the rain?' says the other.

More uproarious laughter follows.

'Oh, oh, oh,' chuckles the first, struggling to catch his breath, 'wait until I tell Pelagius; his sides will split!'

Ruby stands like a stone statue in the wake of the insult.

'Aw, Ruby, I feel bad. That was pretty low,' Peanut says sympathetically. 'I would've stopped you asking them if I'd realised that you were being serious.'

Ruby doesn't say a word.

'Come on, don't be angry,' he continues, holding back a chuckle, 'because I'd sure hate to cop the brunt of that temper of yours.' He ducks to avoid the repercussions of his words, but strangely there are none.

'Actually, it's pretty funny when you look at it,' Kenny dares to say.

'Do you know what's even funnier?' Peanut says mischievously. 'You're worried about a bit of rain, but you forget that you come with a built-in, all-weather force-field. You don't have to get wet if you don't want to, princess.'

Ruby's face goes red. She looks like she wants to curl up and die from sheer embarrassment. Instead she shakes her head and starts laughing at herself. 'I guess I asked for that. What on earth was I thinking?'

'You're good for a laugh, Rubes, I'll give you that much,' Peanut teases. 'I reckon you're a keeper. With you around, we might just get through this nightmare without going completely bonkers.'

'Don't ever change, Ruby.' Max pulls her in for a hug, and the two start giggling.

'Come on you lot, let's get back to our brainstorming,' Jack says with a smile. 'I've got a feeling the rain will be our friend today. I reckon we're going to go out there and wipe the floor with those jerks.'

35

HURLING

JACK

The rain doesn't let up.

When the guards lead the team into the arena, Jack notices that Ruby doesn't put up her shield to ward off the rain.

'I'm no princess,' he hears her grumble under her breath.

He smiles.

Once in the arena, Jack makes his evaluation. He turns to Peanut and then Ruby with a glint of hope in his eyes. He's so lost for words that he can't speak.

'Tell me I'm dreaming.' Peanut looks at Ruby with tears in his eyes. 'Holy crap, Rubes, I'm even too scared to say it, but this looks like a hockey field. Please, God, let it be hockey.'

Jack feels just as giddy. He turns to Kenny, praying he has good news for them.

Kenny gives them a reassuring smile. 'Okay, guys, listen up, it's not exactly hockey, but it's near enough. If you look at the nets at either end of the field, you'll notice goal posts above them. I'm pretty confident this is hurling. We've discussed this at length already. It's like hockey, in that the players use a wooden stick—a hurley—to hit a small ball—a *sliotar*—between the opponents' goalposts. You can either hit the ball over the crossbar for one point or into the net for three points.

'The game is played very much like we know it, where you strike the ball with the stick, but in hurling you can also use your hand to slap the ball, and you can use your feet to kick it, too. There are no rules against striking the ball in the air with your stick, nor anything about catching the ball in your hand and running with it, but for no more than four steps. I'll mention, too, that shoulder charges, blocking and hooking are allowed.'

Jack smiles. 'Awesome, Kenny.' He looks at the others. 'Any questions?' They shake their heads. 'Okay, I'll be quick, we don't have much time. Kenny, will you be okay in goals? I want Ruby centre-forward and Peanut left-inside where they play best. Max and I will defend. I can't promise anything, Kenny, but we'll do our best to stop the balls getting anywhere near you.'

'Hey, I can only do my best.'

'Remember what we talked about yesterday; go hard, because I guarantee they won't be holding back,' Jack warns them. 'All we need to do is get the ball to Ruby. She'll be unstoppable with her shield. Peanut, use your invisibility to confuse and distract them.'

'But how will we know where he is?' Ruby asks.

'You'll still be able to see the hurley, so just look out for a floating stick,' Peanut says with a cheeky grin.

Ruby gives him a dirty look. 'Smart-arse!'

'All right then, princess, how about I just call out so you know *exactly* where I am? That should take the guess-work out of it, right?' Peanut says with a smirk.

Ruby rolls her eyes.

'One more thing,' Jack adds quickly, 'stay alert to the twins' telepathy. I don't need to remind you how dangerous they could be. Now, if I'm right, Edra's their most valuable player. Ryker won't have such an advantage this time. Hockey requires speed and accuracy more than anything else, and we've got that and more.'

Herodus lines them up before The Ancients. The other team are already there. The rain is coming down a little harder, but it hasn't deterred the spectators from coming in droves to watch the third event.

Jack leans forward and glances across to the South Africans. Ryker is closest to him, so he has a clear view of the damage Ruby's deflected ball made to his face yesterday. It isn't pretty. There's a heap of swelling and bruising around his nose, and his eyes are so puffed up that Jack needs to look twice to see if they're even open.

Way to go Ruby!

'Competitors!' Pius calls for attention. 'The nobles have chosen the ancient Gaelic sport of hurling for today's event. Guards, prepare the *clepsydra*. Players, at your ready.'

The teams assemble to their designated sides of the field. Jack calls his team together for a quick huddle. 'Kenny, quick, what's a *clepsydra*?' he asks.

'It's an ancient Greek water clock. It measures time by the regulated flow of liquid out from a vessel. See that clay pot that looks like a huge urn, it's got a small hole near the bottom. They'll fill it with water and allow the water to trickle from that small hole. When the water has stopped dripping, the game will be over. The team with the highest score wins. But,' he adds warily, 'because of the rain, the urn will continue to fill, and the game might go on for hours.'

'Then it looks like we've got a marathon ahead of

us. But we can do it,' Jack says with enthusiasm. 'Let's go win us a hockey game!'

With adrenalin pumping through their veins, they take their positions.

Jack watches as Ruby, with hurley in hand, meets Edra on the centre line. Even though Ruby is quite tall, Edra still towers over her.

The *sliotar* lies on the ground between them. Both stand ready, waiting for the start of the game.

Just as the horn is about to blow, Edra looks down at Ruby. 'You're going down, princess!'

Ruby's brow furrows and her eyes turn to slits.

Jack's heart stops. 'Ruby, keep it together,' he yells, 'don't let her ...' The sounding of the horn drowns out his warning, but Ruby is shrewd enough to not rise to the taunt.

She summons her shield, which instantly repels Edra three metres away and onto her backside, allowing Ruby to take off with the *sliotar*. She dribbles up to Ryker, shoulder charges him to the ground, passes it across to Peanut, who sidesteps Ulan with ease and strikes the ball past Banji into the net for a comfortable three points.

The crowd go wild.

Jack releases his breath. 'Nice one, Ruby!'

Back at the centre, Ruby looks up at Edra's towering form. 'Sorry, hon, did you say something? I was too busy singing *Survivor*. Do you know it?' And then she brazenly starts humming it for her.

Jack splutters, choking on a laugh. He's loving it.

Edra, on the other hand, isn't seeing it the same way. Her face turns red with rage.

But once again, the horn blows, Ruby projects her shield, repels Edra and virtually repeats the same game play, helping them score another three points before Edra knows what's hit her.

The heckler becomes the heckled.

'Whooohooo! You go, girl!' Jack hoots and hi-fives his new hero.

Across the field, Jack catches sight of Ryker who's practically frothing at the mouth. He storms up to Edra and roughly yanks her aside. She stumbles, trying to keep herself upright, and scowls at him. He blasts her with everything he has, then replaces her in the centre.

Jack is ready to step forward to substitute for Ruby, but she turns to him and gives him a reassuring wink.

Ryker glares down at her. 'I'm going to destroy you, little girl!'

Ruby looks up at his smashed-up face, and just as the horn is about to blow, she points to herself and, with an innocent expression, says, 'This little girl? The one that did that to your face?'

The bully is momentarily stunned. The horn goes, the shield repels, and Ruby is off, once again unchallenged.

But Edra is ready this time. Like a streak of lightning, she's on top of Ruby, causing her to underestimate her pass to Peanut. Edra intercepts, and takes the ball, flying up the wing, heading for a goal. Jack is on course to obstruct her path. They collide. He wins the tackle and smacks it back to Ruby. She looks up, searching for Peanut, but he's nowhere to be seen.

'Rubes, far right!' he calls out.

She sees his stick floating in mid-air and hurls the ball in his direction. Peanut takes off with the ball. The sight of it is almost comical; Jack has to stop himself from laughing. He watches Peanut dribble the ball up to the net, slam it past Banji and into the corner for another three points.

The crowd roar, enjoying the antics on the field.

Back at centre, before Jack has a chance to warn Ruby to hold back from baiting Ryker, he hears her attack him.

'You're such a tough guy, picking on girls like that. Back where we come from, you'd be called a lowlife!'

Ryker lets out a massive roar, picks Ruby up by the throat and throws her across the field.

The crowd fire up with excitement, cheering and egging him on.

Ruby rolls on the ground, coughing and spluttering, clutching at her throat and gasping for air. Jack sprints to her side. Max, too, arrives as if out of nowhere and starts to repair the damage done to her crushed airways.

Jack turns to hunt Ryker down but sees Peanut, furious with rage, tearing across the field with his hurley at the ready. He vanishes, leaving the stick in mid-air, then it swings with force at Ryker and hits its target squarely in the gut. The bully doubles over, winded, then flails blindly at his unseen attacker, trying to ward Peanut off.

'You scum bag!' Peanut bellows. 'I'll teach you to beat up on a girl, you worthless piece of shit!' Peanut delivers blow after blow to his head.

Ryker doesn't know what's hit him.

In the frenzy Peanut materialises and continues to punch until his fists are bloodied.

Jack races over and pulls him off before Ryker has a chance to retaliate. 'Are you insane? He's going to kill you. Get the hell out of here!'

Ryker is seething.

Jack stands face to face with him, ready for the fall-out. He summons his strength of calmness and radiates it over Ryker like a blanket. Instantaneously,

Jack sees the change. Ryker appears confused. His expression conflicted. Then he stumbles backwards as though he'd been struck.

'Let's just play the game, all right?' Jack shouts. 'What the hell are we doing here? Are we going to kill each other for the sake of these people?'

Ryker vacantly searches Jack's face and shakes his head as if to rearrange his thoughts in his rattled brain.

The horn sounds for the next round, but not everyone's prepared.

Max is healing Peanut's broken fists, having just finished attending to Ruby. He sees Edra flash past them, hurley on the ball, rapidly approaching Kenny, who's anxiously defending at the net.

This spurs Jack into gear. It's a race to get to the goals in time to block Edra. She's much too fast; he doesn't think he'll make it. But then he spots Peanut tearing up the field and gaining on her. He, it seems, isn't done trying. He suddenly vanishes.

Edra gains momentum, her eye on the goal. She raises her stick in preparation to strike. Peanut, hurley extended, is almost onto her, but he's too late. Edra whacks the ball straight at Kenny. He dives head-on to block the ball and somehow manages to deflect it out of the goal area, but, unfortunately, straight to Ulan. Quick to take the advantage, Ulan swings hard, connects with the ball, and pockets the *sliotar*, past Kenny, for a three-point goal.

The horn sounds. The crowd cheers.

Ulan falls to the ground, doubled over in obvious pain, clutching her waist, and struggling to breathe.

Although concerned for her, Jack keeps his distance and calls the team to re-group. 'Unlucky, Kenny. Good try, though.'

'Sorry, guys; I didn't see her there. I was too busy crapping my pants, waiting for Edra.'

'It's all good,' Jack tells him. 'It looks like Ulan is injured, and I don't think they've got very much left in them. How are we doing? Ruby, you okay?'

'Yeah, thanks to Max, I am.'

'Peanut, try to keep your cool,' Jack warns. 'You're lucky Ryker didn't rip your bloody head off. Let's just play the game, okay? Kenny, how long do you think is left on the clock?'

'Since the rain has let up, at a rough guess, maybe a little over an hour.'

'Okay, we can do this. Ruby, let's switch, I'll go centre,' Jack offers.

'No, I'm good, Jack.'

'Sure?'

She nods.

'Okay, then, let's go win us a game!'

Back on centre, Ruby with her head held high,

joins Ryker. He looks down at her with disdain. At the sound of the horn, she challenges for the ball, wins and off-loads it to an invisible Peanut. He runs with the ball, avoids Ryker by kicking it past him, and then hits it back to Ruby. Anticipating the move, Edra is there in a flash, but, forced on by momentum, she collides with Ruby's shield. The impact causes Edra to fall back and hit her head with a crunching thud.

She doesn't get up.

Ryker and Ulan run to her aid.

Unobstructed now, Ruby takes the ball all the way to the goals, by-passes Banji, and pockets it into the net.

The crowd cheers.

Edra stirs after a few moments. She sits up, holding her head, in obvious pain and confusion.

Jack carefully approaches them. 'Is she all right?'

'What the hell do you care?' Ryker turns his back to him.

Jack looks on for a moment, then calls his team aside. 'Listen up, guys, they're not doing great. Edra's really hit the ground hard. I can't see her going on.'

The horn, once again, sounds for play to commence.

Jack gets his team to take their positions.

Ryker hangs back, seemingly reluctant to return to the centre. He paces back and forth a few times, clearly struggling with his thoughts. He looks at each of his team mates, then after a moment's hesitation, he purposely walks towards The Ancients and concedes defeat.

The Ancients acknowledge the loss, but the crowd boo and hiss their disapproval— clearly, they haven't seen enough.

'Tough crowd,' Peanut says to Jack.

'I think it's best all round. It'll give us a chance to regroup for tomorrow.'

'I can't imagine them being in any fit state tomorrow, even after a rest.' Peanut says.

'You've got a point there. But at least there'll be a tomorrow.'

'What d'ya mean?'

Jack looks over at the others, who are talking excitedly about the win, and lowers his voice. 'I didn't want to freak everyone out, but you do realise that if we'd lost today, we'd be packing our bags and facing the forest people.'

'We'd be in exile. Geez, I forgot about that.'

'At least now, we've got a chance to equalise. And from what I can see, they're hurting so bad that the next challenge should be in the bag.'

'Should be. Don't count your chickens, mate!'

'Yeah, I reckon you're right, there. Anything could still happen.'

36

PLANTING A SEED

JACK

Back in the chamber, drenched and mud-stained, Jack debates whether they should go to the lake to clean up or stay put. He doesn't want a chance meeting with the other team, so they reluctantly send Peanut out to scope the area.

'And don't take any chances,' Max warns. 'I mean it, just find out where they are and come straight back, okay?'

'All right, already, I get it. I promise not to do anything stupid.'

The moment he's gone, Jack immediately regrets sending him. He stares at the door, wondering if he should follow. But before he can act on it, Peanut returns.

'They're down at the lake, but I don't think they'll be there much longer, Ryker seems in a hurry to get them inside.'

'Then we'll eat first,' Max suggests. 'Let's see if they've brought anything we can stomach.'

'I'm starving. I reckon I could eat an elephant,' Peanut whines.

Kenny grins. 'Be careful what you ask for.'

Shocked, Ruby asks, 'Elephant? No, they wouldn't dare; would they?'

'Come on, Rubes. Man, you're gullible. Kenny's only joking. Right Kenny?' Peanut's smile quickly disappears when Kenny's expression becomes grave. 'Seriously, mate, you were joking, weren't you?'

Kenny chuckles. 'And you called Ruby gullible?'

'Phew, you had me going there for a sec. I can't imagine anyone eating elephant; they'd be too tough, wouldn't they?'

'No, in some cultures they do eat them, but in this type of setting they won't because they're too valuable to kill for food,' Kenny explains. 'They use them for their entertainment instead. What they'll use for our meals is whatever's in abundance, like mice. Dormice are considered a delicacy,' Kenny says straight-faced.

'Okay, enough with the gross information overload, master Google,' Ruby says. 'I think I'll stick to eating things that don't need to be caught, plucked or skinned, thank you very much.'

Max sighs as she shares around some bread. 'I really miss Annie's cooking.'

'I miss Annie's cooking, too,' Peanut moans, then he turns to Jack, who's quiet and deep in his own thoughts. 'What's up? You're looking a bit too serious.'

'What? Oh, just mulling over a few things.'

'Like what?'

'Honestly?' The idea he's been bouncing around in his head is a little half-baked, so he's a bit hesitant to share it, but he gives it a go. 'I've been rethinking the idea of finding a way out of here. I know we decided against it before, but something's gnawing at me.'

'Yeah? Okay.' Peanut clearly wasn't expecting that. 'To tell you the truth, I haven't given it much thought, myself. Have you come up with something?'

'Nothing concrete. The thing is … we've been putting all of our energy into winning these games, but what if we can't do it? I mean, what if we lose again? Right now the other team are hurting, so there's a good chance we won't lose, but like I said to Peanut earlier, anything can happen. Let's be realistic here, the South Africans are ahead, two to one. If they win one more challenge, we're goners. We need to win the next two challenges for any hope to compete against the Realm's Champions. And even if we somehow manage to get there, what if it's impossible to beat these guys? I'm not saying I don't hold much hope for us; it's more that I don't trust them. I seriously think we need to come up with a plan B.'

Max nods. 'You've got a point, but what can we do?'

'I know we said it was a big risk, but I think one of us should try to get back to the gateway. If we can somehow do that, then we can get help. And I'm guessing that we're not the only ones trapped here. There may be stacks of kids that've fallen victim to this place. Remember those missing kids we talked about at school? Who's to say they're not out there somewhere?'

'Hey,' Peanut says, 'imagine finding them and taking them home. That'd be awesome! But that's if they're not dead already.'

'Peanut!' Ruby glares at him, horrified by his tactlessness. 'How about learning to filter the things that pop into that brain of yours?'

Jack shakes his head. 'The thing is, no one deserves to be treated like this, not even someone like that jerk, Ryker. If we can somehow find a way out of here, we could be their way out, too.'

'But they'll kill us if we try to escape,' Ruby says. 'We weren't keen to do it before, why are we thinking to risk it now? What's changed?'

'We have,' Jack replies. 'We've got superpowers, and we've learnt how to use them. We might actually be able to do it now.'

Peanut frowns. 'Even if one of us somehow manages to break out of here, how are we supposed to find our way back to the gateway? The forest is huge. And the damn thing is virtually invisible. You'd miss it even if you tripped over it. I reckon you'd have Buckley's chance of finding it!'

'And that's where my thinking hits a brick wall.'

They fall silent for a moment, taking that in.

'Maybe I can help there,' Kenny offers quietly. 'The day we were captured, I left a trail. I reckon I could find my way back if I had to.'

Four stunned faces simultaneously whip around and gape at Kenny.

Peanut finds his voice first. 'You mean to tell me that while the rest of us were freaking out after falling into an unknown world, then running for our lives from half-a-dozen muscle-clad goons, you had enough wits about you to leave a trail?'

Kenny goes red with the sudden attention. 'Well, yeah. It just came to me.'

'Unbelievable.' Peanut shakes his head. 'Kenny, that brain of yours just blows me away. I mean, how does something like that just come to you?'

'Remember how the guard ripped my shirt when he caught me? Well, somehow that gave me the idea to leave pieces of my shirt as a trail.'

'Kenny, you're a genius!' Jack grabs him in a headlock and rubs the top of his head before releasing him. 'You may have just given us a way out of here. Why didn't you say something sooner?'

'I kind'a got caught up with the challenges, so I guess I forgot,' he says sheepishly.

'Do you really think you could pick up the trail?' Max asks. 'I mean, we've had stacks of rain the last twenty-four hours; the trail might have washed away.'

'That's true.' He shrugs. 'I guess I won't know until I try.'

'So do we send Kenny,' Max asks, 'or is Peanut the safer option since he's most likely to get past the guards?'

'I'm your guy!' Peanut grins, his eyes alive with excitement.

'This is massive,' Jack says, feeling a little unsure. 'There's a lot to think about. As it is, if we lose tomorrow, we'll be thrown into the forest and have no choice but to try and find our way back to the portal, anyway. But if we win, we could be stuck in here for some time, so we might need to look into this other plan a bit more.'

Their silence says Jack's given them something to

think about.

'I vote we sleep on it,' he says. 'We can put together some ideas in the morning. Agreed?'

The others nod.

Although terrified of what the plan means, Jack feels lighter, relieved of the weight of hopelessness. Having a plan B means they're gaining back some control over their fate.

'Now, I don't know about you guys,' he says, 'but I'm hanging for a wash.'

37

'What Have you Done?'

Ulan

The third challenge left the South Africans bruised, bloodied and miserable, and after spending a few minutes by the lake cleaning themselves up, Ulan, Edra and Banji return to their chamber. Thankfully, Ryker takes extra time outside for himself, allowing them to talk freely.

Ulan rests a cool, wet cloth on Edra's forehead, trying to bring her some relief. 'Edra, I'm really worried about you.'

'I'm feeling a bit better; at least the nausea is easing,' Edra assures her. 'And if I keep one of my eyes closed, I'm not seeing two of everything, so that kind of helps. But it's this headache … It feels like my head's going to explode.'

'You really copped it,' Banji says sympathetically, 'no wonder it hurts.'

'I'll be okay, but Ulan, you're a mess. What's going on?'

Ulan glances towards the door. Tears sting her eyes. 'Guys, I can't do this anymore. I'm in agony, here. I really tried today, but it near killed me.'

'And that's putting it lightly. I know how bad you really are.' Banji runs his hands through his hair in frustration. 'That's it; you're done! And I don't care what Ryker thinks, anymore. Edra and I will just have to try harder. Right, Edra?'

'Of course. We'll work it out.'

'Where is he anyway?' Banji asks. 'Not that I'm complaining, but he's been gone a while.'

'He's in a pretty bad way,' Ulan says. 'He looks worse than I've ever seen him. He can barely open his eyes now. He really copped a beating from that guy. What possessed him to attack the girl?'

'I reckon he's losing it,' Banji says. 'Whatever's going on in his head, he needs to stop because he's going to ruin it for all of us.'

Just then, they hear a commotion down the passageway, the sounds of muffled cries and frantic struggles gradually coming closer. They stand ready, anticipating some form of conflict, but what they see as the door opens, leaves them shocked beyond belief.

'Ryker! What the hell have you done?'

38

PEANUT THE HERO

JACK

Jack lies on a rock, drying after a swim. The rain has passed, leaving hardly a cloud in sight, and the warmth from the sun seeps through to his bones, lulling him into a state of calm.

His thoughts focus on a getaway plot, unfurling strategies. The more he considers Peanut for the job, the more it makes sense. *Thank God for Kenny. What a genius!* His forward thinking has given hope to an otherwise hopeless plan for escape.

In his mind's eye, Jack envisages Peanut slipping quietly past the guards and backtracking all the way to the gateway using Kenny's clues. Then he sees the return of Peanut, the hero, smashing through the portal with a truckload of military personnel, ready to kick arse and save the day. And in the end, due to the impact of such a huge contingent, more than five innocent victims are rescued. From the collapse of the Realm Empire, dozens of missing kids are discovered, saved and reunited with their long-lost families. Ryker and his group included.

Yeah, we'll even save that jerk!

Jack can't help but smile with an outcome like that. He can picture Peanut now, revelling in his success. *And I bet he'll expect to get all the credit.*

'Has anyone seen Max?' Kenny asks suddenly.

Jack's daydream bubble bursts. Overcome by dread, he staggers to his feet, his stomach twisting in a knot. 'Where's Max? Ruby, is she with you?'

'No.' Ruby's eyes grow wide with fear. 'I thought she was behind the boulder getting dressed.'

'Max!' Jack yells. 'Max!' No reply. 'MAX!'

They run to the boulder, but there's no sign of her.

'Peanut, go inside and see if she's there. Hurry!'

Jack, Kenny and Ruby run around in a frenzy, calling out for Max. But there's no answer.

Peanut returns moments later.

'Anything?' Jack asks. But he already knows.

The confirmation comes when Peanut looks him in the eye and shakes his head.

'Jesus! They've taken her!'

39

DESPERATE TIMES CALL FOR DESPERATE MEASURES

MAX

Heart pounding painfully, Max thrashes about, trying to free herself from her abductor's suffocating hold. She tries to bite the meaty hand that obstructs her breathing, but the more she fights, the tighter the grip.

'Stop!' he threatens, 'or I'll crush the last breath out of you, and then you'll be useless to anyone!'

She freezes, frightened out of her wits, but her gaze darts around, frantically searching for an escape.

One of the twins, Ulan, approaches Max's captor

like you would a rampant beast—hands held up in a non-threatening manner. 'Ryker,' she says in a quiet and gentle voice, 'look at me and listen carefully. What you've just done, we can undo. But you've got to let her go.' She's being careful not to anger him. 'I've read her thoughts. She'll help us if you don't hurt her.'

Ryker's strangle-hold on Max lessens, and the pain from her crushed throat becomes somewhat bearable.

Ulan tries again. 'Ryker, it doesn't have to be like this.'

Max raises her eyes and sees the look of pure evil in Ryker's glare. The intensity paralyses her with fear; those eyes are the windows to the soul of the devil himself.

'Please, Ryker.' Ulan begs.

And then his look changes, and softens somehow. Max can see his inner turmoil.

After a few moments of silence, he seems to come to a decision. 'I'm going to put you down, and when I do, you're going to fix us. Got it?'

Max, her eyes wide with fear, nods her understanding.

He releases his hold.

She bounds from his grasp and dashes across the other side of the room, trying to put distance between them. 'You're insane! Get the hell away from me!'

Ulan jumps between them in a protective manner. 'Ryker, listen to me, and trust what I'm about to say. They're innocent victims here, just like us. She's a good person. And what you're doing isn't right.'

Isn't right? It's called kidnapping! And to think we were coming back for you once we got out of here. Fat chance now, you jerk!

'They're planning to escape! And they're going to get us out too!' Banji says excitedly.

Max is horrified and goes cold, knowing her thoughts have been invaded. She squats in the corner with her hands pressed against her ears, eyes tightly shut, and mentally sings *Survivor.*

'Ryker, get out!' Edra shouts. 'You've made a mess of things.'

'No!' he roars. 'We've suffered enough. She's going to help us, and she's going to do it now!'

Edra stands tall, making her already impressive height more intimidating, and positions herself next to the twins with her arms folded across her puffed-out chest.

The three friends stand resolute.

'Leave. Now.' Edra warns him. 'You've gone too far this time. You're irrational and your decisions are jeopardising our chances of getting out of here. We're a team. We make decisions together. You're not your father. We will not take orders from you!'

Ryker stops. His expression says he thinks Edra has clearly overstepped a boundary. Seething from the uprising, he turns on his heel and storms out.

The mood shifts dramatically.

'What a nightmare. He's completely out of control.' Edra rubs restlessly at her temples. 'What do we do now?'

Ulan puts her arm around Edra's waist. 'Look, he just needs time to calm down. He'll get it eventually. Deep down, he knows that what he's done is wrong.'

Max realises with a shudder that Banji has been studying her intently. His stare makes her feel uncomfortable. She can't believe how easily he accessed her thoughts earlier and wonders whether he knows about Kenny's trail.

'They've left a trail,' he exclaims.

What the hell? Shut him out!

Banji is beyond ecstatic. 'Do you realise what this means? Oh my God, there's finally some hope. They just might be able to do it. They'll definitely have a better chance than what we ever did, especially when one of them can slip past the guards without being seen.'

'Maybe there's hope for them, but there's none for us,' Ulan says bitterly. 'You read her mind, Banji, Ryker's ruined any chance of them helping us now.

And I don't blame her. Why would anyone come back for us after what he's done? I can tell you now, they won't have a bar of it when they realise what's happened, especially Jack. Ryker's made a target for himself by taking his girl.'

What? Who's she calling Jack's girl!

Max suddenly feels disorientated and lightheaded. But her confused thoughts take a back seat when she sees Edra slowly approaching her.

'My name's Edra,' she says. 'Ryker won't hurt you. We won't let that happen. Look, it's hard to believe, but he's normally nothing like this. Being trapped in this place does that to a person. We've been waiting for someone to fall through one of the gateways so we can challenge them for our freedom. It's been four agonising years since we've had that chance. And now that you're here, that time has come; we could finally be going home.'

Max watches them carefully from her crouched position and listens to what they have to say. Edra's explanations answer a lot of her hunches. She refrains from engaging with them and lets Edra talk, hoping that she'll let slip something useful. She considers what Banji has already revealed—that they've tried to escape before.

'Yeah, we've tried several times.' Ulan reads her thoughts. 'And with what your team has, you guys might be able to pull it off. And Edra,' she warns her team mate, 'be careful what you reveal. She's still our rival.'

Max snaps shut her thoughts and buries her face in her lap.

'Yeah, it gets a little annoying, but you'll soon get used to them being in your head.' Edra laughs.

Max closes her eyes and tries to block them out anyway.

'You won't get far doing that,' Banji tells her. 'I'll warn you now, you'll exhaust yourself trying. I'm afraid we'll penetrate your every thought eventually. Anyway, now that you know about us, it's only fair that we ask about your group.'

Max concentrates harder on blocking their mental penetration.

'We know you're a healer and that the tall red-headed guy can go invisible; your leader has strength and is immune to pain; and of course, the other girl has her infamous shield. But what about your other teammate? It's been bugging me. I need to know. What does he bring to the team?'

Max presses her palms harder over her ears and tries to block out all thoughts of Kenny and his genius mind.

'Oh, but of course. It makes sense now.' Banji almost laughs.

'Wow!' Ulan says.

Max is gobsmacked. *How the hell did they get in?* She isn't going to win this battle; she can see that now.

Edra looks from one twin to the other. 'Okay, will one of you tell me already? I hate it when you two do this.'

Ulan laughs at Edra's look of hopelessness. 'He's the reason they know so much; he's like a human search engine.'

'That explains a lot,' Banji says with relief. 'It's taken us years to become so well-informed.'

'Max, is it?' Ulan says as she walks closer. 'Just as Edra said earlier, we've been trapped here for a long time. There were five of us in the beginning …' she looks over her shoulder at Edra, who withdraws, appearing disturbed by the conversation. She continues hesitantly, 'We started off much like you did. We had to compete against another team—a group of four kids—victims of the same portal you fell through. This is what The Ancients do; they wait for what they call "Innocents" to fall through the gateways, and then pit them against each other. The winners, as you know, face their super-team, the Invincibles. The losing team are exiled into the forest, where we're told you'll face mortal dangers. So we fought these kids and progressed to the final challenge where, suffice it to say, we were beaten. And in the throes of the task …,' Ulan struggles to go on, 'well, we lost our friend, Jaeger. We've been imprisoned ever since.'

Max looks across to Edra who is clearly struggling to keep it together. Max can't imagine the hurt they've been through. Losing one of her friends would be unbearable. Her heart warms to them a little.

She then considers Ryker; would they, too, turn savage eventually if they were to remain in this hell-hole?

'Ryker isn't normally like this,' Ulan assures her. 'His intentions, although misguided, are only because he's super worried about us. I imagine it stems from his powerlessness to save Jaeger back then. Max, we're all carrying injuries, and, although he'll never ask it for himself, Ryker just wants our suffering to stop.'

Max watches as the three of them then have a silent conversation. Edra looks imploringly to Ulan, and appears to communicate something of importance, because after a short hesitation the twins nod in agreement.

Edra then approaches her. 'None of us have a choice here; we need to finish this. So if you agree to heal us, we'll make sure that Ryker lets you go. And I'll give you my word, if we somehow beat the Invincibles in the end, we'll come back for you guys, because you've shown us that you'd do the same for us. But if you win, all I ask is that you honour that promise to me, too.'

How can she not do this? They're all victims here. But with Ryker's abusive behaviour fresh on her mind, Max is hesitant to make that vow. He's shown nothing but aggression and an obvious determination to annihilate them at any cost. Her internal struggle to make the right decision has her confused.

But maybe there's a better way. Why can't we join forces? It makes sense, doesn't it? Two teams working together, fighting back, challenging the oppressors.

Ulan and Banji exchange curious looks. Max realises they've been reading her thoughts again.

Ulan nods. 'You've got a point; we could do so much more if we worked together on this.'

And if we do, we'd not only be freeing ourselves, we'd also be helping the other victims that are probably still out there.

In disturbingly vivid detail, Max imagines all those poor kids trapped in the realm, lost to their families. She imagines them living like savages, fighting to stay alive. Max realises that the kids Ulan was talking about earlier—the kids they competed against—are probably the kids that went missing from home five years ago.

Oh my God, we need to find them.

How can she not help? The decision is suddenly easy. 'Okay, let's make a pact. We'll work on this together. I'll talk to my team, and you get Ryker to come around, and we'll make some plans. Deal?' Max smiles, knowing that she's made the right decision.

Edra, Ulan and Banji appear more than relieved.

With the treaty secured, Max offers to help them with their injuries.

Firstly, she assesses Edra and quickly heals her concussion and double vision. Max then attends to Ulan and is shocked to find that she has a punctured lung from a broken rib. There's no way they would've been able to compete like this.

When she's finished tending to their injuries, a deluge of dread overcomes Max. *I've just fixed them. What's to stop them now from backing out of the deal?* She may have just ruined her own team's chance of beating them in the coming challenges. How could she have been so gullible?

She catches a look shared by the twins and suddenly feels sick to the stomach. Could she be right? Have they just tricked her? She breaks out in a cold sweat. She needs to get out of there, and fast. 'Please, I want to go.'

Edra leads her to the door. 'Of course, and we'll explain everything to Ryker. He'll be okay once he sees that you've helped us. Please don't judge him,

Max; he really is a good person. I only ask that you try to forgive him.'

Max nods. She doesn't trust herself to say another word. She'll agree to anything, so long as they let her leave. Now. Her anxiety levels are skyrocketing through the roof.

Edra leads her out to the garden. They see Ryker sitting on a boulder, deep in thought. When he sees them approaching, he jumps down in front of them.

Max is ready to run.

Edra steps protectively in front of her. 'Ryker, please don't. We need to let her go.'

Ryker says nothing. He turns in anger and charges back inside.

Before Edra follows, she reaches out to embrace Max, then steps away with tears in her eyes, and a grateful smile on her face, her sincerity seemingly real.

Max feels numb and questions her paranoia. She hardly knows what to think anymore. It takes her a few seconds to realise that she's free.

At that moment, Jack and Peanut appear out of the woods, and without hesitation, she runs into Jack's awaiting arms.

'Thank God you're all right.' He pulls away from her, looks her over to make sure she isn't hurt, then tugs her back into a tight hold.

'Okay, you two, enough with the soppy reunion,' Peanut teases. 'Let's get out of here before they change their minds.'

Jack grabs Max's hand and leads them as far away from Ryker's team as possible.

Ulan's words echo in Max's ears as she looks down at their clasped hands—*Ryker has made a target for himself by taking his girl!*

A warm, fuzzy feeling that has nothing to do with healing starts deep in Max's belly. Her heart begins to pound alarmingly fast.

'Am I Jack's girl?'

40

THE DEBATE

MAX

Back in the chamber, before relaying to the others what happened, Max decides that her moment of paranoia was just a figment of her imagination, a delusion brought on by the stress of the situation. So she lets it slide and focuses her energy on building this new-found alliance. She tells them what happened, being careful to sugar-coat the bulk of it, not wanting to create hostility between the two teams before they even get a chance to get started.

'We were worried sick!' Ruby's arms wind so tightly around Max's waist that she can hardly breathe.

'We quickly figured out that they took you, but there was no way we could get in to come after you,' Peanut says. 'It wasn't long before Ryker came out like a raging bull. Man, he was fuming. Jack and I nearly crapped our pants 'cause we weren't expecting him. Geez, Max, what did you do to piss him off? You know you can be real scary sometimes, don't ya?'

Since Peanut is doing his typical diverting-off-on-a-tangent recount, Jack takes over. 'With Ryker away from you, we figured you were pretty safe inside with the others. We debated for a while on what to do next. I wanted Peanut to go in after you and make sure you were okay, but Peanut suggested we wait it out ...'

Peanut does a quick, double-take, and Max is certain, by the look of Peanut's expression, that Jack's version must be somewhat watered down. And of course, in his typical fashion, Peanut doesn't leave it at that.

'Nice recount, mate,' he says, smothering a laugh. 'We "debated", did we? Um, that's an interesting way of putting it.'

Jack gives him a threatening glare. 'Nothing interesting in it. There's no need to go on about things, *mate*; that's how it was.'

'Man, were you even there?' Peanut laughs.

'Let it go, will ya!'

Peanut's taunting has Jack looking very uncomfortable. 'Look, whatever. It's not important, and no one wants to hear the details.'

'Oh, I beg to differ,' Peanut says mischievously. 'In fact, we could do with a good laugh.' He gives Max a wink. 'Anyway,' he returns his attention to Jack, 'the way I remember it, when Ryker came out, you, my friend, went a little batshit crazy—for lack of a better description.'

Jack's expression turns murderous. He looks like he's going to strangle his friend.

Peanut, on the other hand, is in his element. 'Man, you should've seen him. He literally turned into the Hulk. He went ballistic. I literally had to hold him down to stop him from diving onto the jerk and beating the crap out of him. I'm surprised he didn't hear us behind the bushes. I tell ya, I had to use everything in me to hold him down. He became this deranged power-packed killing machine!'

'Righto, that's enough!'

But Peanut isn't finished. 'I don't think so, mate. Where was I? Oh yeah. Jack "did" want me to go in after Max—that part's true. But I knew I couldn't risk leaving him on his own in case he decided to attack Ryker the moment I left. And, no offense mate, but Ryker would have annihilated ya. Seriously man, you need to get a grip. Max was all right in the end, wasn't she? All that agro for nothing.'

Jack turns a bright shade of red and looks like he wants to dig a hole and hide.

Max is dying from embarrassment. She feels she needs to say something but is struggling to recover from what was just said.

'So, Max, they know about our Plan B, huh?' And just like that, Kenny diffuses a potentially explosive situation.

'Um, yeah, they thought it might work,' Max says quickly, thankful for the diversion. 'They figure Peanut's got a pretty good chance of getting past the guards.'

Kenny nods. 'Okay, given that we've got this alliance, maybe we should meet up and hear what they've got to say. What do you think? Will they be in it?'

That niggly doubt rears its ugly head again. Max tries to ignore it. 'I can't talk for Ryker because he wasn't there when we made the pact. The others would be, I guess.'

We shook on it. Quit with the paranoia, will you!

'But from all accounts,' she continues, 'it sounds like Ryker could come around eventually. If I get a chance in the arena tomorrow, I'll approach Edra and ask her.'

'But we need to be careful not to reveal any alliance,' Kenny warns them. 'So we stay just as competitive as before, okay? The Ancients can't get suspicious. They need to believe that we're still fighting to win.'

'Kenny's right,' Jack says, his earlier disagreement with Peanut forgotten. 'Yes, we still need to look like we're sworn enemies, but not only for the sake of appearances, but because we really need to stay in the competition now.'

'What do you mean?' Ruby asks.

'Remember we spoke about this, Ruby, if we lose tomorrow, they'll exile us. Alliance or not, we'll be facing a new kind of threat. We can't afford to drop the ball now.'

'Oh my God, that's right!'

'Yeah,' Jack says grimly. 'I was pretty confident that we'd win tomorrow's challenge, but since they've had their injuries healed, we're back to being on an even playing field.'

A cold shiver runs down Max's spine. And Jack is quick to notice. 'Max, you couldn't help it, okay? You were kidnapped; what else were you supposed to do?'

She makes a conscious effort to believe that. This helps placate her somewhat.

'So tomorrow we need to go out there, play hard and win. It's as simple as that. And if we lose, well, we keep our fingers crossed that we can stay safe out there while we look for the portal.'

'Keep our fingers crossed!' Ruby laughs without humour. 'We'll need more than dumb luck protecting us, Jack.'

'So use it as your motivation for tomorrow's challenge.'

'Great,' she moans. 'No pressure!'

'Come on, Rubes,' Peanut says playfully, 'where's that fighting spirit? With that awesome shield of yours, how could we possibly lose?'

The mood shifts with Peanut's excited confidence—or maybe it has something to do with Jack sneakily projecting his blanket of calm over them—Max suspects it does. Either way, the five friends spend the last few hours of the night talking optimistically about what tomorrow will bring.

With each discussion, Max sees them gaining strength and control over their situation. She forgets her previous doubt and focuses with confidence on all the positives that came from today. Yes, they won their first challenge, but that win pales to insignificance compared to the new-found hope they have in making an unlikely alliance with the enemy. They're not alone anymore. And more importantly, they're one step closer to going home.

41

TRUST

JACK

*J*ack wakes early to a day that's bright and sunny, a complete contrast to how he's feeling. He struggled last night with all the negative energy that potentially could've broken his team's spirit. Thankfully, with a little superhuman intervention, he managed to turn it around.

If only he could be so kind to himself. His head aches from all the scrambled thinking that plagued him in a broken sleep. He tossed and turned half the night, worried about today's challenge. What lies ahead of them, he can only guess at. But what he knows for sure is that there's a big possibility that they'll be exiled into the forest to face God only knows what. *How are we supposed to fend for ourselves against wild animals, or wild people for that matter?*

He doesn't voice his concerns, especially to Max. He can't be so naïve as to wholly and solely count on the promise she made with Edra. Bottom line, he just doesn't trust Ryker. Losing today will mean that Ryker holds all the cards and has total control over dealing them. Jack needs to maintain some control over their own fate. In his own tormented mind, he knows they need to keep their focus on getting rid of the other team by beating them. With them gone, they can decide on which path to take—fight the Invincibles and win the ultimate challenge, or go with Plan B. Either way they need to win today.

Max approaches Jack after breakfast with the same concerns. 'Jack, I'm worried. I'm having second thoughts. I don't trust Ryker—the guy plays dirty.'

He can't afford to let her see him affected. 'Whatever happens, happens, Max. We'll know in the first few minutes of the challenge if they're in with us or not. If they haven't been able to talk Ryker around, we'll just have to regroup and change our strategy.'

'Ryker won't listen to them; I know it. Maybe we should do this on our own. What if I've read too much into the deal? Maybe I got it wrong.'

Jack can't understand what's gotten into her. From all accounts, yesterday's pact was virtually set in stone. This morning's a different story. He knows now that she hasn't told him everything that happened. Something's wrong … and that "something" is Ryker.

'That jerk has a lot to answer for,' Jack says to Peanut later that morning. 'If I find out that he hurt her, I'll hunt him down and rip his head off!'

'Whoa! Here we go again. I thought you'd learnt your lesson after yesterday's debacle. Ease up, buddy. All this agro isn't going to help anyone. Like I said before, you need to get a grip and focus on the game.'

Jack tries to calm down. Peanut's right. They can't afford to go into the challenge with that screwed-up way of thinking.

He spends a good part of the morning psyching himself up. Once his head's in the right place, he focuses on the rest of the team. By the time the guards come to collect them for their fourth challenge, the team is energised and eager to claim their second victory.

They're once again presented to The Ancients. As they approach the podium, Jack searches the arena for a hint to what today's challenge is. The tall walls from the previous game have been pulled down, and the set-up has been reconfigured. He's momentarily amazed at this immediate transformation, but then he realises that with superhuman skills anything can happen. From where he stands, he can't make out the format of the arena. He looks to Kenny for guidance, but Kenny shrugs his shoulders; he hasn't got a clue either. Jack begins to worry.

Side by side, the teams stand waiting to hear from the Ancient ruler. As Pius starts his address, Jack casually looks around the arena, noting, once again, the full stadium, then he turns his gaze to the opposition. He makes the briefest eye contact with Ryker, and in that split-second instance he's surprised to acknowledge that the truce is on. Jack questions the look, thinking he may have imagined it. But to his astonishment, Ryker gives him a reassuring nod.

Max has succeeded in turning the tides around.

Max can't see Ryker from where she is, so Jack tries letting her know. She needs that reassurance right now. He sees her lean a little forward, trying to get a glimpse of Edra, searching for confirmation that everything's okay. Jack wills her to look at him. He can give her what she's searching for; all she needs to do is look at him. And then, right on cue, she does. He gives her a quick wink and a smile. Her eyes light up with understanding.

'The results of the challenges, thus far,' Pius announces, 'are two victories to the South Africans, and to the Australians, one. Today's challenge, *Phaininda*, comes from the Ancient Greeks. Guards prepare the arena.'

The crowd cheer in excitement.

The guards guide them to a playing area the size of a tennis court. It's outlined and divided into three sections with two opposing courts divided by a central white court of smaller width.

Jack looks over to the other team. They're far enough away from them to talk without being heard. 'They look a little confused about this game,' he says, 'hopefully they're not familiar with it. I know we've discussed this game, Kenny, but just run it by us again.'

They don't have time for him to elaborate, so he keeps it simple. 'Okay, here are the rules in a nut shell. Each team starts in opposing sides of the court, leaving the white inner field free. The game begins when a ball is thrown into the inner field, then all players are free to move around the court and try to get possession of the ball. The ball can be passed from player to player, like in netball. To get a point, you need to pass the ball from the outer field to a player in the inner field.

'When a point is won, the winning team starts the next match in the white field with the opposing team having possession of the ball in the outer fields. The team in the centre need to block the other team from entering the white field so they don't get a chance to score, all the while trying to get possession of the ball from the other team. First team to reach twenty-one points, wins. Is everyone good with that, then?'

They nod, all raring to go.

'Remember, we might have an alliance, but we still need to keep playing to win,' Jack reminds them. 'We can't let the guards get suspicious, so we play hard, okay?'

'Got it. Let's whip some butts!' Peanut says with an excited grin.

Jack feels good about this challenge, but before they begin, he gives them some final pointers. 'It might get a bit rough out there, so, Max and Kenny, it might be an idea if you guys stay mostly in the outer fields and feed the ball to the rest of us. Ruby, use your shield to keep the others out of the inner field, especially Ryker, he'll be their main scorer. If you can keep the others at bay, Peanut and I can work together to get the points. We can do this. Let's even the score!'

They take their positions, and the teams stand opposing each other, waiting. The horn sounds, and a guard throws the ball high in the air above the white centre. Ruby charges straight for Ryker, her shield preventing him from catching the ball. Edra and Peanut go head to head, fumbling to gain a hold on the deflected ball. With a firm nudge, Peanut succeeds in bumping Edra to the ground. He scrimmages and grabs the ball, then passes it to Kenny in the outer field. He passes it back to Jack who's set himself up in the centre to win the first point.

The crowd cheers.

Jack collects his team into the white zone. The ball is in Ulan's possession. The horn sounds again. Ulan throws the ball straight into the white zone where it lands safely in Edra's waiting hand. The second point goes to the South Africans.

Peanut's jaw drops. 'Man, she's fast. I didn't even see her move! We can't let that happen again.'

'Peanut, you're quicker than me, you'll have to cover her,' Jack tells him. 'Stick to her like glue. I'll do my best to work my way into the centre.'

The South Africans stand in the white zone. Max has the ball. The horn blows, Ryker comes at Jack from nowhere and knocks him off his feet. Max throws the ball to Ruby, who's still in the outer field. She, in turn, throws it towards Peanut, who's running into the inner field. Edra intercepts the ball and throws it to Banji in the outer field. He returns it to Edra, who's now in position for another point.

Two-one; the South Africans are leading. The crowd cheer, clearly loving the game.

Jack looks across to the other team. He sees a silent conversation going on between them and realises the twins have been reading their game play.

'Guys, the twins are reading our attack!'

Ryker's team take the centre field again. Jack has the ball. While waiting for the horn, he busies himself jamming the twin's receptors by singing. With his eyes, he tells Peanut to fly into the centre. Ruby catches that look and throws herself in front of Peanut at the blow of the horn. Her shield deflects Ryker when he leaps at Peanut, and creates a safe passage for Peanut to enter the white zone in time to catch Jack's throw.

Two all.

The two teams continue to challenge each other on an even playing field. It isn't as easy as Jack predicted. With the twins intercepting their play, the competition becomes fierce.

The score is soon nineteen to seventeen with the South Africans in front by two points. The competition has been gruelling for both sides. Max, Kenny and Peanut are running out of steam. Ruby has been using her shield well, so hasn't copped the same kind of hiding. His own immunity has him in good stead for a lot more if necessary. Across the court, he can see that the other team are almost wasted. The twins have almost given up. Edra's right there behind them. She's been slowing down the last few matches. Even Ryker, although built like a tank, hasn't got that much more to give.

Jack calls the team over into a circle. 'Guys, we've

got this. They haven't got that much left in them. I know you're all burning, but I can help.'

So, shoulder to shoulder, the five friends stand, feeling the warmth of Jack's energy radiating into their aching bodies, renewing their spirit and confidence.

Having lost the last point, Jack's team have possession of the ball. The South Africans stand in the white zone. The team's ready for their next move, their thoughts blocked to the twins' telepathy.

Jack has the ball at the ready, waiting for the horn to sound. He looks across to Ruby and nods ever so slightly. Ruby acknowledges the sign. Ryker, having caught the unspoken gesture, looks ready to bowl Ruby over, while Edra keeps a close eye on Peanut.

The horn goes, followed by pandemonium. With Jack, Ruby and Peanut being targeted, no one's marking Max. She runs into the centre. Jack throws a decoy pass to Ruby; Ryker takes chase and collides with her shield. Edra, who mistakenly assumes that Ruby has the ball and is going to pass it to Peanut, runs to defend against Peanut. But the ball is still firmly in Jack's grasp. Amongst the confusion, he hurls it into the white zone right into Max's waiting hands.

Point to the Aussies. Score: nineteen to eighteen.

Ryker's team gain possession. Banji holds the ball, ready to throw a pass. The horn sounds. Ruby appears as if from nowhere and knocks Banji to the ground, forcing him to drop the ball. Peanut is quick to recover it, and he throws it to Jack who has made it into the white zone before Edra can intercept.

Another point to the Aussies. Nineteen all.

The crowd goes nuts.

Jack's team stand again in the white zone. He sees Ryker, ball in hand, looking to the twins for instruction, but the confusion on their faces says they can't get a read on the tactics—the singing has them distracted. Ryker appears agitated by this, and when the horn sounds, he hesitates a second too long in passing it. All his players are covered by Jack's team: Peanut keeps Edra out of the white zone; Max knocks Ulan to the ground, and Kenny is on Banji like a rash. Ryker doesn't see Jack coming at him until it's too late. Off balance, he loses possession of the ball. Jack scoops it up and flings it to Max who has made her way into goal zone.

Another point to the Aussies, giving them the lead. One more point for Jack's team will clench the game.

The crowd clap in unison, encouraging the teams to dig deep. The game could potentially end on the next play.

Once again, the South Africans have possession. The pressure's on Ryker to deliver. He stands ready with a fierce grip on the ball. The Aussies are in the white zone. The horn sounds, and Ryker passes the ball to Banji, who throws it to Ulan. Ulan goes to throw the ball to Edra, but Ruby's shield covers her, so Ulan redirects the pass back to Ryker. Peanut anticipates the move, becomes invisible and steps between the thrown ball and Ryker's outstretched hands. Meanwhile, Kenny has made his way into the white zone. Edra sees Kenny's move and, realising the consequences, throws herself towards the centre. Jack anticipates her move and tackles Edra to the ground. Peanut materialises, sees Kenny sitting pretty in the goal zone and throws it into his waiting hands.

Game over.

The crowd roars.

42

THE BIGGER PICTURE

Jack punches his fist in the air and lets out a tremendous hoot. He runs into the centre and crash-tackles Kenny to the ground. Not missing an opportunity for a rumble, Peanut dives on top.

The girls squeal with excitement. Ruby grabs Max in a hug and they bounce up and down in hysterics. 'We won; we won!'

'How awesome was that?' Max giggles uncontrollably.

But across the court, Jack can hear Ryker losing it. The other team's copping his anger. This sets off Jack's radar alert, and he watches as they retreat back to their chamber. Ryker stomps away, metres ahead of the rest of them.

As they head back themselves, Jack pulls Max aside. 'Did you catch that? Ryker just lost his nut. What was that all about?'

Max shrugs and shakes her head.

Jack drops it for now. 'How did you go with Edra?'

Her face lights up. 'I think they're on board with the plan. I slipped her a note during one of the tackles, and she seemed okay with it.'

This reassures Jack. Ryker just must be, plain and simple, a sore loser.

'Hey, what about that Ryker?' Ruby runs up to them and rests her arm across Max's shoulders. 'I guess we didn't have to worry about pretending to be rivals. Boy, what a jerk! Are you sure he wasn't "not" pretending? It seemed real to me.'

This makes Jack wary. He needs to hear what Max wrote in that note. Back in the chamber, he wastes no time in asking.

'I told them that we're all in favour of forming an alliance, and that we should meet to talk about it. I said that we'll be by the large boulder by the lake at sunset tonight.'

'Well, let's see if they turn up,' Peanut says, sounding dubious. 'After today's little exhibition, I don't trust your chances there, Max.'

Jack thinks back to that look Ryker gave him

before the challenge. This reassures him. 'I don't know about that, Peanut. As far as I could tell, he seemed to be on board with everything.'

'Really? I wouldn't be holding my breath if I were you.'

'Quit it, Peanut,' Ruby snaps. 'Stop being so negative. If Max says they'll show, then they will. That's it, end of discussion, okay? So,' she says more calmly to the others, 'are we all going? Max, who do you reckon will turn up?'

'I imagine Edra will be there, and Ryker, I guess, since he feels the need to be in control of everything.'

'Maybe not such a good idea if we all rock up. It might get the guards talking,' Kenny suggests.

'You've got a point, Kenny. So who of us should go?' Jack puts it to the vote.

He's in two minds whether to go himself. Although he feels he needs to be there to sus things out, he's not sure if he can trust being around Ryker. The way he's feeling about the jerk, he's likely to mess things up by beating him to a pulp.

'Okay,' he decides, 'I think it goes without saying that Peanut needs to be there, and how about you, Max? After all, it's your brainchild.'

Max recoils. 'Me? No, no; maybe you should go, Jack. I don't think I could face Ryker right now.'

Jack sees panic in Max's eyes. This startles him.

His mind races, wondering what Ryker could've done to her yesterday. His blood begins to boil. And just like that, there's no longer an alliance. Ryker has gone back to being the enemy.

Jack forces himself to look away. He takes a few deep breaths to calm down. But it's useless, he needs to get out of there. 'Then I'll go,' he tells her curtly. 'Come on, Peanut. You coming?'

To Peanut's surprise, they leave immediately.

Jack charges outside, his mind on Max's reaction. He knows she's not telling them everything.

Peanut takes chase. 'Hey, ease up!'

Jack doesn't stop. He just ploughs through the bushes.

'Hey!' Peanut grabs Jack by the shoulder and swings him around to face him. 'Look, I know it kills you to see Max like that, but come on, what's going on?'

Jack let's out a controlled breath. 'You saw it too? She's bloody petrified of him. What the hell happened yesterday? What did that creep do to her? Mate, I'm struggling to keep it together.'

'Listen,' Peanut says calmly, 'we can't let this idiot stuff up what we're about to do. Just keep your focus on the bigger picture. Think about going home. Think about your family. Hey,' he says with a sudden mischievous gleam in his eyes, 'think about the headlines we'll be making. We'll be famous! Man, we won't be able to go anywhere without everyone knowing who we are. Our Friday nights will be booked up for months!'

'What?' It takes a moment for Peanut's words to hit him, and when they do, Jack shakes his head and laughs. *Only Peanut would think about girls at a time like this.* 'What about Ruby? You gone cold on her or something'?'

'Ruby? No way! She's part of that bigger picture I was talking about.' He grins and waggles his eyebrows.

'Okay, I'll bite.'

'Ruby doesn't know it yet, but she's crazy about me. And with so many girls vying for my attention when we get back, she won't be able to resist. She'll realise that she can't live without me. I'll have her in no time, hook, line and sinker.'

Jack laughs. Peanut and his logic. What kind of crazy goes on in that head of his, he'll never know.

Without realising it, they've arrived at the meeting place. Jack does a quick surveillance of the area and finds that they're alone.

They wait.

43

THE ALLIANCE

ULAN

Back in the chamber, following their second defeat to the Aussies, Edra has just shown them a letter given to her by Max, and all hell has broken loose. Ryker won't have a bar of any alliance now.

'Ryker, please,' Ulan begs. 'What's your problem? Last night we'd all come to an agreement, and now you've gone and done a complete one-eighty. I don't understand. What's changed between then and now? Don't you see that we can't do this without them?'

'I'll admit it, I made a mistake in trusting them. You're living in a world of fantasy if you believe they'll come back for us once we've helped them escape. After what they did in today's challenge, I'm convinced they won't.'

Ulan frowns. 'What's made you so cynical? Has your view on life been so distorted that you've resorted to trusting no one? Not even us! We've already told you that Banji and I have seen Max's thoughts, and we trust her.'

'Really?' he says with a sneer. 'Then she really must've seen you two coming. What's to say she didn't create this illusion in your head? They're all pretty good at playing mind games, remember. And it's obvious they've mastered the ability to distort your telepathy. Why do you think we lost today?'

Edra jumps to her feet, boiling over with anger. 'Now hang on a second! How can you say that? It was you who kidnapped her, remember? What? You think she set up the whole thing, just to trick us into helping them escape? You're delusional!'

Banji tries to calm the situation by approaching Ryker with quiet logic. 'Look, how many failed attempts to escape have we made? We've tried everything, and nothing's worked. They've got someone who can slip by the guards' defences, and they've already left a trail to help them get back to the gateway. They've got a better than good chance to succeed. Why are you blocking us on this?'

Ryker's expression darkens. 'I don't trust them! It's as simple as that,' he roars. 'The only thing that'll be gained by this "meeting" is that they'll use any information we give them to help in their escape, and then they'll leave us here to rot!'

Ulan cowers from Ryker's outrage. She can't bring herself to look at him, let alone argue anymore.

'We've got one more challenge,' Ryker continues, 'our one and only chance to get to the final round. We're going to do this on our own, like we've done before. We will not rely on anyone else, or their empty promises. We're stronger than them. We're better than them. We can win. It's them who need us, not the other way around!'

'Ryker, you know the challenges we've just had are nothing compared to what we'll be facing in the final round,' Edra says with forced restraint.

But he's adamant. 'Yes, but Edra, we've been in training for four years for this. I know we can do it this time.'

'Even with superhuman abilities, we haven't got the stamina that they have,' Banji argues. 'You saw it today. They've got Jack. Our strength only takes us so far before we're wasted. That's why we lost. And without Max's help, we would've had no hope in competing at all today. Max virtually saved us. Doesn't that speak volumes? Can't you see that we can trust them, and that they're not trying to trick us? We'll be so much stronger if we join forces. We can help each other.'

Beyond reasoning now, Ryker explodes. 'Enough! I've said all I'm going to say! And I forbid any of you meeting with them. Is that clear?' Without another word, he storms out, leaving the others at a loss.

'What the hell just happened?' Edra asks in disbelief.

Ulan feels defeated. 'It's useless. We've read his thoughts, and his mind's made up.'

'So what do we do now?'

Banji looks from his sister to Edra. 'We've got no choice; the decision's been made.'

44

Alliance? What Alliance?

Max

'What! They just didn't show?' Max can't believe it. Jack and Peanut have just returned and revealed that the other team had stood them up.

Her head starts spinning and her earlier paranoia comes crashing back. *I don't get it; we had an agreement. I helped them, and they said Ryker would come around!*

'You went to the big boulder by the lake, right?' she asks. 'Maybe you just missed them. Did you get there too late?'

She struggles to get her head around it. But then, reality hits her square between the eyes. *Who am I kidding? Of course, they didn't show. They needed to be fixed, and I stupidly fixed them. What the hell have I done?*

'There's no mistake, Max, they just didn't show,' Peanut tells her.

She takes a moment for the betrayal to sink in.

'Your pact with Edra was solid; I know that for sure,' Jack reassures her, 'so don't beat yourself up. It's not you; it's that idiot, Ryker. He's got some serious trust issues. He must've changed his mind once we beat them today. What did he think? That we were supposed to just let them win? Whatever, Max, it's out of our control now.'

She knows he's right. The other three were probably on board, but through no choice of their own, they've had to bend to what clearly is Ryker's decision.

'So, okay then, that's the end of it,' Peanut sums up. 'We now know where we stand. There'll be no help from them.'

There's no point tormenting herself over it. She's too exhausted to try to work it out anymore, anyway. It's done. Max ends it there.

'So do we stick to the plan and try to get out of here, then?' Peanut asks.

'I think you're the only one that can make that decision, mate. Do you still want to give it a go?' Jack asks.

Peanut smiles his familiar cheeky grin. 'Yeah, I'm willing to give it a crack. C'mon,' he says, his eyes gleaming with excitement, 'what are we waiting for? Let's get back on track with this.'

Peanut's enthusiasm instantly has the team fired up, and Max quickly forgets her disappointment.

Jack has some ideas ready to bounce off them. He's obviously given the plan some more thought since they last spoke. Max is surprised that he's thinking to make the attempt straight after tomorrow's challenge. His reasoning is because that's when the guards will be least expecting anything.

He calls on Kenny's judgement for guidance. They need to cause a diversion of some kind. What that is at this stage is unclear. They'll start with the bones of a plan, then fill in the details later.

'I agree with Jack that we should do this tomorrow,' Kenny says. 'Peanut, at the end of the challenge, the drawbridge will be down, giving passage to the spectators. This'll be the best opportunity for your escape. Keep in mind that although the guards won't see you exit, they'll notice you're gone. What I suggest you do, once you cross the bridge, is wait outside the fortress walls. The guards will suspect your mission is to make your way to the gateway. What you do then, is simply follow them. They'll take you straight there. That way you won't need to rely on the trail I left.'

'Of course. Genius thinking, Kenny!' Max says, impressed with his uncomplicated logic.

'I think it'll work, but we need to come up with a diversion, one big enough to give Peanut enough time to get past the guards,' Kenny says. 'Has anyone got any ideas?'

They all look at each other, hoping for inspiration.

Peanut has them all stumped with what he says next. 'Kenny, in what century did the Chinese discover fireworks?'

'The early ninth century. Why?'

'Why? Because if we're in a time where they're not used to seeing fireworks, we might be able to distract them enough to allow me to get away.'

Max, Ruby and Kenny look at Peanut like he's missing one pivotal detail—how on earth are they going to get their hands on fireworks?

But Jack and Peanut share a conspirator's smile.

Max catches the exchange. 'Hey, what's going on?'

Ruby eyes them suspiciously. 'What are you two up to?'

'You'll be happy to hear that this "Genius",' Peanut points to himself, 'is blessed not only with good looks, but brains to boot. I'm the perfect catch, Rubes.'

Kenny scratches his head. 'I'm lost; what's that

got to do with fireworks?'

'Well, my brilliant friend, you'll be happy to know … that I've got some!'

'Are you serious?' Kenny exclaims. 'That's awesome, Peanut. If you've got something big and loud enough, we might just have the distraction we're looking for. What've you got?'

Peanut reaches for his backpack and pulls out a box full of fireworks. 'I've got a few big ones; I think that they're good enough.'

'Girandola!' Kenny's eyes light up when he sees them. 'These are perfect, they give off a high-pitched whistle and shoot off sprays of sparks.'

'Who needs Ryker and his failed escape stories? We've got the best strategies, and a bag full of fireworks. What more can we ask for?' Jack laughs.

This has them all suddenly excited and hopeful.

Who would have thought that Peanut and his shenanigans would be the hero in their escape plan?

45

THE FINAL CHALLENGE

JACK

Before they get called up for today's challenge—the final one—Jack gathers the team together for a last-minute pep talk. 'Guys, just remember, with or without our back-up plan, whatever happens, we need to win today so we don't get chucked into the forest.'

'To be honest,' Kenny says, 'I'm putting my money on Plan B and hoping Peanut pulls this off. Who knows what we'll be up against with these Invincibles? One of the guys in the other team died in that challenge, didn't they? So I'm betting it's pretty serious stuff.'

Jack surprises them by saying, 'You know what? In all honesty, I think we've got a fair chance.'

Max shakes her head. 'Kenny, I'm with you. I'm kind'a freaking out about going against them. Jack, how can you say that?'

'The way I see it, Ryker chose to go up against them rather than join forces with us. To me, that speaks volumes. He obviously feels that they can be beaten.' In Jack's mind, it all makes sense; they really do have a fighting chance. All he needs to do now is convince the others that he's right.

When the time comes, guards once again usher the team into the arena to face their opposition for the last time. Jack stops mid-stride in disbelief. If he was expecting anything, it definitely wasn't what's in front of them, now.

'Chariot racing?' Peanut's reaction mirrors his own.

Two wooden, open-backed carts on wheels wait with two horses hitched to each.

Of course, chariot racing as a sport is as ancient as it comes, but it's not exactly a team sport. Jack's thoughts run amok. *How's this going to work. How's everyone supposed to compete?* He turns to Kenny for help.

'Chariot racing has origins as far back in time as 1300 BC,' Kenny begins. 'Typically, a chariot is driven by one charioteer. So I'm guessing that they're thinking of a relay race, where everyone's expected to have a turn at driving. If that's the case, and I hope I'm wrong, then we're in trouble, because it takes great strength to control the horses, and realistically, Jack is the only one who'll be able to manage them. The other team have the same problem, with Ryker.'

Jack's concern isn't so much that he'll need to be their only driver—he knows he can go the distance—it's that he needs to drive at all. *What the hell do I know about chariot racing? What the hell do I know about horses, full-stop?* His only experience with a horse is with one on his grandparents' farm. And that horse was so old it was ready for the knackery.

'Kenny, what else have you got for us?' he asks anxiously.

'The race is usually twelve laps around the arena, and from what I can tell, they've set up racing-chariots as opposed to war-chariots. There are pros and cons to racing-chariots. They're a lighter frame to help with speed, but they're not as sturdy as war-chariots. The driver needs to keep a good balance between speed and accuracy, especially around the bends. Any contact between the two chariots could prove to be disastrous.'

Jack inwardly groans.

They soon learn that Kenny was right; the race

will be carried out as a relay.

'We have chosen the ancient event of chariot racing for today's challenge,' Pius begins. 'Although traditionally not a team sport, I know not how Herodus has arranged it, but a variation of what we are accustomed to may be amusing to us all.'

The rules allow two riders in the chariot at the same time, while the rest of the team wait on a podium at the starting line. After each round of the arena, when the chariot returns, one team member must get off the cart while another embarks. Fortunately, there's no rule regarding the charioteer, allowing Jack to be their only driver.

Max frowns. 'Jack, how will you cope going twelve laps on your own?'

He doesn't admit it, but Jack is more worried about making it around the arena once, let alone twelve times. Luckily, Kenny gives him a quick run-down on how to direct a team of horses.

'I'll lend you a hand when you get tired,' Peanut tells him.

'I'll give it a go, too,' says Kenny. 'Between the three of us, we'll somehow manage.'

But Jack is no quitter. He only hopes that he doesn't stuff it up on the first go. Kenny said the chariots weren't sturdy. If he goes down on the first turn, then there goes the competition—over, before it even begins.

Both teams stand together on the podium. Ryker leers down at Max, clearly biting back words of offense.

Jack protectively grabs Max by the shoulders and moves her out of harm's way, then eyeballs Ryker. 'You're going down!'

Ryker turns to face him. They stand toe to toe, ready for combat. Ryker is at least a head taller than Jack and twice as wide, but he doesn't intimidate Jack in the least.

'You think you can take me on?' Ryker laughs.

'I'll take you on any day of the week,' Jack growls through gritted teeth. 'How about it? Man to man? But hitting girls is more your thing, isn't it?'

Ryker looks past Jack to Max. 'Don't underestimate that spitfire. I've got infected scratches from where that she-cat drew blood.'

Jack sees red. He chargers Ryker and shoves him in the chest. 'Touch her, and you'll be praying for mercy!'

Ryker loses his balance momentarily. The look of shock on his face gives Jack the confidence he needs. Gone are any earlier doubts; he can do this.

Peanut and Kenny stand by Jack's side with their arms crossed against their chests.

Ryker starts to laugh. 'I'm not going to waste my

energy playing your stupid games. I'll destroy you where it matters.' He turns his back to them and casually walks away.

Jack's control snaps. But before he knows what's happening, Peanut and Kenny are on him, dragging him as far away from Ryker as possible.

Peanut stares him down, 'Mate, you need to get a grip!'

'But did you see that? The arrogant jerk! I'm going to make him pay for what he's done!'

'Jack, save it for the challenge,' Kenny yells at him.

He looks over to Max, whose eyes are wide with fear. He can't bear seeing her so scared.

Man, you've got to pull your head in!

He takes a few deep breaths to calm himself. 'Yeah, okay. You're right, I'm an idiot. Let's just win this and go home.'

'Now you're talking. So let's go get 'em!' Peanut's enthusiasm is what Jack needs right now—and just in time.

The guards bring the chariots to the podium. Ryker is quick to climb onto the first cart, clearly confident to get this started. He secures the reins around his wrists and waits for Banji to position himself behind him.

Jack and Kenny prepare themselves on their

chariot. Jack mimics Ryker's hold on the reigns. Guards then lead the horses to place the chariots in position on the track. 'Get ready for a rough ride, Kenny. Make sure you get a good foot grip,' Jack says.

'Don't worry about me, just concentrate on what you need to do. Now remember, start off slow until you've gotten a feel for the horses,' Kenny tells him. 'Ryker will take off, being the arse that he is, but don't feel you have to keep up. Speed doesn't always win. He's more likely to make mistakes and risk tipping the cart by pushing it.'

'Gotcha. I won't do anything stupid.'

'Let's hope Ryker's not so smart. With an ego the size of his fat head, he might just do anything to stay in front.'

Jack's wired and ready. Adrenalin pumps through his veins, urging him to tackle this challenge with everything he has.

Ryker's horses become agitated, and he shouts at them to settle, but this has the opposite effect, and the animals become increasingly restless. He tugs at the reins, becoming angrier and succeeding only to add to their confusion.

All the commotion he's creating spooks Jack's horses a little, too. So he casts a blanket of calm over them, and they start to settle. He turns to look at his team waiting on the podium. Max is deep in conversation with Edra and Ulan, and there doesn't appear to be any animosity between them. If anything, Edra's body language shows remorse. Max's expression shows genuine concern.

That idiot's got a lot to answer for!

Ryker's team looks mutinous. Seeing this makes Jack even more determined to beat him.

Both teams jump at the sound of the horn. Jack fumbles with the reins, and his horses rear and meander aimlessly. Ryker takes off like a shot, his experience making a mockery of Jack's attempts. But Jack doesn't allow that to affect him; in fact, it makes him more determined to succeed. With his focus back on track, he quickly gains control of the horses and guides them down the straight in a fast canter.

He watches as Ryker approaches the first bend. He takes the turn dangerously fast, causing one of the wheels to lose contact with the ground. Jack's almost certain the cart's going to tip over, but by some miracle, Ryker manages to righten it. His horses thunder down the straight, kicking up dust in their wake.

Jack takes the turn carefully, at a fast but safe pace. He tightens his grip on the reins and calls for Kenny to hold on. Once that's done, he urges the horses to break into a gallop, and they oblige, increasing their speed. They power down the track, and before long,

Jack is on Ryker's tail.

Ryker eases up a little as they head into the next bend, and his team arrive safely at the podium first. Banji quickly jumps off the chariot and helps Edra get on.

No time is wasted. Ryker is off again before Edra has found her footing, but she recovers quickly, grabbing the sides of the chariot in time to secure herself. 'Ryker! Watch out; you're going to get us killed!'

Ryker doesn't appear to hear her. If he has, he doesn't acknowledge her. He's clearly on a mission.

Jack pulls into the podium seconds after Ryker has left. Kenny jumps off and Ruby gets on while the horses are still in motion. Jack pushes on, tearing up the straight, his team of horses—clearly well trained for the sport—responding well to his commands. Jack catches Ryker on the next bend. Ryker's horses go a little wide, and Jack seizes the opportunity to cut in front of them and gain the lead. With a flick of the reigns, he encourages his team to speed up, and they tear up the track, galloping at full pelt.

The ground trembles as the horses thunder up the straight, all four horses breathing heavily as the teams try to beat the other to the next bend. Ryker runs his team dangerously close, causing the carts' wheels to scrape briefly. Ryker nudges forward. Jack falls back a little, seeing the bend is close ahead. Ryker cuts in front of Jack and almost tips again on the bend. He straightens the cart and arrives, once more, first at the podium. Edra and Ulan exchange while the chariot is still moving.

Peanut stands ready as Jack pulls in. Ruby hops off as he quickly jumps on.

'You're doing great, mate; are you okay to keep going?'

Jack doesn't stop. 'All good, Peanut. This is awesome! These horses are amazing; they're doing most of the work on their own. Just hold on; we're coming into the turn.'

The chariot begins to sway dangerously. Jack has gone into the turn too quickly.

Peanut grips the sides. 'Jack! Watch out!'

'Throw your weight to counterbalance the tilt!'

'We're not going to make it!'

'Keep pushing!'

Jack pushes with all his might against the cart's side, urging the chariot to set right. He closes his eyes, anticipating the inevitable crash, but the chariot, somehow, straightens.

'Man, that was too close!'

'Sorry, mate. Now hold on; I'm going to catch him.' Jack pushes his horses on. They draw near and in no time overtake on the straight, then he sneakily cuts in front of Ryker's team on the turn, forcing him to slow to prevent a collision. Jack closes his eyes again, waiting for the impact. But nothing; somehow they're safe. Jack barely makes it to the podium before Ryker.

Max is on the chariot even before Peanut alights. Banji exchanges with his sister.

'Jack, you've got to slow down,' Max yells at him. 'You barely made it back that time.'

'It's okay. Don't worry; I've got everything under control,' Jack says with a grin.

He confidently guides the horses again into a fast gallop, and they tear down the straight. Max grips so hard onto the sides of the chariot that her knuckles are white. The erratic motion tosses her from side to side like a rag doll. As they near the far-end turn, Jack can hear Ryker fast approaching, hooves rumbling close behind them.

'Hold on, Max; this is gonna be close!' he calls out.

Jack glances behind. Ryker's horses are virtually breathing down Max's neck. Ryker cracks the whip several times and shouts loudly, urging his horses to go faster. The ground beneath them trembles from the thundering hooves, and Jack feels spray from the horses' mouths on the back of his neck.

Coming into the turn, from the corner of his eye,

he can see Ryker's horses nudging dangerously close. Jack pulls back on the reins to prevent a collision. But Ryker doesn't slow down, and one of his wheels lifts. The momentum sways the cart sideways. Ryker throws himself to the other side to counterbalance the chariot, but Banji, no longer able to hold on, is thrown clear of the cart. Jack uses all his strength to pull back on the reins, signalling his horses to stop.

Ryker loses control. His chariot tumbles to the ground in a wreck, taking his horses down with it.

Jack's horses rear at the sudden chaos underfoot, and he's completely powerless to avoid what happens next. All the weight of Jack's horses comes crashing to the ground, trampling, with a sickening crunch, the cart, and the limbs and bodies of the victims below.

The crowd cry out with gasps and screams of horror—some cheer.

Jack jumps off the chariot and busies himself calming his horses before they crush Ryker further. A few gentle words, and the animals settle to his soft touch. He drags them away from the carnage, then races back to Max who's at Ryker's side, stone-faced, looking down at his mangled body in disbelief; he's almost unrecognisable, twisted and tangled in a mesh of broken chariot and trampled horses.

Ryker's horses struggle to free themselves from their restraints, causing more mayhem. Jack realises that he needs to calm and free them first in order for Max to get to Ryker safely. This proves to be a nightmare of a challenge since one of them has broken its leg in the fall and is protesting wildly in pain. He blankets them with his calm, and then in a desperate rush, he pulls the fallen horses, best he can, away from the wreckage. Once he has them settled, he runs back to help Max tear away the broken debris, frantic to reach Ryker's motionless body.

Max wastes no time in assessing the situation. 'He's got a pulse, but just barely.'

Ryker's body lays in an awkward position, clearly broken. His head is crushed, and his pupils are dilated.

'No!' Max's eyes widen in panic. 'I'm losing him!'

Jack is oblivious to the crowd gathering around them. He doesn't hear the gasps of horror as both teams look on. There's little hope.

'God, help me!' Max places her hands on Ryker's head. Broken bone and matted hair are mashed together in a bloody mess. 'Come on!' she screams, willing herself to hurry.

Jack sees the bleeding almost immediately start to subside, and the bones begin to fuse and take form. God only knows how much damage there is to the brain.

'Something's wrong,' Max cries out in sudden

alarm. 'He's stopped breathing. 'No, no, no. Come back!' She pounds on his chest, throwing her whole weight behind the life-saving compressions.

'Tell me what to do!' Jack yells at her.

'Push down, hard, both hands, here,' she shows him exactly how to place his hands over the breast bone. 'Thirty times, fast. Count out loud so I know when to give mouth-to-mouth.'

While Jack administers the compressions, Max prepares Ryker's head and neck.

'… twenty-seven, twenty-eight, twenty-nine, thirty,' Jack stops, and Max begins.

With her mouth on Ryker's and her fingers pinching his nose, she blows two deep breaths into Ryker's lungs. Then she instructs Jack to repeat his compressions while she places her hands over Ryker's head and continues to heal the brain trauma.

'… twenty-nine, thirty.' Jack stops.

Max blows two more breaths. 'Again!'

Together they work on Ryker, never letting up, knowing his life is in their hands.

Max suddenly reaches out for Jack to stop. He looks at her, alarmed.

She stares vacantly into his eyes.

His heart sinks.

And then, in a quiet whisper she says, 'I can feel a faint pulse.'

He's back! Jack falls back on his heels, exhausted, and looks at Ryker's chest, rising and falling with each unaided breath.

Ulan and Edra clutch each other, quietly crying. Banji has his arm around them terror in his eyes. Ruby and Kenny stand silent by their sides. There's a deathly silence amongst them as they watch on. The crowd, too, look on and wait to see what's going to happen. Miraculously, within minutes, there're signs of Ryker returning to consciousness. His eyes eventually flutter open, and he makes an attempt to lift his head.

Ulan and Edra fall at his feet.

The crowd cries out in disbelief.

Suddenly, the horn blasts, commanding attention. The crowd becomes silent. Herodus' authoritative voice cries out, 'Barricade the exits; close the drawbridge. We have an escapee.'

Jack jumps to his feet and scans the arena. He sees Kenny; he sees Ruby; he looks down at Max.

But where's Peanut?

46

A Lightbulb Moment

Peanut

Someone's down, but from where they're standing on the podium, Peanut can't see who it is. He jumps off and pelts down to the scene of the accident, his heart pounding out of control. He prays to God that it isn't Jack or Max. He and Edra reach the carnage at the same time. The others arrive moments later. They stand horror stricken at the sight of Ryker's mangled body. Jack has been frantically working to clear a path for Max to get to him.

'Jesus, what a mess!' he whispers.

An eerie silence falls over the arena. The only sounds are those made by Max as she tries to force some life back into Ryker's motionless body, and Jack compressing down onto Ryker's chest, trying to kick-start his heart.

Peanut's at a loss as to what he can do to help. He looks around for a way to be useful. All eyes are on Jack and Max.

And then it occurs to him; he needed a diversion, and now he has one.

Without a second thought, Peanut steps back behind the group, trying not to draw attention to himself, and vanishes. Without a word he quietly slips away, aware that someone might hear him in the dead silence.

By the time he reaches the drawbridge, his chest is aching from his racing heart. His anxiety levels have reached an all-time high. He stops to consider his options. He needs to pass the guards blocking the exit without being detected. Just then, the guards collectively move into the arena to see what all the commotion's about.

Not stopping to question this unexpected opportunity handed to him, Peanut makes his escape.

As he's crossing the drawbridge, he hears a horn blast from within the arena followed by Herodus' announcement. In a panic, he makes a run for it.

He darts deep into the forest, ducking and weaving, jumping over fallen trees and roots. Branches tear at his face and arms, but he doesn't let that slow him down.

When he thinks it's safe to stop and plan his next move, he does. He crouches behind a bush and urges his heart to quit racing so he can think straight. All that adrenalin still has him ready to run. He tries to listen out for the sound of a chase, but he hears none.

He debates whether to lay low and wait, like Kenny suggested, or look for the pathway while he's got this chance to go it alone. He gets up and tentatively looks around for Kenny's clues. He wanders a little further, scoping the ground while keeping his eyes and ears peeled. But before too long he's ventured deep into the forest. He hasn't found any sign of Kenny's torn shirt, and now he's lost.

He silently blasts himself for not staying put and tries to retrace his steps, but only manages to get completely disorientated. 'Geez, I'd make a lousy Boy Scout. I should've just stuck to the plan.'

Something tightens around his ankle and with a swift jerking motion drags him high up into the trees. He gasps for air at the unexpected shock, and it takes a moment for his head to stop spinning enough for him to realise that he's dangling upside down, suspended from a tall tree, trapped in a snare of some kind.

A nearby rustling reveals an unexpected sight. To

Peanut's shock, he sees a small man wearing nothing but a hessian sack. He's filthy, with long, matted hair and a short beard. The spear in his hand makes him look half-crazed and barbaric. The man gazes up in Peanut's direction, looking perplexed. Peanut guesses the reason for his confusion—he can see the weighted rope, but can't see what's suspended in the snare. Peanut remains silent.

'What is this trickery? Who goes there? Show yourself!' the man commands.

Peanut tries not to move.

'I know you are there, I can sense you, stranger!'

Peanut says nothing.

'You cannot fool me; I have the power of foresight,' the little man says. 'Today I saw a vision that my snare will provide for me today, and it has. What sorcery do you possess to thus conceal yourself?'

Determined not to be found, Peanut remains quiet and still. But that plan falls to the wayside the moment he sees the savage preparing an attack. He raises his long spear, aiming it straight at him.

What the hell!

Peanut holds back a squeal and starts to swing erratically. Despite his panic, he tells himself it's not because he's freaking out but that it's a deliberate tactical manoeuvre.

'Speak or I will be forced to spear you!'

Heart thumping, Peanut continues to swing. It takes everything he has not to scream for help. *This is it … this is how it ends!* Tears sting his eyes.

The wild man takes aim.

Dear God, please, I'll do anything if you make him miss. I'll stop calling my brother a moron. I'll help mum with the cooking. I'll put back that twenty bucks I borrowed from Dad's wallet. I'll even donate a kidney.

But then he remembers he's invisible.

Idiot! How's he supposed to get ya when he can't see ya?

He relaxes a bit more when he sees there's only the one spear. The odds of getting caught have dramatically shifted in his favour. He watches on with a little less trepidation now as the forest dweller steadies his hold and takes aim at his moving target. All of a sudden, he releases the weapon and, to Peanut's horror, it lands with unprecedented accuracy directly on the unseen mark.

47

῾Is it a Trick?

Guards throw Jack into the chamber with the others and bolt the heavy door shut. He sits up against the wall and tries to take in all the madness of the last hour.

He notices Max trying to wipe the dried blood from her hands by rubbing them on the straw, then up against the rough stone walls. Her actions become manic. She's delirious. Jack comes up behind her and holds her near-raw hands in his own to stop her from hurting herself any further. She struggles to free herself, but Jack holds firm. He wraps his arms around her, securing her in their safety. She turns to bury her face in his chest and breaks down crying. He holds her until the shock of what just happened, subsides.

She's exhausted—completely wasted. Feeling her start to waver, he reluctantly loosens his hold and lays her down before she collapses, then gently places a kiss on her brow before letting her go. He remains close by her side, holding her bloodied hands. She's asleep in moments.

Ruby smiles at him. 'I hope Peanut's okay.' She sighs. 'I feel sick to the stomach knowing he's out there on his own.'

Jack knows that pain. His gut is tied up in a knot too.

No food comes that night. And neither does the offer to go out in the garden.

Jack lies on the straw next to Max, closes his eyes and begs for sleep, but his mind explodes with images of what happened in the arena.

A rustling sound outside the window stirs Jack out of his inner turmoil.

'Pst! Pst!'

The persistent sound makes him sit up, his ears on high alert, adrenaline speeding his heart. *Could it be Peanut already?*

'Pst! Max!' The voice comes from the window.

The others sit up to listen.

Jack jumps up and moves to the window. In the light of the moon, he sees the silhouette of someone just outside. It's Ryker.

'What the hell do you want?'

Ryker comes out from the shadows and up to the window. 'I need to talk to Max. Please, before you say anything, I need to apologise to her … to all of you, for what I've done. I'm ashamed of my behaviour, and I know I don't deserve your forgiveness.'

'Okay, you've said it. Now get lost.'

Ryker lowers his head. 'Look, Edra warned me not to come, and I get it. I deserve nothing less, but you've got to let me talk to Max; it's urgent.'

'Say what you have to say; she can hear you.'

Max, awakened by the commotion, cautiously approaches the window. Jack pulls her to his side.

'Max, you need to come,' Ryker begs. 'They've got your friend. They've beaten him, and he's in a pretty bad way.'

'What? No!' Ruby collapses in a heap.

Max leaps for the bars on the window and starts screaming, 'I need to get to him. Help me out of here!'

'Quick; I can take you to him. There's not much time.'

Jack doesn't stop to think. He grabs the bars and shakes them with everything he has. He feels them give a little. 'Help me!' he yells to Ryker.

Together, with a bit of effort, they manage to

pry the bars loose and free an opening big enough to allow Max to pass. It's a tight fit, but with sheer determination, she manages to squeeze through.

No time is wasted. They take off into the garden.

Jack watches them disappear into the darkness, his heart racing and breathing laboured. He prays she reaches Peanut in time.

And then reality hits him. His heart seems to stop. He feels as if the blood in his veins becomes ice, and he turns to stone. He's just handed Max over to Ryker, her abductor. 'What the hell have I done? Max!'

Startled, the others look at him, not yet seeing what he sees.

'It's a trap!'

Ruby gasps.

'What?' Kenny's eyes widen in alarm.

Jack snaps. He dives for the window and tries to ram his body through the opening. Kenny grabs him from around the waist and fights to pull him back. Ruby tries helping by tugging at his legs, but Jack puts up a fight. He kicks and screams like a madman, but together they manage to tackle him to the ground. Kenny throws himself on top of him and pins him down by the shoulders.

'Get a grip!' he screams at him. 'He's come to help Peanut!'

'No! It's a trap!'

Kenny fists Jack's shirt and shakes him. 'You're wrong! Why would he do that after what you and Max did for him? Think about it!' He shakes him some more. 'Look, Peanut needs Max. Focus on that.' Kenny keeps at him until he sees the logic register in Jack's eyes, and then he relaxes his hold and falls back, exhausted.

Jack stares up at the ceiling, seeing nothing. He shuts his eyes to block out everything around him and forces himself to focus on anything that'll distract him from his destructive thoughts.

'She'll be okay, Jack,' Ruby whispers as she lays down beside him and rests her head on his shoulder.

All Jack can do is pray to God that she's right.

They wait.

48

TOO LATE?

MAX

Max runs as fast as her legs can carry her, fighting her exhaustion and trying not to be distracted by destructive thoughts. Her focus is to get to Peanut in time; nothing else matters. She runs blindly through the garden, whipped and beaten by bushes at every turn.

Ryker comes to an abrupt halt just outside a chamber window. She smacks into his solid back, almost knocking herself out with the impact. He grabs the bars on the small window and begins to loosen them just as he did earlier. Without Jack's help, the process proves to be more of a challenge.

Max is hysterical with worry. She begs him to hurry.

And then, finally, the bars come free.

Ryker picks her up and helps her through. Max falls to Peanut's side ready to assess him. What she sees makes her jerk back and gasp in horror. He's hardly recognisable. His face is swollen and bloodied. His body lays in an unnatural heap. She looks at his injuries and knows exactly what they've done to him. She can't hold back at the horror she's seeing. She starts to sob uncontrollably.

Ryker watches. 'What is it? Are we too late?'

She can't answer; she's too distraught.

'Max!'

She struggles to contain herself. Her heart has been smashed into a million pieces. 'How could anyone be so cruel?'

'Is he still alive?'

She nods.

'Then help him! I know you're hurting right now, but you've got to be strong. He needs you.'

Ryker's words hit her like a slap to the face. How can she be so selfish at a time like this? Bracing herself for what she needs to do, she swipes at her tears and pushes through the shock of seeing Peanut so broken. Her hands hover over his body, quickly assessing the damage. Heat radiates immediately from her fingertips, and the healing process begins.

Ryker watches in silence.

She doesn't stop. She methodically runs her hands over the areas that need attention most.

'Jesus! What have I done?' Ryker stares at her hands in horror.

She looks down to see what he's seeing. Her hands are covered in dry blood—Ryker's blood. She looks at her clothes, stained with the same.

'Max, save him, like you saved me.' Unbelievably, tears run down his face.

She can't spare Ryker any attention. Her focus is on Peanut. She gets back to it, working tirelessly over his injuries. Slowly the blood clots, and the swelling and bruising begin to disappear. She hears the click of broken bones being mended. But she doesn't stop, not until she's satisfied that Peanut is whole once more.

And when that's done, she falls by his side and allows herself to cry.

Soon there's nothing but silence.

'Maxine,' Ryker calls out quietly. But there's no response. She's fallen asleep. 'Yes, rest; you deserve that much,' he whispers.

❧

Sometime later, Max stirs, waking to someone calling out her name.

'Max, Maxine, you need to go back,' Ryker whispers. 'We can't let the guards find you here.'

Mention of the guards jolts Max wide awake. She looks down at Peanut and sees him sleeping peacefully. 'You'll be okay now, buddy,' she whispers, tenderly touching his face.

She moves to the window, jumps up and tries to pull herself through, but can't. She's still exhausted.

'Try again,' Ryker says. 'I'll grab you this time.'

Max takes a run-up, jumps, then grabs hold of the window's edge. Ryker takes her wrists and carefully pulls her through. He holds her gently by the waist and lowers her safely to the ground. Their eyes meet for a moment.

Max quickly looks away, suddenly feeling very uncomfortable.

Ryker clears his throat.

'Thank you,' she says quietly.

She watches as Ryker replaces the bars in the window, then they walk silently through the garden. Ryker stops by the lake and offers Max some time to wash the dried blood from her hands and face.

By the time he gets her back, it's well into the early morning.

'Max!' Jack calls out anxiously. 'Are you all right? How's Peanut?'

Kenny and Ruby are by his side in seconds.

Ruby's eyes are puffy from crying. 'Max, how is he?'

'He'll be okay. He's resting now.'

'What happened? You've been gone for ages?' Kenny asks, worried.

'It took a while to heal the injuries.'

'I'll help you back in if you like,' Ryker offers.

She nods.

He gently picks her up, helps her through the window, then leaves as soon as he's secured the bars.

Jack watches Ryker walk away. 'Weird; he almost seems human.'

Max doesn't want to think about Ryker. She's just thankful to be back.

Jack pulls her into a hug, and his warmth relaxes her. 'How bad was he?' he asks.

'He's good now, Jack. That's all that matters.'

'Max, tell us everything,' Ruby begs. 'Jack lost it when you left. He thought it was a trick, that Ryker was kidnapping you again. And to be honest, I kind'a freaked out, too.'

The thought of that possibility had never occurred to her.

'He's changed.' She hesitates a moment, remembering his tear streaked face. 'It's really weird; I think he might be genuinely sorry for what he's done.'

'He must be, because he risked getting caught coming here tonight,' Kenny reminds them. 'He could've left Peanut there to die.'

The images of Peanut's broken body come back to haunt her. Tears prickle her eyes. She turns away and vows never to let them know how close to the truth that is.

49

RYKER'S MISSION

RYKER

The following day, Ryker wakes determined to make amends with the other team. What he did last night was only the beginning of his redemption. His near-death experience left him knowing that he needs to fix his mistakes.

He thinks back to what he witnessed last night: Max's gut-wrenching anguish at seeing her friend totally broken; the blood, his blood, tainting her healing hands; and then later, Max, curled up asleep, exhausted from her efforts. These images had the power to move him.

There was something fragile about the sight of her lying there, finally finding peace. Seeing this brought him an inexplicable sense of happiness, an overwhelming tightening sensation in his chest from knowing that he'd helped. And he's thankful that he could get to her in time. If he hadn't come across Peanut when he did, he'd be dead now. The hidden escape hole he'd made years ago that he uses to roam the garden at night for alone time was Peanut's saving grace.

But today's a new day, and Ryker is on a mission to set things right.

'Guys, I've been a dumb-ass,' he says. 'No doubt about it. And I'm sorry. I know that's not enough, and I can't take back what I've done, but I can promise to make up for it now. I was wrong about them, and you were right. I should've trusted you. I'm ready to fix this. All I ask is that you trust me in what I'm about to do.'

He sees doubt in the look his friends exchange and confusion on the twins' faces as they struggle to read him. 'Come on, guys, give me another chance.'

Edra looks at the twins. Some unspoken agreement is made between them. 'You stuff this up, Ryker, and I'll personally make your life a living hell.'

He laughs. 'Agreed.'

'She's not kidding,' Banji tells him. 'And I'll help her.'

'Me, too,' Ulan says.

'Okay, I get it. Don't worry; you couldn't do

any worse than what I'd do to myself. So,' he says, 'as you know, yesterday's nightmare challenge wasn't completed. So this is what I propose to do.'

After telling them his idea, and seeing their sceptical reaction, he makes them a promise. 'I give you my word. You're my only priority. I'll keep you safe. You've got to trust me.'

After a hesitant pause, Edra shakes his hand, securing their agreement.

Ryker immediately relaxes. They're united once again, and this lifts a heavy weight off his chest. 'I'm feeling good about this already.'

50

THE GIFT

JACK

Once again, no food is brought to the chamber the next morning. Nearly two days without a scrap of food to eat or some water to drink. Jack does his best to curb their hunger pains. To his relief, the guards come eventually and give them access to the garden, and better still, some news. They sit by the lake talking about the unexpected forfeit by the other team.

'So that's it; we've done it,' Kenny says. 'One more hurdle and we can go home.'

'Looks like it. But what about the others?' Max asks. 'What'll become of them now?'

'I guess they'll be exiled, if they haven't been already,' Jack says. 'Man, I'm glad it's them and not us.'

'Call me nuts, but I kind of feel sorry for them,' Ruby says. 'I mean, how will they cope? They've got no food or shelter, and what about the forest people?'

'You know what? We really dodged a bullet there,' Kenny says, relieved. 'They could've demanded a rematch since none of us actually won that challenge. Something must have happened for them to bow out. Maybe it's like you said, Max, that Ryker has changed.'

'Well, all I can say is thank God he came to help last night,' Ruby reminds them. 'Oh, poor Peanut. Max, he'll be okay, won't he?' she asks for the hundredth time.

Max laughs. 'He'll be back to his annoying self in no time; you wait and see.'

'What's going to happen to him now?' Kenny asks.

'I hope they let him go.' Ruby sighs loudly.

A sudden movement from beyond the bushes alerts them that something or someone's approaching. Ruby jumps protectively in front of her friends with her shield ready.

'I always knew you were sweet on me, Rubes,' a cheeky voice calls out.

'Peanut!' Ruby squeals and races to him. She throws her arms around him and hangs on tight with a hold that looks like she's never letting go.

'Hey, ease up.' He laughs. 'I'll need Max to fix my broken bones again if you keep this up.' He gives Jack a wink, then secures his hold on her.

'I'll give you broken bones!' She makes a show of pretending to strangle him.

'So you're okay?' Jack asks. 'Max didn't say much.'

Peanut lets go of Ruby for a moment and reaches out to pull Max into hug. 'Come here, you. You're my guardian angel, you know that? Ryker told me what you did last night. Thank you. I really mean it.'

Max holds onto him tightly. 'So you saw him?'

'Yeah, he came to my window early this morning to make sure I was okay. He didn't think I was going to make it. To tell ya the truth, neither did I.'

'What?' Ruby exclaims, horrified. 'Max, you didn't tell us he was that bad.'

'Hey, chillax, Rubes. I'm good now, aren't I?'

'Thanks to Max, you are,' a voice calls from the bushes.

They turn to see Ryker and Edra coming towards them.

Jack instinctively positions himself in front of his friends.

'It's all good, Jack. We're here as friends; you have my word.'

Jack relaxes his stance, but doesn't drop his guard

completely.

'We can't stay; the guards will be looking for us soon. And since we won't have a chance to talk again, we've come to wish you good luck.'

Good luck?

'I've given Peanut some information that you'll need going into battle with the Invincibles. He'll fill you in later.'

Jack's guard drops a little more, and his curiosity spikes.

'I want to congratulate you,' Ryker continues. 'In the end, the best team won. I think that under different circumstances, we could've even been friends. I've got a feeling that we'll meet again.'

Ryker offers his hand and Jack hesitantly accepts. An unspoken pact is sealed with that handshake.

Edra hugs Max goodbye. 'Thank you for everything. We're able to go knowing that we'll have half a chance out there because of you. When you win, come back for us, okay?'

Max takes Edra's hands in hers. 'Stay safe, and we will, I promise.' With one more hug, they part ways.

Jack watches them leave with mixed emotions. Edra's parting comment makes him think that they've got half a chance to win this. He turns to Peanut, anxious to hear what Ryker has told him. 'Okay, so what now?'

'Man, my head's spinning from all the stuff he said. You're not gonna believe it,' he begins. They all sit by the lake as Peanut fills them in.

'So, yeah, there're five Invincibles, each with ridiculous superhuman powers. There's this old guy, Athos. His strength is immortality. He can't die, no matter what you do to him. They've got no idea how old he is. They stopped counting ages ago. Ryker said not to let his grey hair and beard fool us. He's as fit and as strong as an ox, and his mind is as sharp as a whip.

'Then there's Shant. He's got the power to control the weather. Ryker warned not to underestimate him. Beowulf is the third one. He's got this cool thing where he communicates with animals. Can you believe it?'

Jack's head spins with information overload. Peanut keeps shocking him with more and more near-impossible challenges that they're going to be up against. And there's still another two that he's yet to hear about.

'Vyvian is the only female in the team,' Peanut continues, 'and guess what? She can fly! Man, how sick is that? And the one Ryker said to really watch out for is Archimedes. He's got the power to control your thoughts!'

'Geez, not more brain invasion!' Ruby whines.

'Yeah, sorry, Rubes. Ryker said that in their

battle, he stuffed them up big time. They had trouble working as a team because he constantly interfered with their mind set. At one stage, he had them turning on one another, causing them to lose focus on the challenge.'

Jack struggles to get his head around all of this.

'Did he say anything about what the challenge might be?' Kenny asks.

'Oh, yeah, about that, he said that the challenge is different every time. But listen to this … when they were up against them, they had to compete in a gladiator challenge. He said that they were put into the arena with, not only the Realm's best, but also … wait for it … a whole heap of wild animals!'

If Peanut wanted a reaction, he certainly gets it. Pandemonium breaks loose.

'Wild animals?' Max turns to Jack in a panic. 'How are we supposed to deal with something like that?'

'You've got to be kidding.' Ruby grabs Peanut's arm, looking for some reassurance.

'And that's how they lost. Beowulf was in his element. He had total control over the animals. One of their team mates was mauled to death by a lion! I tell ya, I felt sick in the gut when he told me that.'

'Oh God, no! Those poor kids!' Max's eyes go wide in horror as she looks at him.

Jack's heart sinks. How the hell are they supposed to do this? More to the point, how is anyone ever meant to win? He doesn't get it. What was Ryker thinking? Choosing to go up against the Invincibles instead of forming an alliance with them? Jack was half way ready to believe that they had a chance, that beating them was doable. But after hearing what happened to the other team, he's suddenly not so sure. Superpowers or not, he'd be struggling to even convince himself that they have a chance, let alone reassuring the other four.

They turn to him for answers. He looks at their desperate faces and feels sick to the stomach knowing that they're depending on him for that glimmer of hope when right now he can't even think straight.

But maybe Kenny can.

'Kenny, we need you to pull a rabbit out of a hat. Yeah, we've all seen the movies, but surely these gladiator battles aren't anything like that. Tell us what it was really like.'

Kenny looks down at his feet, clearly reluctant to answer.

Jack's gut clenches.

'As much as I'd like to, Jack, I can't sugar-coat this,' Kenny says. 'Gladiator spectacles were the most brutal and bloodiest sports ever. Typically, the gladiators would fight each other, man against man, until the opposition couldn't fight back. But it wasn't unusual for them to be pitted against wild animals.'

The colour drains from Max's face. 'How is anyone supposed to compete with that?' She turns again to Jack, her eyes begging him to tell her that everything's going to be all right.

He can't look at her—it's killing him seeing her so defeated. He looks at each of his other friends, fighting hard to remain their beacon of hope. But, no matter how deep he digs, that positive energy from within struggles to ignite.

And this must've shown on his face because Max bursts into tears. 'It's hopeless; it's over!'

And that's when he knows he needs to fight back. He needs to show her there's hope. 'What? No, Max, it's not. We're not done, yet.'

'Yeah!' Ruby protests with him. 'I've got news for you; there's no way in hell that I'm giving up. I wanna go home!'

Ruby's sudden anger spurs Jack on further.

'But—' Max begins.

'No buts, Max,' Ruby says forcefully. 'You forget, we've got my shield. There's nothing out there that can penetrate that.'

'Yeah, Max. What's gotten into ya?' Peanut gives her a questioning look. 'With Ruby's shield and my invisibility, they won't stand a chance. We'll be all over 'em.'

'And that's with just us two. What about what Jack can do?' Ruby adds, her eyes shining.

Jack is so caught up in their enthusiasm that he nearly misses Ruby's tribute. He stops, not quite getting her meaning.

Ruby rolls her eyes. 'You might not be able to talk to the animals, but you can do something that Beowulf won't be expecting … you can psych them out, and stop them from attacking.'

'And what if we use our mind-blanking technique on Archimedes? That'll screw him up.'

'Hey, good point, Kenny.' Peanut high-fives him. 'Anything's worth a try, right?'

Thanks to his friends, a hopeless situation has taken a turn for the better. Jack feels super positive about things again. He squeezes Max's hand. 'Hey, are you alright?'

Max looks down at their clasped hands and nods. 'I've had my stupid melt-down, so, yeah, I'm good and, more importantly, back on track. Now let's go kick some butts!'

That's my girl!

Her sudden energy gives him more strength, and he jumps straight into talking strategy. 'So, Peanut, do you know if we've got time to prepare for this final battle?'

'Yeah, Ryker said that The Ancients wait for the day after the new moon, whenever that is.'

'I can tell you.' Kenny stops to make a mental calculation. 'Okay, so it'll be in nine days from today.'

'Nine days! Why so long?' Ruby says. 'I'd rather get this over and done with.'

'I'm kinda glad we've got a few days up our sleeve,' Peanut says with a sudden mischievous gleam in his eyes. 'It'll give me time to snoop around and find out a bit more about these superfreaks. Hey, maybe I can get past the guards again. You know—'

'No!' They all yell at once.

Peanut laughs. 'Relax; I'm kidding. You think after that last beating, that I'm gonna try that anytime soon?'

Lucky for Peanut, Jack has a sense of humour, otherwise he'd be ready to belt him.

'But I reckon I'll give snooping another crack. Who knows, I might just find out—'

Jack and Kenny grab him and drag him to the edge of the lake.

'Hey!'

They lift him up.

'Come on, guys, put me down. I was joking about that, too. Come on … '

But he doesn't finish his protest because they throw him head first into the water.

The others stand around laughing.

Peanut comes up spluttering, and the mischievous grin on his face has the girls squealing and running for cover.

Max darts past Jack. Big mistake. He grabs her before she gets too far. 'You, my friend, need a bath. You stink!' He picks her up, laughing, and carries her to the side of the lake.

'You wouldn't dare!' she threatens. 'If I go in, you go in!'

She clings to him for dear life. And sure enough, as Jack nears the edge of the water, he loses his footing, and they both tumble in.

They come up laughing.

Ruby doesn't get far. Peanut is out of the water quicker than she can scream, 'Peanut, no!'

He grabs her, hauls her over his shoulder, slaps her bottom for good measure, then unceremoniously throws her into the lake.

While Peanut is holding his sides laughing at Ruby's demise, Kenny sees an opportunity and takes it. He runs up behind Peanut and knocks him back into the water.

Game on!

They spend the rest of the day just being kids.

Later, as they lie drying in the sun, relaxed and sleepy, Jack's curiosity gets the better of him. 'So,

Peanut, what happened? How did ya get caught?'

'Oh, man, I was hoping you wouldn't ask,' he says, mortified. He hides his bright-red face in his hands and shakes his head. 'I feel so stupid. I'm almost too embarrassed to tell you.'

Jack grins. 'Now I've got to hear this.'

'Okay,' Peanut braces himself with a deep breath. 'The plan started off like a dream; we needed a diversion, and Ryker provided it. As soon as I saw the opportunity, I vanished.'

'You're pretty quiet when you want to be,' Kenny teases.

Peanut chuckles. 'Yeah, I surprised myself, too. The place was so quiet you could've heard a pin drop. But that only added to the pressure. And do you know something, I nearly choked. I won't lie, I nearly didn't do it. My heart was thumping so loud, I was sure everyone could hear it. When I realised that no one noticed me gone, I high-tailed it out of there.

'When I got to the drawbridge, the guards were so caught up with what was happening in the arena, I simply walked past them. Too easy! I was out in the forest before I knew it, so I ran like a bat out of hell. And then the unthinkable happened ...' He looks away from their eager faces. 'I got lost. I was so caught up with getting away that I wasn't watching where I was going.' He looks up. 'Stupid, huh?

'And it gets worse,' he continues. 'Just wait until you hear what happens next.' He chuckles to himself. 'In my pathetic attempt to get away, I got snared in a trap, just like a wild animal.'

'What? No way!' Jack wasn't expecting that.

'Yep. I was dangling by one foot, high in the sky, feeling like a bloody idiot.'

Ruby gasps. 'Oh my God!'

'I knew then that I'd stuffed up our chances of escaping because of my stupidity.' Peanut is so embarrassed; he can't look at any of them in the eye.

'Then what?' Jack asks.

'Well, I didn't have to wait too long before one of the forest people came across me.'

'No.' Kenny's jaw drops.

Ruby grabs hold of his arm. 'You must've been scared out of your wits. What did he do when he saw you?'

Peanut smiles at her naivety. 'I was invisible, remember?'

'Go on,' Jack says impatiently.

'Hold ya horses. Geez, talk about pushy!' He gives Jack a dirty look for ruining his moment with Ruby. 'Anyway, as I was saying, this guy comes out with his spear in his hand.'

Max grimaces. 'I think I know what's coming.'

'Yeah, I reckon you would, Max,' he says. 'You

would've seen the results last night. Anyway, the little guy looks up, but he can't see me, 'cause I'm invisible, right? But he's not stupid; he knows he's caught something, so he calls out to me. Of course, I stay quiet, hoping he'll go away.'

'But how did he know you were there in the first place?' Kenny asks.

'Oh, he's got this freaky sixth sense where he can see into the future, so he literally saw me coming.'

'Cool power,' Kenny says in awe.

'Yeah, but as much as I tried to explain the situation, the problem was that he didn't really understand what I was talking about. Half the time he was scratching his head trying to work out what I was saying. And what made things worse, he didn't trust me, even after I argued with simple logic, telling him that he would surely have seen from his visions that I wasn't there to mess with him. But he was a persistent little pain in the neck, and before I knew what was happening, he raised his spear, took aim and gouged me in the foot.'

Ruby gasps.

'Yeah, I couldn't believe it either. For someone who can't even see his target, his aim was bang on the money. Pretty impressive, hey?'

'And then?' Max leans towards him.

'Well, that kind'a did it. I gave myself away

because it hurt like nothing else. Then I tried to negotiate with him—you know offered to save him and his friends if he let me go, but the traitor wouldn't have a bar of it. He said something about having a sick family at home and that he needed to trade me for supplies. And then, yada-yada-yada, he calls the guards and I cop a hiding for running away. That's it. End of story.'

Peanut sheepishly looks up, waiting for them to blast him for his stupidity. 'I'll tell ya something for nothing; at the time, the pain in my foot from the spear was nothin' to the way I felt for letting you guys down.'

'Wow!' Ruby stares at him, gobsmacked.

'Wow, all right. I really messed up.'

Jack feels numb. He can't believe it. They were so close. All Peanut had to do was lay low and wait for the guards to take chase. Yeah, he messed up. Jack rubs his forehead, unable to say anything supportive, but the look of embarrassment on Peanut's face softens him. He sighs. 'You stuck your neck out for us, mate, and none of us can be disappointed with that. Right guys?'

'We're just happy that you're okay.' Ruby settles closer to Peanut's side and clasps his hand affectionately in hers.

Peanut's eyes almost pop out of his head. He

exchanges a knowing look with Jack and waggles his eyebrows.

Jack laughs.

Suddenly Peanut's stomach growls so loud that everyone can hear it. 'Bloody hell, did ya catch that? Come on, let's go eat. I'm starved.' He pulls Ruby to her feet and heads for the chamber. 'What's for dinner? Maybe it's roasted armadillo with a side of stewed liver and mashed sheep's brain? What do ya reckon? Yum, can't wait!'

51

Mr Brightside

Ryker

The guards march the defeated challengers across the lowered drawbridge and dump them outside the confines of the fortress. They carry their meagre belongings and some food that Ulan had the foresight to stash away in a hessian sack.

Ryker stops and draws in a deep breath. 'Ah, the smell of freedom.'

'Don't get too relaxed, Ryker; our freedom will only be defined by our ability to survive out here amongst these savages,' Edra says tersely.

'Such a pessimist, Edra. We answer to no one anymore. Doesn't that lift the burden of the last four years from your heart?' he teases.

'I'm a realist, Ryker; we've been dumped in the

wilderness without protection and with very little food. Our only comfort at the moment is that it isn't raining.'

Ryker sighs deeply and looks at his friends with a smirk on his face.

Ulan frowns. 'What's gotten into you? I think that hit to the head did something to you. Doesn't it bother you that we've nowhere to go, and that our lives are in danger?'

Ryker continues to grin. He's not surprised that Ulan isn't getting a clear read on him. He's experimenting with the telepathy jamming technique that Jack's team adopted against them, to see how well it works.

'What's with that look?' Her eyes narrow in suspicion.

And it's working like a charm. I should've done this ages ago. I could've got away with a bit more private time!

'At least you're in a good mood. I like The Killers, too. Is *Mr Brightside* a favourite? I haven't heard ...' she stops mid-thought, then looks at her brother, who's cottoned on at the same time.

'Ryker!' they cry out simultaneously.

'Come on.' He grins. 'Let's find some shelter, and then I'll tell you my plans.'

Banji, who's been wallowing the whole time,

perks up. 'You've got plans? I hate that I've missed that! What's going to happen? Come on, tell us. I need to hear something positive right now.'

'All in good time, Banji. All in good time.' He chuckles.

There's a plan. Of course, there's a plan. Ryker wouldn't jeopardise their safety knowing there was a good chance they'd lose against the Aussies.

He laughs to himself as he watches them all buzz with enthusiasm. Edra's lost the look of trepidation, and Banji is no longer indulging in misery. He smiles, knowing that now their outlook on their situation doesn't seem so dire.

They search the forest until they find four solid trees nestled close together. They'll provide a good base for a makeshift elevated tree house. While he sends the others to scour the area for long, broken-off tree limbs to form the floor of the tree house, he goes about forming a structure to support the floor. Using the natural V's from each of the four tree trunks, he secures four long tree limbs with some vine he finds growing on the forest floor. To cut these vines into usable lengths, he fashions a cutting tool by striking two rocks together to form a sharp edge.

The treehouse floor is high enough to keep them safely off the ground, away from wild animals. And they'll access the tree house by rope. He asks Edra and Ulan to construct a rope using three lengths of vine plaited together.

They work tirelessly to his commands, not questioning his knowledge and skills. They know about Ryker's past-life training.

He's a machine. Ryker doesn't stop until he's satisfied they'll be safe at least for tonight. Tomorrow he'll work on creating a canopy to shelter them from rain.

Just before nightfall, Ryker works on the final touches, then goes with the others to find some water. Once done, they're ready to ascend the tree house. Ryker starts climbing the massive tree using nothing but a vine strapped around his waist. He virtually bunny-hops all the way up. Once up there, he lowers the secured, plaited rope the girls made earlier, and one by one, pulls them up to safety.

They sit and share a humble meal of bread and water.

'Ryker, the suspense is killing me,' Banji says. 'It's so weird not being able to get into your head. Can you tell us what's happening now … please?'

Ryker stretches, yawns and makes to lay down for a sleep. 'Maybe in the morning. I'm a little tired now,' he teases.

'Ryker!' they yell at him.

'Okay, okay. Do you want the whole forest

knowing we're here?' He smiles. 'Look, I'll be honest, I can't take the credit for what we're going to do. It's the Aussies I need to thank for their ingenious thinking.'

'What do you mean?' Edra asks.

'Remember, Banji, you told me the other team left a trail?'

'Sure. Oh. Why didn't I think of that?'

'We're finally going home,' Ulan whispers in a strangled voice.

'I don't want us getting ahead of ourselves,' Ryker says. 'Anything can happen. What if we can't find the trail?'

'But Ryker, your training will help, won't it?' Ulan asks hopefully.

'I'm quietly confident, Ulan, but what if it doesn't? We need to remain realistic about this. And keep in mind that even if we do find it, it won't lead to the portal we fell through four years ago. It'll take us back to theirs, so we'll end up in Australia.'

'I've always wanted to visit Australia.' Ulan giggles.

'So what's going to happen next?' Edra asks.

'The plan is to set out early tomorrow morning, find some food, then go in search of the trail. We stick together. We don't go anywhere alone, agreed?'

Come first light tomorrow, they'll begin their

search. Now they need to rest.

Ryker is confident that he's built them a safe-haven. The only way up is by rope, and that rope is now rolled up on the floor next to him.

Although they're sleeping in the open, the canopy formed by the treetops blankets them well enough. They lay on their hessian sacks looking up at the stars that peek through the branches, and one by one they breathe in the same deep scent of freedom that Ryker described earlier.

52

Medwin

Ryker

The next morning while searching for food, they come across a small running stream nestled in a shallow clearing of trees. Ryker fashions a stick into a spear and skilfully catches a few fish, he then builds a fire to cook them. And how he does this has his friends stare at him in awe. After cleverly gutting the fish with the makeshift cutting tool he made earlier, he places them on a few large river stones he threw on the fire earlier, now heated enough for the fish to be cooked on.

They're sitting around the fire enjoying their meal, and talking of Ryker's extraordinary abilities when Ulan suddenly perks up, alarmed. Banji does the same.

'What is it?' Ryker's senses go on high alert.

'Someone's in the bushes, watching us,' Ulan whispers.

Banji answers Ryker's unspoken question. 'By the large tree to the left.' He closes his eyes in concentration. 'I think he's alone.'

'Be sure,' Ryker says.

Banji confirms that he is.

'And he's hungry,' Ulan adds.

Ryker slowly stands, the spear clenched tightly in his hand.

'What are you doing?' Edra whispers in alarm.

'Don't worry, Edra. Leave it to me.' Ryker walks calmly to the stream and settles himself on a rock. After catching several more fish, he returns to his friends and, in a raised voice, says to the stranger, 'You're welcome to join us. We're peaceful people who mean you no harm.' He takes a moment to clean the fish, then throws them on the heated stones and waits.

Sometime later a short man with long black hair and a beard comes out from behind a large tree. He approaches cautiously, a spear in his hand.

'Come, join us,' Ryker again offers.

'How is it that you knew of my presence?' the man asks suspiciously.

'I heard you,' Ryker lies.

The man comes closer and stares warily at Ryker.

Ryker can see the scepticism in his look. 'I have excellent hearing,' he quickly adds, then tries to distract him by turning his attention to the fish he's cooking.

'And I have the power of foresight. I do not doubt your hearing, but I sense something awry with your half-truth.'

Ryker blasts himself for lying. 'Forgive me, I merely wished to draw you out and offer you food and friendship.'

The small man studies Ryker for a while. 'My foresight has prepared me for you today,' he confesses. 'It told of a meeting with strangers who were to bring about great changes.'

'Is that right?' Ryker asks casually while inwardly bubbling with excitement.

'That is so,' the man replies. 'I had another premonition only two days ago, and it, too, came to pass.'

Ryker's interest spikes. *Could he mean he met with Peanut?* He takes care to rein in his excitement. 'Interesting. You have an uncanny gift there, my friend. I'm curious to know more.' As Ryker waits to hear what the man has to say, he carefully drags the hot stones from the fire, and using a thick strip of bark, scrapes the cooked fish onto a large leaf and offers it to him.

The man readily accepts it and hungrily begins to eat. Between mouthfuls he relays his story. 'It was a most unusual experience, one I am still having difficulty trying to fathom,' he begins. 'He had escaped from the fortress and spoke of salvation. He invited me to join him, but at the time I could not be swayed.'

Ryker sees an opportunity to form an alliance with this man. 'I know of him, and what he said is true. We, too, are preparing an escape. And we can help you and your friends, if you like.'

The man looks from Ryker to the others and appears to be assessing his sincerity.

'How many people live in the forest?' Ryker asks.

'There are over one hundred dwelling here,' the man replies, his eyes wary.

'Is that so? Is there enough food for so many?'

The man narrows his eyes in suspicion. Ryker suspects he's questioning his motives, so, he offers him more fish. 'Only, I imagine that food is scarce, and that competition for it is fierce.'

'Food is indeed in short supply. Your ability to catch fish is extraordinary. I admire your skill.'

Ryker considers the stranger for a moment: the way he dresses; the way he speaks. 'Tell me something, how long has it been since you competed in the challenges?'

The stranger's expression indicates confusion.

'I mean, how long have you been living in exile?'

'I have lived my whole life in the forest, as did my mother. I have never competed. As for my father, he was in the challenges many years before I was born. He died an old man when I was a small child. I do not remember him.'

Ryker initially has trouble comprehending what that means. Could it be that there have been people stuck in this realm for well over a century, generations created from people who'd been exiled over the years?

Ryker's determination to escape heightens. 'I'm going to make you a promise: once we're free, we'll return to help you escape this place. We'll take you back with us to where food is plentiful, and your family and friends will be safe.' Ryker stands to leave and offers his hand. 'I thank you, my friend. You have opened my eyes to the reality of what's happening here.'

The man hesitates, looking unsure of what the gesture means.

'This is my promise to you,' Ryker explains. 'We seal the promise with a handshake.'

The man cautiously takes Ryker's hand in his and then smiles, showing his acceptance of the alliance. 'I sense that this is the beginning of a new and better life.'

'I couldn't agree more. My name is Ryker, and these are my good friends Edra, Ulan and Banji.'

'And I am Medwin. I will wait for the day when our paths will cross again.'

Ryker leads his team back towards the treehouse, his thoughts buzzing from the unlikely alliance they've just made.

Edra breaks his train of thought. 'Can you believe the magnitude of this?'

Ryker shakes his addled head. 'I know; it's huge. The fact that these challenges have been going on for forever is mind-boggling. We need to stop it. Come on, let's look for that trail.'

53

THE SOUND OF THE TRUMPET

JACK

They sit by the lake on the eve of the final task. Jack can't believe that it's been only a little over two weeks since they found themselves trapped in this ancient realm. It seems to him a lifetime ago that they were setting up tents and playing a friendly game of volleyball.

His mind races and, for the millionth time, he wonders what tomorrow might bring. It's been over a week since the last challenge, and they've spent most of that time preparing themselves for the inevitable. Thankfully, for whatever reason, the guards have relaxed their vigilance over them, allowing them more freedom in and out of their chamber.

The sun has almost gone down. Before long, they'll be in complete darkness. They'll have a New Moon tonight.

'Hey, guys, let's head inside; it's getting dark,' Ruby says, rubbing her arms from a sudden chill.

They prepare to leave, but Max stops. 'Did you hear that?'

'Hear what?' Ruby whispers anxiously.

They all stand still for a moment, listening.

Jack can't hear anything unusual. 'What did it sound like?'

'You're going to laugh, but it sounded like a trumpet.' She closes her eyes and listens again, then shakes her head. 'Funny, I must've imagined it.'

'Shh! I just heard something.' Ruby grabs hold of Max's arm to shush her.

Again they stop, silent.

'There it is,' Ruby says softly.

'I heard it, too!' Kenny says.

Jack hasn't heard anything. But then the sound comes a little louder, and he finally hears it. 'Hey, you're right. But a trumpet? That's weird.'

The sound, now being carried on a light breeze, becomes clearer.

'What the …? That's an elephant!' Max says in disbelief.

They hear it again, more distinct this time.

'Whoa!' Peanut's eyes grow wide. He listens harder. 'There's more than one, and they're coming closer.'

Jack feels his anxiety rising. The elephants must have something to do with tomorrow's challenge. He can hear them clearly now, and there's definitely more than one.

'No-no-no-no-no! We're going to have to fight wild animals!' Max cries out in a panic. 'It's the same challenge all over again. You know what? I don't think I can do this. I'm done. I'm out of here!'

Jack grabs Max by the arm to stop her escape. He places his hands on her shoulders and gives her a gentle shake. 'Hey, look at me. Max, we've got this.' He smiles at her. 'We just need to keep our heads, okay? And right now, you're kind'a losing yours.'

Max stares at him, breathing heavily.

'Now calm down. Take a deep breath.' He waits for her to settle. 'So we're good?' he gently asks her.

She slowly nods.

He pulls her into a hug. 'That's my girl. You'll see, everything'll be okay.' He lets out a deep sigh. They can't afford to fall apart this close to the final.

'But it might not be a whole heap of animals.' Peanut steers the conversation back to something more constructive. 'What if it's "just" elephants?

Could that happen, Kenny? We haven't heard anything else, have we?'

'Well, yeah,' Kenny says as he delves into his archives of knowledge. 'The Ancient Romans used elephants in challenges. They called them the Beasts of Carthage, and the challengers were called Bestiaries, or beast fighters …' Kenny stops mid-sentence. From the expression on his face, his thoughts have taken a detour.

'What's going on in that brain of yours, mate?' The smile on Jack's face disappears when Kenny doesn't answer.

He's so deep in his thoughts that he's oblivious to everyone's sudden anxious attention. Then, without warning, Kenny grabs Peanut by the arm. 'Hey, you got a minute?' he asks, then drags him away, deep into the garden.

Jack watches them disappear, unsure whether to follow, but before he can utter a word, Kenny calls out to them. 'We'll be back in a few. See you inside, okay?'

'What was that all about?' Ruby asks.

'I don't know, but if Kenny's hatching a plan, I'm not gonna stop him,' Jack replies.

'Shouldn't we be worried?' Max asks.

'Um? Nah. It'll be all right … I think.' But Jack doesn't sound too convincing.

'Guys, it's Kenny's brainwave we're talking about, not Peanut's, so it'll be okay,' Ruby reminds them.

Max snorts. 'Come on, let's go inside. We'll find out soon enough.'

And just as they sit down to eat what the guards have left for them, the boys return, both grinning with mischief.

Jack can't wait to hear what they've been up to. 'So are you two going to let us in on your little secret?'

'Who? Us? A secret?' Peanut says innocently.

He and Kenny remain tight lipped.

'Come on, we're dying here,' Ruby says. 'Give!'

Peanut shrugs and pretends to be at a loss as to what they're talking about.

'I can't talk to you like this!' Jack says, flustered. He turns to Kenny instead. 'Kenny, mate, what's going on?'

'What? Nothing. I just wanted to show Peanut something,' Kenny replies with a mischievous smile.

Ruby groans. 'Great. Now there's two of them.'

Max giggles. 'Kenny's gone over to the dark side.'

'You're kidding, right? Kenny, I'm your mate, remember?' Jack tries to guilt it out of him.

Peanut starts to laugh. 'Will you relax! We're just pulling your leg. Geez, talk about being neurotic. Now, what's to eat? I'm—.'

'Starving! Yeah, we know, already,' the girls say in

unison.

Jack shakes his head and laughs. He opens the food hampers, curious to see what "culinary delights" the kitchen has sent them. 'Wow, they've sent us a feast!'

'Yeah?' Peanut goes to investigate. 'They're probably banking on it being our last supper.'

Ruby's head whips around, a look of pure panic on her face.

'It's a joke!' he says quickly. 'I'm just kidding! Geez, what's wrong with you lot? Rubes, babe, get a grip.'

'Not funny, Charlie!' she snaps at him.

Jack smothers a laugh.

'Hey, when the guards from the kitchen come to collect the baskets tonight, can we tell them to leave them?' Kenny asks, unexpectedly. 'You know, just in case we become peckish during the night.'

'Say what?' Ruby stares at Kenny, suddenly distracted from Peanut's earlier joke.

'What? I'm a growing boy.' Kenny looks offended.

'Wait a minute; what's happening here?' Jack looks from Peanut to Kenny and then back again.

The two say nothing, just smile an identical lopsided smile.

Jack gives up because he knows that look, and is well qualified to know not to prod any further.

So the huge hampers, half filled with food, remain.

They talk tactics the rest of the night. And when they've gone over their strategies enough times to be able to do them with their eyes shut, Jack suggests that they turn in. 'That's it. There's nothing more we can do now.'

He lays awake for a while, mulling things over in his head. Peanut lies next to him, tossing and turning, struggling to settle. Then Jack hears him get up, and before he has a chance to ask him if everything's okay, the chamber door opens, and Peanut disappears.

What the hell!

He jumps up and follows. After quietly passing the sleeping guard outside, he bolts through the passageways, hoping to catch up to Peanut.

It's pitch-black outside with hardly any visibility due to the new moon. Jack stumbles his way through the garden, making a racket.

'Geez, mate, you're making enough noise to wake the dead!' Peanut whispers angrily.

Jack jumps, frightened out of his wits. 'Geez, yourself! Give a bloke some warning next time,' he yells, clutching at his chest. 'You nearly gave me a heart attack! Where the hell are you, anyway?'

Peanut makes himself visible. 'Sorry, mate, I forgot. What are you doing out here?'

'What am I doing? I could ask you the same thing! What are you and Kenny up to?'

'Look, we figured it wouldn't go down well with you guys if I snuck out again,' Peanut confesses, 'but we needed to find out more about the elephants.'

'So what's the plan?'

'No real plan, just to sneak out and find a tree that I can climb that gives me a view outside the fortress.'

'Okay, so let's go.'

They head off deeper into the garden, and stop when they reach a point where they can hear the elephants just beyond the fortress wall.

Peanut indicates a tree he thinks might give him a good view, but the limbs are too high off the ground. 'Can you give me a leg up?'

'Yeah, but there's no way you'll reach. Maybe if you stand on my shoulders.'

Jack squats on his haunches, Peanut climbs on, and then Jack hoists him up towards the lowest limb. It still amazes him how easy it is to do such things.

'I'll admit it,' he says, 'I'm going to miss being this strong when we leave this place.'

'Yeah, I know what you mean. This disappearing thing's been pretty cool. But if I had to pick between giving it up and going home, I'd give it up in a heartbeat.'

'Same.'

'Hey, what if we get to keep 'em!' Peanut gets so excited with this thought that he loses his balance, and Jack has a job and a half to keep him from falling.

'Hey, watch it!'

'Sorry.'

'How 'bout you concentrate on getting us out of here first.'

Peanut carefully stretches up on Jack's shoulders, but there's still no way he can reach. 'Mate, I fall short about a metre. Maybe I'd have a better chance if you jump up that last bit.'

Jack slowly bends his knees in preparation for the jump, and then, with an enormous effort, he springs up as high as he can.

From the unexpected force of the jump, Peanut cracks his head on the bough, then falls to the ground. 'Yow! Shit, that hurt!' Peanut rubs the top of his head.

'Sorry.' Jack chuckles. 'I hardly know my strength.'

'Now I need Max to fix this headache you've just given me.'

'Suck it up, princess!' Jack teases. 'C'mon, let's try again.'

So with Peanut once again balanced on Jack's shoulders, the two try again, and this time he makes it.

'What can you see?' Jack asks eagerly.

'Give me a sec, I need to climb a little higher.'

Jack watches as his friend disappears into the darkness. He sits and waits, listening to the rustle of the leaves as Peanut continues to climb. About ten minutes later, he hears him descending, and he's soon dangling in front of Jack ready to jump down.

'What's the go?' Jack asks.

'I could barely see them, but yeah, there's a herd of elephants in an area just off the arena. At a guess, there's probably a dozen of them.'

'Man, a dozen?' Jack says, surprised. 'Maybe you were right earlier. With that many elephants, they might not be using any other animals.'

'Yeah, but I don't get it, what's the task, then? Are we gonna have to kill them? Because I'd hate to do it. And how the hell do you kill an elephant, anyway?'

'Nah, I don't think that's what we're meant to do. I wonder how the Invincibles fit into it.' Jack is stumped. He can't imagine how this is going to pan out.

'Whoa,' Peanut says. 'Do you remember that scene out of *Lord of the Rings - The Return of the King*? You know, the one where there's a battle with those dead people and the huge war elephants. Do you reckon they'll use the elephants like that?'

'Geez, they'd better not!' Jack says horrified, remembering the scene. 'We'd be like lambs to the slaughter!'

'Hey, I'm just saying. It might be nothing that gruesome. We'll ask Kenny.'

ↄ

The next morning Peanut and Jack fill the others in on what they found last night. And after putting it to Kenny, they discover that Peanut's guess wasn't that far off the mark.

'A war elephant,' Kenny tells them, 'is trained for combat. Its main use is to charge the enemy, break their ranks and instil terror. They're typically guided by soldiers sitting in large, protective carriages, harnessed on the elephant's back. These soldiers are generally armed with spears, and bows and arrows.'

'So what you're saying,' Max begins calmly, 'is that the Invincibles will be riding these huge beasts while we scurry around like mice trying to avoid getting stomped on and being bludgeoned to death by their spears? Sounds like a fair fight, NOT!' She grabs Jack's arm in a panic. 'What hope have we got?'

'Max is right!' Ruby cries. 'How do we do this? How does anyone ever win?'

'Girls, it'll be okay,' Peanut says. 'I promise.'

Ruby turns on him. 'Are you completely nuts? Weren't you just listening! We haven't a hope, Peanut!

Absolutely none.'

Peanut laughs, grabs Ruby by the waist and starts spinning her around.

Jack doesn't get it. Has Peanut lost the plot?

'Peanut, stop,' Ruby squeals, now laughing. 'What's gotten into you, you loony?'

Peanut exchanges a look with Kenny and smirks. Jack's seen that mischievous, lopsided grin way too many times to not know that he's up to something. And he's right.

'Kenny and I have a plan,' Peanut explains. 'And a bloody good one at that.'

The madness stops. All eyes turn to the two mischief makers, and suddenly there's a glimmer of hope.

54

BRING IT ON

JACK

The time has come. They have a plan, and they've gone over the various scenarios dozens of times. Jack knows they're ready for anything. His confidence blankets the rest of the team. This is it. There's no turning back. Losing is not an option.

Herodus once again leads the five victors into the arena. The crowd roars.

The first thing Jack notices is that the drawbridge has been lowered. Barricading the exit is a dozen or so guards, standing resolute.

He looks up and, as expected, sees The Ancients seated on their raised platform overseeing the event. He takes a moment to look around. The stadium is filled to capacity, with eager faces looking down at

388

them, everybody anticipating a great battle.

But where are the Invincibles? Their opposition is nowhere to be seen. Jack's anxiety kicks into a higher gear.

Herodus leads them to stand before The Ancients. He raises his hand, commanding everyone's attention. The silence that follows makes Jack sick to the stomach. It's now or never.

'My Lords, our five remaining competitors have fought valiantly and have earned their place to challenge our own champions'

The crowd erupt, cheering and clapping. Their excitement amplifies when their ancient leader stands to address them.

It takes him a moment to regain the silence. 'My people, welcome. We have anticipated this day for many years. A long time has passed since our champions have been challenged. Today, my friends, you will witness a great mastery of skills. We have chosen a challenge that promises to enthral and excite you all.

'Challengers, your task today is simply this ... to cross the lowered drawbridge.'

Jack waits to hear the rest of it, but that's it. He's done.

'Simple? Yeah, right,' Peanut coughs on a laugh. 'Pull the other one.'

Jack smiles, the burden feeling a lot lighter now. He looks at the girls. The same look of "I call bullshit on that one" is written on their faces. He almost starts to laugh.

'Let the games begin!' Pius announces.

The crowd stand ready and shout with excitement.

Jack looks in every direction, anticipating a blind attack, but there isn't one. No Invincibles, no elephants … nothing.

'What's going on?' Kenny asks, looking around in alarm.

Then they hear, in the distance, the trumpeting sound of elephants on the move.

Jack lets out a slow, nervous breath, and takes a moment to settle his nerves. He looks at Kenny. 'We all know what to do.'

The crowd hear the beasts approaching and erupt in a boisterous cheer. They stand and eagerly await the appearance of the giant warriors. The guards barricading the entrance, part, preparing for the grand entrance, and the arena falls into a deathly silence.

The trumpeting bellows grow louder.

The five challengers stand ready, their eyes fixed on the drawbridge, waiting to see what horror approaches.

Then, all of a sudden, they're there.

The crowd erupts.

Five huge war elephants enter the arena, each one carrying a rider in a protective carriage. Each rider is dressed for the part, wearing headdresses and draped in animal hides. Armed with bows, arrows and spears, they look quite the ancient warriors.

'Looks like it'll be a fair fight,' Peanut says sarcastically.

'Don't look now; the odds have just gotten worse,' Max adds, alarmed.

And sure enough, coming up the rear are more war elephants—too many to count.

'What?' Ruby grabs hold of Max's hand in a panic.

There must be at least two dozen elephants. Jack senses everyone's confidence plummet. 'Guys, keep it together, okay? We know what we need to do. Stay close to Ruby. Ruby, no pressure but how are you doing?'

Ruby takes in a deep breath. 'Okay, let's do this!'

Jack turns to Peanut. 'You ready, buddy?'

Peanut's face lights up with mischief. 'Bring it on!' And then he vanishes.

The ominous giants approach with one rider leading the herd. He's calling out instructions and the animals are responding.

Beowulf!

An overwhelming feeling of despair comes over Jack, but he quickly realises the source. He shakes his head and locks eyes with one of the Invincibles. 'Block your thoughts, everyone. Archimedes is up to his tricks already,' he warns. 'Keep focused!'

Jack concentrates all his efforts on stopping Archimedes' attempts to manipulate his mind. The words to his favourite Nirvana song fill his head, and he studies Archimedes's reaction to gauge whether or not it's making an impact. The Realm champion's look of confusion gives Jack hope.

Archimedes turns his attention to the others, and again his reaction is the same.

It's working!

The elephants close in and start to encircle them. Suddenly Beowulf breaks from the pack, appearing to initiate the attack alone. And before Jack has a chance to call out a warning, an abrupt change in the atmosphere and an increase in air movement alerts Kenny to what's about to happen.

'Shant's conjuring up a storm! Ruby, your shield! Now!'

The four friends huddle together, and Ruby produces her shield, cocooning them in its dome in the nick of time. The wind picks up at a fierce pace, and whips violently around them. The Invincibles fire arrows and spears only to realise that the shield is impenetrable.

From the protection of their bubble, Jack sees the arena through the haze of a sand storm. The spectators cower, struggling to watch the events unfold while shielding their faces from the hazardous debris.

The elephants begin to run amok.

Jack can see Beowulf's rage. He commands Shant to stop. 'Cease your efforts, you fool! You are creating mayhem with the animals!'

This infuriates Shant. 'So your scheme was to go it alone and claim all the glory? Move aside, and let me finish what I have begun.' In one swift motion, he conjures up several bolts of lightning, striking them repeatedly at Ruby's shield. But the shield holds fast.

The sudden explosive attack makes the elephants more erratic, and the realm champions struggle to calm their rides. Mayhem reigns. Beowulf yells for Shant to stop. Vyvian flies into the sky and pelts arrows from every direction. Each Invincible tries to outdo the other.

'Enough!' Beowulf bellows. 'Archimedes, what use are you? How is it that they remain united? To destroy the shield, you need to divide their alliance!'

Archimedes shakes his head, at a loss. 'I do not understand it. I have no control over them. Somehow they are blocking my efforts.'

Jack's confidence soars.

'Remove the animals!' Shant orders Beowulf. 'I have an idea.'

Beowulf glowers at him, clearly not impressed with the command. They stare at each other, neither one prepared to back down.

Jack holds his breath, quietly hoping that they lock horns.

But Athos defuses the situation. 'Beowulf, grant him this. We achieve nothing by arguing.'

Beowulf, clearly against his better judgement, orders his elephants to move away.

Shant doesn't waste a second. With his arms raised, he conjures up a mini tornado, and the rotating column of air vacuums the four helpless victims into its funnel-shaped centre. It lifts them high into the sky, swirling them within, and then rips the group apart.

Ruby's shield now only protects her, and the team tumbles uncontrollably within the tornado.

Vyvian seizes the opportunity. She takes off, flying up and around the whirlwind while firing her arrows into the funnel. Jack sees arrows whipping past him and prays she misses her target … but too late. Jack refocuses and yells at Ruby to regain control. She struggles to right herself and at last succeeds. But then, suddenly, she doubles over, holding her head, blocking her ears.

Archimedes!

'No! Ruby, don't listen! Don't let him in your head!' Jack struggles to keep her in his sights. 'Ruby, shut him out!'

An arrow flies into the tornado and hits Ruby's shield. The impact of the arrow on the shield is nothing, but it has a huge effect on Ruby. She shakes her head and lets out an almighty roar. 'Nooooo … I'm a survivor! You won't beat me!'

With an intensity that belies every other attempt she's ever made, Ruby's shield bursts open to encompass her friends once again. The tornado combusts from the impact of the shield and dissolves into a mere cloud. The sphere holding the four friends falls safely to the ground.

Shant looks on in disbelief. Wild with anger, he conjures heavy dark clouds until a blanket of gloom shadows the arena. A warm current of air whirls upwards, then bullets of ice dart to the earth, pelting at Ruby's shield. But the hail simply bounces off.

A sudden explosion, followed by the hissing and

crackling of brightly coloured sparkles, startles and confuses the crowd. They look upwards, searching the sky. The darkness above glows with light. The Invincibles, the guards and The Ancients look on the streaks of coloured fire and smoke with fear.

With some effort, Jack stops himself from laughing. The look on their faces is priceless. Piercing whistles and more explosions light up the sky again. The Ancients cower and duck for cover. The Invincibles don't know where to look. Thanks to Peanut, the fireworks do their job. They have everyone looking upward, distracted.

A series of noisy ground crackers create more chaos with the elephants. Startled, they crash into each other in a frenzy, trying to escape the threat. In their desperation, some of the elephants start ramming into the stadium, forcing the crowd to scatter in hysteria. The building begins to crumble under the attack. Spectators by the hundreds trip over each other to avoid being crushed in the mayhem.

To Jack's relief, Peanut appears at the entrance of the arena carrying a familiar covered food basket— one that holds the remnants of last night's meal, and something more, something crucial for their escape plan. He throws open the lid and releases hundreds of frenzied mice that have been trapped in there.

Pandemonium breaks loose. The sudden onslaught of scurrying vermin makes the elephants shriek with fear. With riders on their backs, they stampede out of control and head straight for the Nobles. A tragedy is about to unfold right before their eyes, and Jack can see that the realm's heroes are powerless to stop it. But he doesn't wait to witness the outcome. The opportunity to escape has been paved.

'Get the hell out of here! Now!'

55

THE DECISION

MAX

Max can't believe what's going on. Everything's happening at once. Peanut has succeeded in creating the distraction they needed to get away. All she has to do now is run.

As she's heading for the drawbridge, she does a quick head-count. Kenny has already crossed ahead of her. Behind, Peanut hesitates only to help Ruby who has tripped in her hurry to get away. Jack is running at the rear, but looks safe. Her gaze darts everywhere, scouring the exit for any threat. She holds her breath as she passes, but there's nothing. Their escape, miraculously, goes unchallenged.

'Kenny, keep going; we're right behind you,' Jack yells. And very quickly they disappear, swallowed by the depths of the forest.

Max doesn't stop. She keeps up the vigorous pace and manages to stay hot on Kenny's tail. Every now and then, she turns to make sure no one is falling behind.

Jack stops and bends over, clutching his chest, trying to catch his breath. Max calls for the others to wait and runs back to him.

He laughs. 'Bloody hell, can you believe it? We made it!'

She doesn't know whether to smack him or kiss him.

'Peanut, you were brilliant!' He laughs again. 'And, Kenny, you're a genius!'

It's then that Max notices Jack clutching at his side and fresh blood saturating his shirt. The tail of a broken arrow protrudes from the red stain. 'Oh my God! Jack, you're hurt!'

He calmly holds her back from flying at him. 'It can wait; we've gotta keep going.'

'What the hell, Jack?'

'Not now, Max!'

'But, Jack!'

'I can handle it, okay?'

The sound of a fast-approaching movement nearby snaps her back to the crisis at hand.

'Run!' Jack grabs her hand and makes a run for it.

Like a rag doll, she gets dragged behind him. She trips and stumbles, and fights to remain upright. She finally manages to yank her hand free from his hold and runs for her life. She's deep within the woods when a familiar voice calls out to them, stopping her dead in her tracks. It's Ryker.

His unexpected appearance is a massive relief. Max holds her hand to her heart, willing it to calm down, and waits for the others to catch her up. 'Thank God, Ryker, we thought you were the guards.'

Through great drags of breath, he calls over his shoulder as he disappears into the forest, 'They'll be here soon enough. Follow me!'

Max hesitates a moment to check on Jack.

'Stop it!' he grabs her hands in his. 'I can't feel it, remember? Just keep up with the others, okay? Now go!'

He shoves her gently to follow the others, and against her intuition, Max does as she's told. Logic tells her she can't stop to think about it now. It's crucial that they put some distance between the guards and themselves. Adrenalin once again pumps through her veins, urging her on.

Ryker is relentless, his pace gruelling. Thankfully, after what seems like ages, he starts to slow. But Max quickly realises that his actions are with purpose. His movements become more cautious. Her senses go on high alert.

Ryker turns to them, and between deep gasps of breath, he relays in silent gestures that up ahead is the gateway protected by four guards. He motions for them to not make a sound.

Max tries to slow her breathing.

A soft rustling sound around them reveals more surprises. Edra, Ulan and Banji emerge quietly and join them. Max smiles with relief and lets go of the breath she just drew in.

Peanut gestures to Ryker that he'll go forward to investigate before they go any further.

Ryker shakes his head, assertively. 'We don't have time,' he whispers. 'It won't be long before the other guards get here.'

'I'll create a diversion to draw them away from their post,' Peanut says.

They hesitate for a second, collectively thinking what might work as a diversion.

'Do you have any more fireworks?' Kenny asks.

'Far out; ya don't ask for much, do ya?' Peanut whines but hastily rummages through his backpack anyway.

Max prays for a miracle, and her heart rate spikes when she sees him lift his head and smile that mischievous smile that everyone has come to know.

'Come to daddy!' He pulls out a two-metre roll

of Tom Thumbs.

Max's eyes pop and she barely suppresses an excited squeal. She reverently clasps her hands together, looks heavenward, and mouths a silent thank-you to the Fireworks Gods.

Jack and Peanut exchange an enthusiastic high-five.

'Okay.' Jack takes control. 'That'll cause the diversion we need, but we need to act quickly. Tom Thumbs go off real fast. Peanut, you'll need to set them off deep enough into the forest to give us all time to get away, but not so deep that you'll have trouble getting back in time.'

'Gotcha. No worries!'

But before he gets a chance to take off, Ruby grabs hold of him. 'Now don't do anything stupid, all right? No mucking around; you come straight back.' The kiss she plants on him causes a befuddled expression, but it's soon replaced with a big goofy grin.

'Get going!' Jack growls under his breath and gives him a shove back to reality.

Before he leaves, Peanut turns and gives Ruby a cheeky wink. 'Rubes, you won't have time to miss me!' And then he vanishes.

Ryker instructs them to remain together and be ready to run on his command. They move in a little closer, and Ryker motions for them to squat and conceal themselves. He then indicates to Jack, with a nod of his head, the direction of the gateway. Jack peers ever so carefully around the tree he's hiding behind. Max, too, leans forward a little to have a look. Four burley guards sit lazily in front of the floating, transparent gossamer veil. It's barely noticeable and would be easily missed if not for the guards marking it.

Max lays low, waiting, listening for the diversion and mentally preparing for the sprint.

From her position she has a clear view of Edra and Ulan, huddled together behind a boulder. Ulan has her eyes closed, and Edra holds her hand in support. Max's heart aches for them. They've only had each other these past four years. The bond they share is strong.

Max looks around for Ruby. She spots her standing deathly still behind a tree. She too has her eyes closed, taking deep calming breaths. Max smiles, knowing her too well now. If only she realised her worth, she wouldn't be so jittery. In Ruby, she has a friend for life. She knows this to be true. What they have is steadfast, something that will endure each and every experience to come.

Banji is concealed slightly off to the side of the group, looking overly anxious. Max frowns at him sympathetically. He must have everyone's thoughts bouncing around in his head. She's thankful that she only has her own to contend with.

Max then searches for Kenny. She can just see him peeking from behind a tree. He looks ready to take flight. She smiles, seeing the irony of it all. The one that originally didn't give himself any credit is now her biggest hero. If it wasn't for him, they wouldn't be minutes away from finally going home. The trail, the fireworks, the mice and the mayhem … all thanks to the genius that is Kenny.

Max smiles, then looks to find Jack. Her breath hitches when her eyes lock onto his. There's a tenderness in his look. Her face flushes with heat. He winks at her then silently laughs. Max can't help but smile back. There's comfort in their familiarity.

Max shyly lowers her gaze, but loses her composure when she sees, once again, Jack's blood-stained shirt. The panic in her eyes has Jack remember the offending arrow.

But too late, the sound of the diversion reverberates throughout the forest. Max looks at the gate keepers, who stand in alarm. The head guard gestures to the others to go and investigate while he remains to protect the gateway. The three guards take off in the direction of the noise.

When they're deep enough in the forest, Ryker motions Jack to help him charge the remaining guard.

But Kenny intercepts, having spotted the urgent

interchange between Max and Jack. 'Jack, I'll do it. Get Max to fix you.'

Jack looks like he's about to argue.

'Go!' Kenny growls under his breath before taking off to help Ryker.

Max watches as Kenny fearlessly tackles the guard around the legs from behind, forcing him to topple to the ground face first. Ryker pounces on top of him and knocks him out cold with a blow to the head. In the far distance, they hear the sound of rapidly approaching footsteps—the guards from the arena. They need to move.

Max grabs Jack to assess the situation. There's no time to spare. Her heart jumps into her throat when she realises how critical his injury is. The arrow is pressing dangerously on his aorta. Any sudden jolt, and Jack will rupture the vital blood vessel and die. She can't just patch him up; she needs to remove the arrow, and fast. But there's no time, and she knows it.

Without wasting another second, Max yanks the broken arrow out with a strength she didn't know she had. The heat in her hands surges to the wound and seals off the potential life-threatening bleed, but her determined focus on the site drains her strength. She's close, so very close to finishing. She looks up wearily, trying to gauge the amount of time they have left.

'Kenny, grab the girls and go!' Ryker yells.

'What about Peanut?' Ruby cries.

'Ruby, we have to go, now!' Kenny grabs Ruby and pushes her through the veil. He hesitates for a split second watching Ruby vanish before him, before helping Ulan and Edra.

The guards fast approach. One comes into view and races towards Ryker, wielding a machete.

'Go!' Ryker yells as he pushes Kenny through the gateway in time to defend himself against his attacker.

While Ryker fights off the guard, Banji dives through to safety.

'Just a few more seconds, please God, give me the strength to finish this,' Max pleads.

Ryker quickly and efficiently disarms the guard and they then engage in a more even fight without weapons. The guard charges him, but Ryker is ready. He delivers a debilitating side kick to the guard's abdomen. The guard bowls over, winded. Ryker grabs him in a head lock and pounds his fist repeatedly into his face. After several blows, the guard falls limp to the ground. Ryker looks up to locate Max and Jack. They're out of time. He needs them to pass through. Now.

Several more guards appear, but Max hasn't finished. Jack is still critical.

There's no way Ryker will be able to take on this many at once, but suddenly the charging guards mysteriously all topple over, conveniently tripped by a tree vine that appears out of nowhere. An invisible Peanut has granted them a few more precious seconds to complete the healing.

'Jack, take Max, and go!' Ryker roars.

Jack grabs Max's hand, then searches blindly for Peanut.

'Jack, move it! What are you waiting for?' Peanut yells as he materialises before him.

'Take him,' Max calls out weakly as she falls back, breaking her contact with Jack.

Peanut yanks Jack to his feet and without a second thought throws them both through the veil.

The fallen guards have recovered, and they're mere moments away. Max looks from them to Ryker. She's too weak and too far from the portal to get there in time. She wills him to leave and save himself, but he needs to act now.

She watches his indecision. He turns to look at the curtain beckoning him. He needs only to fall back and disappear from this Ancient world forever.

The guards are upon him.

Max's heart thumps in her chest.

With a deep-etched look of panic, he looks back at her, then turns to the veil …

Done.

His decision is made.

❦

The story continues in the sequel, *Realm Travellers - A Parallel Dimension,* scheduled for publication at the end of November 2020.

A Note from the Author

Did you enjoy my book?

If so, I would be very grateful if you could write a review and publish it at your point of purchase. Your review, even a brief one, will help other readers to decide whether or not they'll enjoy my work.

Do you want to be notified of new releases?

If so, please sign up to the AIA Publishing email list. You'll find the sign-up button on the right-hand side under the photo at www.aiapublishing.com. Of course, your information will never be shared, and my publisher won't inundate you with emails, just let you know of new releases.

About the Author

M J Raco, a mother of three and grandmother to one, lives in South-Western Sydney, Australia. She has dedicated over thirty years of her life to helping save and restore the sight of thousands of patients in Australia and Fiji.

She takes inspiration from the words of Ralph Waldo Emerson: 'Do not go where the path may lead, go instead where there is no path and leave a trail.'

www.ingramcontent.com/pod-product-compliance
Lightning Source LLC
Chambersburg PA
CBHW030700190726
48286CB00001B/112